COLD

AROUND THE

HEART

COLD

AROUND THE

HEART

Michael Prescott

Cold Around the Heart
By Michael Prescott
Copyright © 2013 by Douglas Borton

ISBN-13: 978-1484074176

The road gets dimmer and dimmer;
Sometimes you can hardly see;
    But it's fight, man to man,
    And do all you can,
For you know you can never be free

—Bonnie Parker, "The Trail's End" (1933)

prologue

The blood trail was easy to follow in the deep white snow.

Her quarry was leaking badly now, but still making pretty good time. She could have caught up with him easily enough, but because he was armed, she was holding back, staying close to the trees, offering him no clear sightline. She didn't know how handy he was with that crossbow, and she didn't want to find out.

He was a bow hunter, and he'd been stalking deer until she began stalking him. On this snowy weekday the Barrens were empty; she had seen no other hunters, had seen no one at all. She and her prey were alone in a chalk-white forest, watched only by the trees.

He couldn't help leaving tracks, of course—deep ragged pockmarks in the hills of snow where his boots clomped down. But the scarlet thread of blood was easier to see in the failing daylight. She only hoped she finished things before dark. Using a flashlight would make her an easy target.

Really, the job should have been over by now. Had it gone as planned, she would be back in town, sipping cocoa at the Main Street Diner and thawing out after her exposure to the January chill. But because he had the bow, she hadn't wanted to get too close. She'd tried a kill shot from a distance, crouching in a blind, her target hovering over the gun sight. With a long gun she would have made the shot, but with the pistol it proved too great a challenge. She nicked him in the shoulder on her first try, got him in the leg as he was scrambling away.

She wouldn't have thought a man with two slugs in him could

get very far, especially when one of the rounds had lamed him. But the will to survive was a remarkable thing. For more than an hour she'd chased him through the Barrens as the winter sun became a pale smear of saffron in the western sky. She had seen him raise a cell phone to his ear a couple of times, but she couldn't get a signal out here and she was betting he couldn't, either.

He was slowing now, his reserves of energy giving out.

She wondered if he'd gone bow hunting often. She wondered if he had killed many deer, and if so, if he had tracked the wounded animals, following their blood spoor. Probably. Karma was a stone-cold bitch sometimes.

The sun was a blister on the horizon when she found him in a clearing. He lay on his back in the deep powder like a man trying to make a snow angel. The crossbow was by his side, but his hand wasn't on it.

She couldn't tell if he was alive or dead. She approached slowly. When she was a yard away, she saw his eyelids flicker as a puff of breath drifted clear of his mouth.

She put her foot on the bow and eased it sidewise, out of his reach. Then she just stood there, looking down. She knew he was seeing her only in silhouette, a wild-haired apparition limned by the dying sun.

"Help me," he said in a sandpaper rasp.

She shook her head. "Sorry."

It was a lie. She wasn't sorry.

He tried to make sense of what was happening to him. His pupils darted, frantic, in the frozen mask of his face.

"Who are you?" he asked at last.

"My name's Parker. Jacob Hart hired me."

That ought to make things reasonably clear. She watched as comprehension widened his eyes.

"I'll pay you more," he said. "I'll pay double. I'll pay anything."

"You got one thing right, buddy. You'll pay."

She steadied the pistol, targeting his heart.

From this distance she couldn't miss.

1

On Tuesday, August 21, Bonnie Parker hung a sign on her office door that read GONE FISHING. It was no joke. She had a rod and reel in her car, a beat-up but still serviceable Jeep Wrangler she'd purchased secondhand six years ago at the start of her career. She drove the Jeep to a lake on the edge of town and sat on the grass in the shadow of a looming radio tower that broadcast death metal music to the greater Millstone County listening public. For five uninterrupted hours she lounged with her back against the tree, the pole in her hands and a line in the water. She got no bites. It didn't matter. She hated cleaning fish. If she'd caught one, she would have thrown it back.

People who didn't know her sometimes asked why she lived in a small town on the Jersey shore, where the only action after midnight was the checkout counter at the twenty-four-hour A&P. They pegged her as a city gal, but the truth was, she'd spent enough time in cities during her teenage years, crawling like a flea in the mangy underbelly of urban life. But didn't she miss the excitement? She told them she got enough excitement in her job. *I'm a PI*, she would add, invariably clarifying, *a private investigator*. If necessary she could supply them with edited and sanitized anecdotes, complete with funny endings.

Truth was, not all her cases had funny endings, and not all of them could be sanitized. And she was much more than an ordinary PI. But people didn't need to know about that.

By six o'clock she was drowsy after a long day of doing nothing. She reeled in her line, packed up her gear, and steered the

Jeep into town, or what there was of it.

The downtown strip of Brighton Cove was four blocks of gift shops, eateries, and real estate offices. There was a consignment shop where she bought hats, and a sporting goods store where she bought ammo. One of the more unprepossessing buildings housed her detective agency, which she'd named Last Resort—an anteroom with two ratty garage-sale chairs, and an office with a scuffed-up desk, a mildewed sofa, and a window overlooking her parking space in the side alley.

She didn't look out that window very much anymore. Not after what happened last March. She'd thought the passage of time and the change of seasons would bring closure, but the summer was nearly over and, for her, nothing had closed.

On days when she wasn't working, her habits were obsessively regular. Sure, it would be safer to vary her routine and keep potential enemies off balance, but she kind of enjoyed daring fate. Besides, if a bad guy had her number, she was probably screwed no matter what she did. So it would have been no surprise to anybody that at precisely six fifteen PM she parked at the curb outside the Main Street Diner.

The little coffee shop boasted a menu every bit as imaginative as its name. Cheeseburgers and pies were the staples, but every evening a chalkboard tented beside the door advertised the dinner special. Tonight's special was scallops. There were other offerings on the menu, but she didn't look at them. She always had the special. She was so predictable that Lizbeth, the waitress, didn't even bother to take her order anymore.

Lizbeth let her seat herself at her usual spot, a corner table by the window with a view of the entrance and a wall at her back, and then delivered Bonnie's usual summertime drink, pink lemonade. She would have preferred a Jack 'n' Coke, but liquor licenses were hard to come by in Jersey, and no eatery in Brighton Cove had one except the Mute Swan, a snooty, overpriced restaurant in the Prince Edward Hotel, and everyone knew the hotel's proprietors were mob-connected.

At the table she took off her hat, a cute little Panama number. She felt strongly that everybody should have a thing. Her thing was hats. There was no deep reason behind it. She just liked hats.

She sipped her drink, gazing into the pink depths of her glass. When she looked up, she saw Dan Maguire in the doorway. He strode up to her table and set his hands on the chair across from hers.

"Seat's taken," she said.

"I don't see anybody using it."

"Wow, I just can't put one over on you, can I?"

He sat. "Sometimes, Parker, I get the feeling you don't want me around."

"Nobody wants you around, Dan. Something on your mind?"

"You're always on my mind."

"Didn't Willie Nelson sing about that?"

"I dunno. Did he?"

Brighton Cove's chief of police was not a music buff, evidently. "He did. But I'm guessing he meant it in a romantic context. Unless he was thinking about the IRS."

"Yeah, old Willie is a tax cheat, isn't he? But I guess there are worse things to be. Aren't there?"

"How should I know? I've led a very sheltered life."

"Not sheltered enough. You don't fool me, Parker. People look at you with your sweet little cheerleader face. They don't think you're dirty. But you are dirty, and we both know it."

"You're way off, Dan."

"Am I?"

"Yeah. I was never a cheerleader. I played field hockey."

"And you played dirty, I'll bet." His smug smile was nauseating.

She brushed a blond wisp off her forehead. "You know, sometimes I almost get the impression you don't like me."

"I don't like it when people break the rules in my town."

"So it's your town now? You've been chief for less than a year and already you're acting like you founded the damn place."

"I'm paid to keep order. That means keeping a lid on crime."

"Biggest crime in this jerkwater burg is a flock of geese jaywalking across South Street."

"Gaggle."

"What?"

"It's a gaggle of geese. And you're wrong. We get crime here. Just last night there was a break-in at Starkey's."

The sporting goods store. "What'd they take, a bat and a Wiffle ball?"

"I get it. You don't respect the law."

"That's not it, Dan. I just don't respect you."

"That mouth of yours will get you in trouble someday."

She shrugged. "I like trouble."

His fingertips drummed the tabletop. She wondered if he stayed up late thinking of new ways to be irritating. "So," he asked, "where were you that night in March, anyway?"

Usually she didn't bother to hide her feelings, but she could be inscrutable when she wanted to be. She used her poker face now. "You really want to have this conversation again?"

"The case is still open. And it has your stink all over it."

"I wasn't aware I had a stink."

"I can nose you out a mile away."

"Guess I'd better change my deodorant."

Dan Maguire was forty years old, but his hard, squinty eyes reminded her of her grandfather, a dogged, wiry, sunbaked brown nut of a man who'd worn himself out with physical labor in a lifelong struggle against poverty. She'd known her Pop-Pop only glancingly; her upbringing was too chaotic to allow time with relatives, and he died when she was ten. But she remembered the day when he took her aside and said he saw himself in her—the same tenacity and determination. The words scared her, because she didn't want to be like him, hard and unfeeling. But he'd been right, hadn't he? He had seen who and what she was.

"Parker? You still with me, or did you find someplace better to be?"

"Anywhere away from you would be a better place, Dan. It would pretty much have to be."

"You're not winning me over with your charm."

"I'd have to be a snake charmer to do that."

"Now that's just unfair. I'm not the one who's cold-blooded." He smirked at his own cleverness. He did that a lot. It was just one of his many appealing traits.

She sighed, bored with him. "Did you have something you wanted to say to me?"

"Where were you that night?" he repeated, persistent as a dog working a bone.

Lizbeth arrived with a plate of scallops. Bonnie let it cool in front of her.

"Maybe we should be talking in the company of my lawyer," she said.

"You haven't got a lawyer."

"I could get one."

"No need. This is just an informal chat."

"Aimed at putting me behind bars."

"You wouldn't necessarily do time. Not if you could convince a jury it was self-defense. So ... where were you that night?"

"Home alone."

"Curled up reading a good book?"

"It wasn't that good."

"No one to vouch for your whereabouts. No one to back up your alibi."

"Why would I need an alibi?"

"Why indeed?" He let a pause hang between them before asking, "Know who I ran into today?"

"I don't give a rat's little pink dick who you ran into."

"Mrs. Gillian Hart. Small world, huh?"

"Small town, anyway."

"She was at Granger's Farm, buying a wreath."

"Little early for Christmas."

"A wreath for a grave."

"Oh."

"I asked her about you."

"Kinda figured you'd already done that."

"Sure. But I asked again. Thought her memory might be better."

"Is it?"

"Nah, she still doesn't know you from Adam."

"Sounds definitive."

"Funny thing, though. In a town this small you'd think everybody would know everybody."

"Mrs. Hart and I travel in different circles."

"Yeah, I'm sure that's true. She would have no reason to come in contact with you, unless she required your services."

"And she told you she didn't."

"I've found that people who require your services often forget they know you when official inquiries are made."

"If they forget, how do you know they ever hired me in the first place?"

"Someone does. You make a living, don't you?"

"That's not a crime."

"Depends on how you go about doing it. Of course, lately business hasn't been so good, I guess."

"It's not bad. Despite your best efforts."

"My efforts?" His puzzlement was badly feigned.

"I know you're behind it, Dan. It has *your* stink all over it. Malicious gossip is potentially actionable, you know."

"Geez, Parker, it's not like I'm trying to run you out of town or anything. Not like I think you'd be better off relocating out of state. It's not like that at all."

"Good to know."

"I want you to stay close so I can nail you."

"What does your wife think of that ambition?"

"I know Gillian's lying. I know her husband hired you. And I know you killed him."

Bonnie fixed her gaze on him. Her eyes were deep blue and

she knew how to use them. Her stare could unsettle most men, but Dan just sat there and took it. "If I killed her husband, wouldn't she want to cooperate with you and help put me away?"

"There might be reasons she doesn't want to cross you. You're a killer, after all. Bonnie Parker, gun for hire." He studied her with ostentatious interest. "That's an interesting name you've got. I always thought it was familiar. Other day it came to me. Faye Dunaway."

"Never heard of her."

"Sure you have. You're named after a notorious criminal."

"My dad liked outlaws."

"Then you've done him proud, haven't you?"

She sipped her lemonade. "Keep riding me, Dan."

He leaned across the table. "It suits you, too. You're just like her—a pure sociopath. A person incapable of normal human emotion."

"I know what a sociopath is."

"That's because you are one," he said triumphantly. Yes, it was quite the devious verbal trap he'd lured her into.

"You're so full of shit, Dan."

"I don't think so. I've got your number. You're a freak of nature, like a serial killer."

"Serial killers are all played out. I like to stay ahead of the trends."

"I've met mobsters, made men—there are one or two in this town. I've known gangbangers who'd open fire on a crowd in a drive-by."

"Nice class of people you associate with. Goombahs and street lice. It suits you."

"My point is, they're nothing compared to you. They've got some humanity—at least a spark. I look into your eyes, I don't see any spark at all."

"Maybe you just don't light my fire."

"I don't think there's a fire to be lit. I think, on top of everything else, you're a sexless, frigid bitch."

"Ooh, that's really hitting below the belt."

"I'm watching you, Parker. I'm watching all the time."

"You didn't happen to see where I left my earrings, did you? I've been looking everywhere."

His hands curled into fists. "I'm going to get you. It'll take time, as all worthwhile things do. But I will get you."

"Good luck with that."

"All it takes is one slip. You'll get careless and spill something to a friend. The friend will talk. And that'll be that."

"I don't have any friends."

"Well, isn't that sad? Guess you scared them all away."

"What's scary about me?" She let the question dangle unanswered, then jerked forward. *"Boo!"*

He flinched—couldn't help himself—and she laughed.

"Who's looking sad now?" she asked.

"Screw you, Parker."

"Yeah, you wish, buddy boy. In your friggin' dreams."

He got up, peeved at his inability to rattle her. Before leaving, he took one more shot. "Ever visited the Edna Mahan Correctional Facility in Union?"

"I'll put it on my to-do list."

"You should. Get a preview of your next twenty years. A twelve-by-twelve cell with a bull dyke for a roommate. An hour of exercise in the yard every day."

"I thought you said the jury would be swayed by my self-defense plea."

"I said it was possible. It's also possible you could go away for the duration. If this state still had the death penalty, you could even get the needle."

"Good thing they repealed it, then."

"Sure is, Parker. You have such delicate wrists. It might be hard to find a vein."

He left. She stared down at the plate of scallops, not so hungry anymore. But to leave them uneaten would be to give him a kind of victory. She ate them all, feeling them slide down her throat like cold dead things.

"You and Danny don't get along so well, do you?" Lizbeth asked when she refilled the lemonade glass.

Bonnie wondered how much the waitress had heard or guessed. How much anyone in town really knew. "He's an asshole."

"Don't I know it. Thinks he's God's gift. Always been that way. I knew him since I was a kid. He grew up next door to me."

"Yeah?"

"His family had this dog, a Dalmatian. Pepper, her name was. Do you know they kept that dog locked in a shed out back, day and night, all year long? And they never cleaned it out. I mean, she must've been ankle deep in her own shit. It was Danny's job to feed her. He'd open the shed a crack, toss in some dog chow, and you'd hear him slam the door, *bam!* Animal cruelty is what it was."

"Nobody reported it?"

"You know how it is in this town. No one wants to make waves. And with his dad on the force ..."

"Yeah. I know how it is."

"That's the thing about Danny, though. He wasn't just lazy or careless about the dog. I think he got a kick out of keeping her shut up in there. I think he liked it."

"Great guy to have as chief of police."

"I wouldn't cross him, that's for sure. He's not the brightest, but he's bullheaded as all get-out. And I think he still likes it—slamming that door."

Bonnie thought about that as she finished her dinner. What she'd learned about Dan didn't come as any shock. Cruelty and evil rarely surprised her; she didn't hold a high opinion of human nature to begin with.

Still, while she might not like people all that much, she did like animals. And what Dan Maguire had done to his dog Pepper really toasted her Pop-Tarts.

She left Lizbeth a nice tip, as always, then took a stroll to the pet store down the street. In the alley behind the store, she found plastic bags of animal waste in a trash bin. She took a good-sized bag and sauntered over to the police station on High Street, just off Main. Dan's car was in the parking lot. His personal car, a shiny new Buick Regal. It was locked up tight, but the front window on the driver's side was open a few inches.

"You can smell my stink, huh, Danny boy?" Bonnie tore open the bag. "Well, smell this."

She poured the bag's contents through the gap in the window, piling up a noxious brown hill on the leather seat.

As she walked away, flies were already swarming around the Buick, fighting for a piece of the action, and life was good.

2

Pascal had enjoyed cutting the woman's throat.

There was an art to it. Too deep a cut would produce a fountain of arterial spray from the carotid. The mess would be considerable. Pascal disliked messes. Too shallow a cut, on the other hand, would leave the victim with enough strength to cry out and perhaps fight back.

An amateur would simply jam the blade into the neck and rip it sideways. This was mere butchery, of no aesthetic value whatsoever. The expert, the man who took pride in his work, understood the importance of self-control. The knife, like any other weapon, was an extension of one's own body, and the body was the avatar of the mind. A calm and focused mind would do neat and careful work.

Pascal had been supremely calm as he touched the knife edge to the woman's throat, applying the perfect degree of pressure while he guided the blade in a light semicircle that opened a deceptively thin seam in her white skin. It had looked like nothing, that seam, barely more than a paper cut, except for the sudden spill of blood in a thin but steady flow. She had clutched her neck, trying to speak, her eyes huge and frightened, her throat weeping red tears. And he had watched, appraising his work with a connoisseur's eye and judging it good.

That was yesterday, in Manhattan. The job had gone well, leading him one step closer to his objective.

It was seven PM when he arrived in Brighton Cove and checked into the only motel on the highway, the Coach House, an

L-shaped cluster of single-story units huddled behind a dilapidated Vacancy sign. As the establishment's sole amenity and selling point, the sign boasted CABLE TV.

He parked the Lexus outside the office and dinged the bell at the registration desk, summoning the sweaty overweight manager. He paid in cash, requesting a room without neighbors—a request easily met, as the motel was largely empty. There was a moment when Pascal looked up from his wallet to find the manager studying him with shifty, worryingly alert eyes. But it was only a moment, and then the man's features relaxed into indolent indifference.

Pascal gave it little thought. His face often drew stares.

In his room, he laid his suitcase on a wheezing luggage rack. Inside were several changes of clothes, recently laundered at a public laundromat, neatly folded and stacked. Years of traveling had made him an expert at packing with maximum efficiency. There were also multiple pairs of black leather gloves, sheepskin leather lined in cashmere, identical to the pair he was wearing. He wore gloves nearly always. He had to.

In addition to the suitcase, he carried a duffel bag stocked with gear. The contents of the bag made commercial air travel impractical. He relied on an expensive but discreet service that could send a private aircraft to any landing field in the western hemisphere on short notice.

His work had taken him all over the world. He loved cities, the rush and crush of crowds, the anonymity of urban life. In a provincial backwater such as this, a man with his features stood out too sharply. He disliked being noticed, preferring to pass unseen and unremembered.

Still, his appearance had its advantages. Some of his employers had been known to call him El Diablo, and he did not think the nickname was spoken entirely in jest. They regarded him with something akin to superstitious fear. That was good. Fear was always good.

Most of his assignments had taken place south of the border.

Seldom had he visited the United States, and for that he was glad. He despised the effete degeneracy of this country, the softness of its people, their arrogance and complacency. Their ancestors had been men of parts, but these moderns were bloodless parvenus. Eunuchs—infantilized, permanently needy, shirking responsibility, fearing hardship—the useless products of a fin-de-siecle culture.

He was a man of a different spirit and a different age. To his employers he might be a devil, but when he looked into the mirror he saw a wandering privateer, a knight errant. Every era had its freebooters, its bandits, its mercenaries—the men who belonged to no country, who survived by strength and skill, shifting for themselves, accepting isolation, deprivation, and danger. Those few were truly alive. The rest were bloated slugs battening on pap —the burghers and rentiers. Today there were more of them than ever, and fewer men like him.

He had visited a fortuneteller once, a white-haired lady in a Sao Paulo apartment crawling with cats. She told him he had been a knight in the Crusades. Fired with zeal, he had slaughtered the infidels in many battles before falling at the gates of Jerusalem. Toward the end of his life, she said, he had begun to doubt the virtues of war. Had he lived, he might have become a spiritual seeker. But it was not to be—not in that lifetime. Perhaps in this one.

He could not say how much he believed of her story. But he did think he was moving along a spiritual path. He might be a monster—most people would say so—but if so, he was a self-aware monster. Like Prospero taking ownership of Caliban, he could say of himself, "This thing of darkness I acknowledge mine."

Whether or not the fortuneteller had read him truly, he was certain this lifetime was not his first. He saw his essential self as a river flowing through many lands. Different terrain, different people crowding the banks, but always the same river, the constant current of his being. He had worn other lives like so many suits of clothes, and there were more lives to come, a wearying succession of them, with never an end. He did not think there was a higher purpose or ultimate meaning to it all. He did not think it was part of a master plan. It was just how things were. There was no point to it, except to exist and to go on existing, forever and ever, amen.

People called him crazy when he talked like that, so he had learned not to talk of it. He knew, though. What the dull-witted understood as reality was no more than a glimmer of light on water. True reality was not the object of contemplation, but the mind that contemplated. He had known only one other person who understood. She had been lost to him for years, yet she was still more real than anything around him, more truly present than any passing strangers. His Beatrice, his Galatea, his morning and evening star.

He hung his suit in the closet and placed a few items around the room, but left most of his belongings in his luggage. In the event of a hasty departure he would have no time to repack. His satchel, bearing several items of a high-tech nature, remained stowed in the Lexus. He did not expect to need it. From years of experience, he had developed a sixth sense about such things. He knew when he was on the verge of success. He could feel it in his nerve endings, taste it at the back of his throat. His intuition had never failed him. It would not mislead him now.

Soon, very soon, his work would be done, and he would be on his way out of this decadent country, and for the first time in his life he would be free. Finally—free.

His gloved hands flexed, and he felt his mouth stiffen in a smile.

3

The Tenth Avenue Freeze-out in Miramar was an ice cream parlor named after an old Bruce Springsteen song, which the locals would know, because while to most people Springsteen might be just another washed-up sexagenarian rocker, around here he was a graying, frog-voiced demigod. The place offered a variety of sundaes and cones with Springsteen-inspired names like The Boss and The E Street Shuffle, none of which made any sense in the context of ice cream. Bonnie ordered a Thunder Road, two scoops of dark chocolate in a sugar cone.

She hung out in the parking lot, working on the cone and chuckling occasionally as she imagined Dan Maguire's reaction when he found a load of dog poop in his car. She was a big chuckler, did it a lot. At times it was more like a chortle. Like now, for instance.

She'd needed a pick-me-up. Things had been rough lately. Her income was down, way down. The chief's whisper campaign was working. As word got around that Bonnie Parker was involved in some ugly business that had gotten a client killed, she found herself less likely to get the small, everyday jobs any PI could handle—spying on a wayward spouse, tracing a runaway kid. Milk runs, but they paid the bills.

Without the usual scut work, she was reduced to waiting for another one of her special cases, the kind that called on her particular, unadvertised skill set. Not that she was exactly itching to put another notch in her gun, but, hell, a girl had to eat.

She could hardly advertise her custom services in the Yellow

Pages, and her clients, knowing they were accessories, weren't likely to talk; but somehow word got around. There were rumors. In a small town there were always rumors. The previous police chief, a graying grandfatherly type who knew how the world worked, had been willing to look the other way. Dan Maguire was less understanding. He didn't like anyone freelancing on his turf.

She found herself licking the cone faster in a losing battle to consume it before it dripped all over her arm.

Anyway, another job would come along. There was a steady demand for her expertise. Since opening her PI shop, she'd taken care of five people. One of the five had been put down in self-defense, and the other four had been eliminated proactively, so to speak. What the hell, if the government could start a preemptive war, she was entitled to do some preempting of her own.

Things would work out. Or she would end up dead, and all her worries would be over. It wasn't so far-fetched. She was twenty-eight years old and figured there was an excellent chance she wouldn't make it to thirty. Like her namesake, she seemed fated to die young, and not in bed. But like the original Bonnie Parker, she would have had a hell of a run.

***

On her way home from Miramar, she took a detour to Atlantic Avenue, parking a few doors down from number 44, the home of Mr. and Mrs. Andrew Wright and their daughter, Sienna, a sophomore at Holy Cross High School.

She got out of the Jeep. The tree-lined street was growing dark. The trees creaked in the wind, heavy branches swaying.

Next to 44 Atlantic was a vacant lot, large and overgrown. She hiked through a tangle of pine trees and holly bushes, binoculars swinging from her neck.

A fence divided the Wrights' backyard from the empty lot. Back in January, Bonnie had climbed the fence, shimmied up a tree outside Sienna Wright's bedroom, and forced the window. No one had been home, making it easy for her to install a UHF transmitter inside the smoke detector in the ceiling. The detector was hardwired into the main current, and she had run the bug off the current also.

The transmitter had a range of two hundred yards, more than adequate to reach the oak tree where the receiver-recorder mechanism was concealed in a knothole. The receiver ran on a lithium-ion battery which had to be changed weekly.

She replaced the battery, then yanked the 2GB thumb drive from the receiver's USB port and slapped in a new one. The old one went into her pocket.

Before leaving, she raised the binoculars and scoped out the upstairs window on the far left. The curtains were open and the girl was inside, talking on her cell phone. She looked relaxed and happy. Bonnie smiled.

A lot of the time she found herself feeling dirty. But not now.

Watching Sienna, she felt clean.

***

Her place on Windlass Court was as compact as a gingerbread house in a fairy tale, but with a bigger mortgage. The house was originally a single-family residence, but sometime in the '70s, when real estate values started to soar, the owner had the inspiration of dividing it in two, making a duplex out of it. Bonnie owned the west side of the building, which put her marginally farther from the ocean than her next-door neighbor, Gloria Biggs.

Proximity to the ocean was not much of a selling point in any case, since the house was located eight blocks inland, a hundred yards from the railroad tracks. At night, instead of hearing the roar of the surf, she could listen to the rumble of commuter trains and the occasional howl of the town fire siren. Good times.

She parked the Jeep in the garage, which was rigged with a high-intensity overhead light that came on when the door opened. The light allowed her to see every inch of the space before she pulled in. Unlike other people, she didn't pile up cardboard boxes or old furniture in her garage. Clutter was dangerous. It offered concealment for the kind of person who wanted to be concealed.

The garage was separate from the house. She walked along a

path that had been overgrown with shrubbery when she bought the place. She'd convinced Mrs. Biggs the yard would look neater if all those sprawling, messy plants were cleared out and replaced with a few flowerbeds. She didn't give a crap about landscaping. She just didn't want somebody jumping her from behind a hedge.

Mrs. Biggs was outside now, watering the flowers. The watering can had lady bugs painted on it. Mrs. Biggs' sweater—yeah, she wore a sweater in August—was also adorned with lady bugs. Big lady bug fan, was Mrs. Biggs.

"Hey, Gloria," Bonnie said, sketching a wave.

She looked up from her roses. "That man called again."

Bonnie stopped. "Did he? What'd he say this time?"

"He wants to know what you did with the gun. The thirty-eight, he said. That's a revolver, isn't it?" She might be seventy-something years old, but she was still sharp as hell.

"Yeah."

"He said it could be in a landfill or a lake, or you might have held on to it. He told me to ask if you have it hidden in the house."

"I don't."

"No need to tell me. I wasn't actually asking. And there was one other thing."

"Okay."

"He said he knows why you did it. You were protecting the girl."

She crossed her arms. "He said that?"

"Yes. Just that way—the girl. No name. I asked, what girl? He only laughed and hung up. He's a sly one, isn't he, or at least he thinks he is."

"Caller ID?"

"Unknown party, same as always. I star-sixty-nined him, but all I got was a recording that said the service wasn't available for that number."

It wouldn't have mattered. He had to be using a burner—a throwaway cell phone, the kind that couldn't be traced. The only hope of IDing him was to hear his voice. Bonnie had thought about asking Mrs. Biggs' permission to hook up a recording device to her landline. But she didn't want her neighbor more involved than she already was.

"Okay, thanks, Gloria. I guess you're wondering what this is all about."

"None of my beeswax. Which is exactly what I tell people when they ask about you."

"People ask?"

"Oh yes. I say you're quiet and you keep to yourself."

That was what neighbors always said about the killer in their midst. "Sorry if I'm making things awkward."

"Not at all, dear. I'm happy to have you around. It's like having a superhero next door."

"I'm no hero, super or otherwise."

"Well, it's certainly more interesting than living next door to a CPA or an insurance salesman. There's just one thing that puzzles me. It's a rather personal question, if you don't mind."

Bonnie braced herself. Here it came. How could a young girl like her get mixed up in such bad business? Why didn't she find a more respectable line of work, or settle down with a husband? Didn't she know she was throwing her life away?

"Go ahead," she said warily.

"For the life of me, I can't figure out why you don't just pop this guy. He sure as hell sounds like he's got it coming."

Bonnie laughed. "Well, it would help if I knew who he was."

"Oh, I see. But once you identify him, then—bang?"

"No comment. Take care, Gloria. And if that creep calls again, tell him to get lost."

"Oh, I couldn't do that. But I *will* tell him to fuck off!"

She went back to watering her rose beds. Bonnie walked on, but not quickly. She was thinking.

Mrs. Biggs was right, of course. If she ever did identify the guy, there would be only one way to handle him, and it ended with a bang. Kill or be killed was the oldest rule of the animal kingdom, and the one most strictly enforced. You could bitch about it, but you couldn't get around it.

The guy had been calling Gloria Biggs once or twice a week for the past month. He knew things about Jacob Hart. The extent of his knowledge became clearer with every call. Sometimes she thought it might be Dan Maguire, playing some kind of weirdo mind game, calling Mrs. Biggs because he was afraid Bonnie would recognize his voice. And Dan would have read the autopsy report, of course, so he'd know about the .38. But there was no way he could know about the girl.

No one knew about her, no one who was still alive.

Except ...

Bonnie shook her head slowly. She didn't like the explanation she'd come up with, but it was the only one she had.

She had reached her front door, but it no longer interested her. She wasn't going inside, not yet. She had another stop to make in town.

Moving swiftly now, she retraced her steps to the garage, climbed back into her Jeep, and aimed it toward the beach, heading for 1212 Ocean Drive, the residence of Mrs. Gillian Hart.

4

The Hart house was the most expensive property in town, a rambling Edwardian pile known as a "cottage" in the local lingo. A century old, it dated back to the days when Brighton Cove was the getaway of choice for wealthy Philadelphia merchants who built feudal manors to celebrate their own awesomeness.

Bonnie parked across the street by the boardwalk, where her aging puke-green Wrangler was less likely to draw attention. She crossed Ocean Drive. The sun was brushing the horizon, and the weather was turning. Gray clouds boiled in the northern sky. She never paid any attention to weather reports; she liked surprises. It looked like tonight would be stormy. Probably the rain wouldn't come soon enough to prevent the fireworks down at Point Clement, a Tuesday night tradition in the summer. She never attended anyway. The only fireworks she liked were the Hollywood orgasm kind.

A pair of recumbent stone lions guarded the front steps of the Hart residence. They looked surly. No doubt they served as an effective deterrent to Girl Scouts hawking Thin Mints. Near the lions stood a bronze jockey holding a lantern. He had been a little black guy once, but at some point in the property's history someone had repainted him as a little white guy, making him a hair less politically incorrect.

She rang the doorbell and waited. It was time she and Gillian Hart had it out.

The door opened on a squat, squarish housekeeper with a

round Aztec face and suspicious eyes. "Yes, I can help you?"

"Is Mrs. Hart at home?"

"Who I say calls?"

"Bonnie Parker."

"You wait please."

The door shut. Bonnie waited. At least the lady had said *please*.

She passed the time adjusting her hat.

The door opened again, and the housekeeper was back. "She have guest."

"Sure she does."

"Is true."

"I don't care if she's entertaining the Queen of Sheba."

"She does not see you," the woman said firmly. "You go away."

"I not go away," she said, slipping into the housekeeper's speech pattern. "You tell her I'm not leaving until we talk."

"She say you no go, she call policeman."

That was a poor bluff. Gillian Hart couldn't afford to bring the police into this.

"Listen. You tell Mrs. Rich Bitch if she doesn't let me in, I'm gonna cool my heels on her front porch till the neighbors start to talk. Tell her she's got an appointment with me whether she likes it or not. And tell her she'd better like it. *Comprende?*"

The housekeeper looked scared. "You wait."

"I wait," Bonnie told the closed door. She figured if the gatekeeper still refused to budge, she would muscle her way inside and track down Mrs. Hart on her own. The house was big, but not that damn big, and there couldn't be that many places for a grown woman to hide.

The housekeeper returned in forty-six seconds. "She see you. Five minutes. Then you go."

"Whatever." Bonnie figured she and Gillian had more than five minutes' worth of conversation to get through, but she wasn't going to quibble over details.

The housekeeper led her through the foyer. Bonnie had never been inside this house. She had expected dusty heirlooms and faded oil paintings of disapproving ancestors. Instead, there were angular chairs, glass coffee tables, and soft music, something mellow and New Agey, playing through an unseen speaker system. Down one of the hallways she heard a murmur of voices—a man and a woman. Maybe Gillian really did have company, not that Bonnie gave a crap.

She was escorted to a glassed-in sun room at the rear of the house, looking out on a landscaped yard where croquet matches were sometimes played. The view through the glass walls was dimming, the sun edging toward the horizon.

"She come," the housekeeper said, leaving. She seemed glad to get away.

Bonnie circled the room, taking in its details. A recliner, a pair of rattan straight-back chairs, a bowl of fruit—real, not wax. A housefly batting its tiny brains out against the glass panes. And on the wall, a photographer's portrait of the late Jacob Hart.

She had enough self-control not to flinch from the photo. It startled her, though. In the portrait he looked exactly as he had on the day he'd visited her office. She remembered how he'd made a comment about the agency name on the door.

"Last Resort? Is that what you are?"

She couldn't tell if he was puzzled or pissed off. "For some of my clients, I'm afraid it is."

"You're not my last resort, Miss Parker. I have unlimited resources. I can go anywhere I choose."

"And yet you came here. I'm flattered."

"I came here because you're convenient. You're the only private investigator in town."

But she knew he was lying. He hadn't picked her for convenience. He was aware of the full range of services she offered, and he thought he would have need of them. She could tell. She could see it in his eyes—that desperate, cornered look.

He wasn't a fat man, which was too bad, because he really

should have been. He would have worked well as a bad guy in an old movie, the obese malevolent crime lord with his fingers tented on his belly. He might not have the jowls and the belly fat, but he had the rest of the act down pat—the sly smile, the half closed eyes, the phony courtesy, the bored demeanor.

His wife had come with him, the two of them starchily dignified, looking out of place in her shabby digs. She knew them by reputation, two of the wealthiest locals, and in Brighton Cove that was saying something. They were in their late sixties, childless, known for their charity work in New York. He had expanded a family-owned grocery store into a chain of upscale bodegas, Hart & Hawthorn; the name persisted, though Mr. Hawthorn, the father's partner, had long ago sold out his share. The stores offered a variety of exotic produce imported from Latin America. Bonnie had bought some stuff there. The cherimoyas were pretty tasty.

Jacob did nearly all the talking. He made a pretense of being calm, almost bored, as he explained his predicament. Months ago he fired one of his top people, a certain Kurt Land, for embezzlement. Land denied everything, and the parting was ugly. Now Land had found a way to get even. He'd held on to some company documents pertaining to a financial indiscretion, a matter that wasn't necessarily illegal but couldn't be made public—Jacob didn't go into details—and he was blackmailing his former employer. Jacob had paid him off once already, but predictably Land had come back for more. It was now apparent to Jacob that he would never be rid of the pest—that was what he called him, "the pest"—unless other arrangements could be made.

Bonnie had no love for blackmailers; they ranked only slightly above rapists, kidnappers, and email spammers on her list of undesirables. A greedy blackmailer who didn't know when to quit was the worst kind. "I can talk to him," she said.

"I'm not hiring you to talk, Miss Parker. Kurt Land won't be satisfied with any amount of money. That's obvious. He'll go on milking me until he's drained me dry. We need to make him go away."

And there it was. The kind of statement that always made its way into these conversations when her special skills were in demand.

Even so, she took no action until she had satisfied herself that Jacob's story was true. She insisted that he make the next payoff, which she observed from a distance, watching through binoculars. She saw the satchel of money change hands. A week later Jacob came to her with a recorded phone conversation in which Land demanded yet another payment.

"You see? The man is insatiable. He cannot be reasoned with. He hates me for firing him. He's found a way to get revenge, and now he won't stop—until he *is* stopped. You know what I mean, Miss Parker. We are both worldly people. You know what I require you to do."

Gillian wasn't with him that time, and he seemed to feel more free to speak. Bonnie in turn felt freer to answer. "I'll take care of it," she said quietly. "But my services don't come cheap."

"Nothing worth buying ever does."

It took her ten days to find an opportunity to make her move. Her chance came on a weekend when her quarry left his home and hiked into the Pine Barrens, toting a crossbow. She nicked him from a distance, then hunted him through the fresh-fallen snow until he could run no more.

And then everything had gone to shit, and now she was keeping more secrets than usual while Mrs. Biggs fielded telephone calls from a creep who knew things he shouldn't know.

This line of thought was making her edgy. She took out a cigarette and lit it. Yeah, she was a smoker. Parliament Whites. Cancer might kill her someday, but she was betting some random member of the criminal population would get the job done first.

"Put it out."

The voice was Gillian Hart's, and it came from the doorway.

Bonnie turned. "Excuse me?"

"Smoking is not permitted in this house."

"Hey, if I can smoke people, I can smoke cigarettes."

Gillian pursed her lips. "You're most uncouth."

"Wrong. I'm plenty couth, except when I'm being jerked around."

"What is that supposed to mean?"

"I think you know. I'm on to you, Mrs. Hart."

Gillian turned away, seeming more annoyed than rattled. "You'll have to leave now."

"Yeah, that's not gonna happen. Sorry to interrupt your hostessing duties, but you and me are about to enjoy some quality time."

"Do you know what kind of risk you've taken by coming here? A patrol car could cruise past at any moment and see your car parked outside."

"I parked by the beach."

"You've still taken an unnecessary chance. There can't be anything you need to say to me."

"Wrong again."

"You want to talk? All right, then. Convince me you didn't kill my husband."

Bonnie took a long drag on the cig before answering. "I did kill your husband."

"You admit it? Just like that?"

"Just like that."

Gillian gave a delicate shudder. Bonnie ignored it. She knew an acting job when she saw one. In her taxonomy, the human species was divided into sheep and wolves. Gillian wasn't one of the sheep.

"You're a monster," Gillian said. "We never should have hired you."

"No, probably not. I have this way of getting to the bottom of things. I'm sort of a nosy Parker, pardon the expression. If your husband didn't want his dirty little secret to come out—"

"Who are you to talk about dirty secrets? Your whole life is a dirty secret."

"I'm not the one who was being blackmailed. Though I'm guessing that's about to change."

"Change, how?"

"I can't help thinking that's your ultimate objective in setting up those phone calls."

"What phone calls?"

"Come off it, Mrs. H. I know you're behind them."

"I'm not behind anything. You're saying someone else knows about—about Jacob's indiscretion?"

"His indiscretion and a whole lot more. Which means it's gotta be you. Unless you blabbed to somebody else."

"I've never spoken with anyone about this matter. Not once."

She didn't appear to be lying. "Hmm. Well, that's a pickle. 'Cause if it's not you, then who the hell is it?"

"There's no one else. No one." Her eyes narrowed. "Not if you did your job."

"I always do my job."

"Kurt Land went missing in the Pine Barrens, but the search parties didn't find his body."

"That's because they didn't look in the right place."

"Or possibly you made a deal with him. Spared his life in exchange for a payoff."

"What payoff? Your husband got his cash."

"There was ten thousand dollars missing."

"Land must've spent it or socked it away somewhere."

"Or did it end up in your pocket?"

"You think I can be bought that cheap?"

"I think everything about you is cheap."

"Cut the crap. I played it straight down the line. It's your hubby who didn't go by the rules. He hid in the alley behind my office—"

"Nonsense."

"He hid in the alley," Bonnie repeated. Gillian had never heard her side of the story, and she was going to hear it now. "I'd been working late on this really boring case where I had to go through approximately a million emails. That night I didn't leave till after ten. Must've been bleary-eyed from reading all that crap. I didn't see his car parked at the end of the alley."

"This is a fantasy."

"He waited till I opened up my Jeep. When the dome light came on, he had a clear target and he fired. He was a good shot. He didn't miss by much. But I was better. I didn't miss at all."

"Absurd. My husband didn't even own a firearm."

"Yeah, he did. A Sig Sauer forty-five. Nice one, too. Maybe you didn't know about it. There were other things about him you didn't know, remember?"

"No gun was found on his body."

"I took it off him. Couldn't let the police find it. They'd know it had been fired. Then we're talking about a gunfight, and what we want it to look like is a mugging gone wrong. Otherwise it raises too many questions."

"The police found only one bullet at the scene. The one that killed him."

"That's because his shot went into my Jeep. It lodged in the headrest. I dug it out later and dropped it in the Crab River inlet, along with his gun."

"Well, I don't believe Jacob ever had a gun. I believe he was unarmed and defenseless, and you killed him—murdered him— because he'd violated your sense of propriety, if vigilantes have such a thing. You lured him to your office that night and gunned him down in cold blood. And you counted on me to say nothing because—well, because ..."

"We both know why you can't talk. But you're wrong about me. I thought maybe you'd listen to reason, but I guess not."

"How dare you take that tone with me."

"Take a tone? What, you're my mother now?"

"Get out."

Bonnie finished her cigarette and stubbed it out on an end table. "No point blaming me for what went down. It was his play, not mine. He started it. I only finished it."

She started to leave. Gillian's voice stopped her.

"You have a great deal of confidence in yourself, don't you? It will be the death of you. One of these days you'll come up against somebody more formidable than my husband. Somebody who's better than you are."

Bonnie met her eyes. "Bring it on."

"Have you ever visited Jacob's grave?"

"No."

"When that day comes, Miss Parker, I'll make it a point to visit yours."

The words pursued Bonnie as she left the house. She was thinking of the wreath Gillian Hart had purchased today and wondering, for the first time, if it was meant for Jacob—or for her.

5

Pascal chose to dine in elegance tonight. It was a caprice, prompted by the certainty that the job was nearly done, the prize almost his. He wished to salute his good fortune and to meditate on a storied career now drawing to a close. Perhaps such congratulations were premature, but he was in an expansive mood. He felt light and almost happy, a state of mind rare for him.

And so he left the shabby motel and took the Lexus into town, searching for a suitable place to eat.

The black SUV had been his for less than twelve hours. Previously he had driven a rented Lincoln. After taking care of the woman in Manhattan, he had found it prudent to change vehicles. The switch was probably unnecessary; he had no reason to believe anyone had seen his car parked in the woman's neighborhood; but such precautions were second nature to him now.

He abandoned the Lincoln in a different part of town, then stole the Lexus by the simple expedient of ambushing its owner in a parking garage. The victim never saw his face, and except for a gash in his scalp he would be none the worse for the experience. Later, Pascal exchanged the vehicle's license plates for those of another Lexus, reducing the risk of being pulled over by an alert patrol officer with a BOLO list. His policy was to leave nothing to chance.

For twenty minutes he cruised the dark boulevards of the small beach towns. In a community called Miramar, he found an Italian restaurant that appeared acceptable. The decor was understated, the lighting dim, and the menu posted in the window offered a pleasing range of entrées at prices sufficiently high to promise adequate culinary quality. He allowed the hostess to seat him at an out-of-the-way table. As a solitary diner, he would naturally be exiled to some remote corner of the room; such was the unspoken rule at all dining establishments. He did not mind. He valued privacy.

It had been some time since he had indulged his appetite for fine food and drink. When on an assignment he was strict with himself, maintaining spartan discipline. At all other times he walked a middle path between the self-denial of the ascetic and the self-indulgence of the sybarite. He was a connoisseur. He believed in enjoying the good things of body and soul, but always in moderation. Anything could be done well, done expertly, and when done to perfection, it was an expression of eternal truths. Even the simple act of eating could reflect a refinement of spirit and rise to an expression of art.

As could the act of murder, of course. He was no moralist. He drew no normative distinctions.

He spent some time studying the menu and chewing a breadstick, before informing the waiter that he would like the Chilean sea bass. It felt like the proper, patriotic dish for him to order.

"I have not seen your wine list," he added, "but perhaps a good Riesling ..."

"I'm sorry, sir. This is a BYO place."

"A what?"

"Bring-your-own. We don't serve alcohol here. We don't have a liquor license."

"No spirits? Not even wine?"

"Sorry. But there's a liquor store right down the street. You can buy anything there and bring it in."

"I must do my own shopping?" he asked incredulously.

The waiter shrugged. "It's the law, sir."

"Very well. Hold my table."

Pascal found all this most ridiculous. A restaurant in this price range that did not serve wine—madness. But symptomatic of American society, where the population no longer objected to laws that treated them like children. Quite the opposite—they wanted to be coddled and cocooned, diapered and burped by their smiling, officious overlords.

He would not miss this decadent country when he departed. And he would never come back. He promised himself that.

The liquor store was three doors down, a tawdry little shop with blinking lights in the windows and cases of beer stacked on the dirty tile floor. Beer and hard liquor were its mainstays, but there was wine at the back. In a refrigerated cabinet he saw an acceptable chardonnay.

The cabinet worried him, though. He feared refrigerators. Did not use one in his home. Consumed only fresh foods stored at room temperature.

But surely he could reach inside and grab the bottle. He had his gloves on. It would be all right.

He opened the cabinet and retrieved the bottle, and there was no problem. The blast of cold air troubled him briefly, but the gloves did their job, and now he was retracing his steps through the store, toward the clerk at the checkout counter.

But the bottle itself was cold, colder than he'd expected, and its chill began to invade the fingers of his right hand. He switched the bottle to his left. No good. Now he felt it in that hand also, felt it through the glove's leather, or perhaps it was only his imagination, perhaps he was deceiving himself ...

"You okay, mister?" the slovenly, sleepy-eyed clerk inquired.

He tried shifting the bottle back to his right hand, but his fingers wouldn't work and it slipped free and hit the floor with a crack. Nothing dramatic, no explosion of shards, merely a sharp percussive noise and the bottle rolling, a narrow seam open in its side, amber liquid spilling out.

"Hey," the clerk said.

Pascal looked at the spreading puddle on the floor and felt ashamed, like a child who had wet himself. He stepped away from the puddle, toward the door.

"Pal, you gotta pay for that."

Pascal wasn't listening. He could feel the first needles of pain probing under his fingernails like bamboo shoots. He knew what was coming. He had to get out.

"You break it, you bought—hey!"

Out the door, down the street, running past the restaurant with its stupid, incomprehensible policies, onto the side street where he had parked the Lexus. He needed all his remaining coordination to insert the key into the door lock and then into the ignition slot.

The SUV rumbled to life. He pulled away from the curb and drove east for a mile, arriving at the boardwalk, where he parked. He turned up the heat, set the blowers on high, and struggled to peel off his gloves.

His hands came into view, the skin shading from dead white to cyanotic blue. For the moment all circulation past the wrists was cut off. The pain was an electric burn.

He held his bare hands in front of the vents, letting hot air wash over them in a healing stream. The car's interior grew hot, unbearably hot and close, stifling in the summer night, but he didn't care. His hands needed warmth. Like hothouse flowers, they must be cleansed of the fatal chill.

After several minutes the pain began to subside. His hands tingled as blood began to circulate again. The attack had been blessedly short-lived. He was not always so fortunate. Some attacks could last for several hours. One terrible episode had tormented him for a full day.

He had consulted doctors around the world. All agreed that he suffered from a rare circulatory malady in which exposure to cold caused the blood vessels of his hands to spasm, restricting blood flow and leading to pain, numbness, and loss of muscular control. During a severe attack his fingers could become spastic, useless.

That was all they could agree on. Every possible underlying cause had been considered. Hypothyroidism, Raynaud's disease, scleroderma, diabetes ... Tests ruled out each possibility, leaving him with a mystery ailment that persisted despite all his efforts to find a cure.

He had tried natural remedies, overcoming his skepticism of such things. He had applied homeopathic ointments and gobbled ginkgo biloba capsules. He had even visited a healer once, a shaman with a reputation for working miracles.

Nothing had helped. His only relief was obtained by wearing gloves to protect his hands and warm them. In private, sometimes, he removed the gloves to massage his fingers. His hands were ugly things, scabby with old cuts and slow-healing sores; his poor circulation left him vulnerable to ulcers of the skin and impeded the healing of even minor lacerations. But he had grown accustomed to their appearance.

What he never quite got used to was the cold. Even sheathed in black leather, his hands were cold. Sometimes merely chilly, sometimes freezing. He felt the cold always, and on rare occasions when another human being touched his bare fingers, that person felt the cold, as well. One woman—the one special woman of his life—had told him that it was like taking a corpse's hand. She had not said it unkindly, but her words stayed with him.

At times he wondered if he was not a corpse already, or some eldritch thing between cadaver and man. He wondered if the essential coldness of his nature, the very quality that made him so good at his job, had not migrated to his hands, as it would, in time, migrate to other parts of him, creeping over him and through him until eventually, like Shakespeare's dying Falstaff, he would be cold all over, as cold as any stone.

He shook his head, retreating from such thoughts, and focused on practicalities. He could not return to the restaurant, of course. It did not matter. He had lost his appetite.

For now he needed rest, an hour or more of rest in a darkened room, to calm his mind and soothe his nerves.

Before commencing the drive to the motel, he pulled on the gloves to hide the ugly travesties of his hands. He couldn't help smiling at himself. All this, because he had insisted on wine with dinner—because he had been in a celebratory, even romantic mood.

"You are an old fool, Pascal," he said aloud in his native language, emphasizing the point with a cluck of his tongue.

Forty-six was not old for any normal man. But it was ancient for a man in his line of work. He had outlasted all his rivals. He might as well have been a hundred years old, and just now he felt those years, a century's worth.

"It is good that this is the last job," he whispered, putting the Lexus into gear.

Yes, good for the knight errant to hang up his scuffed and dented escutcheon, his creaking and tarnished armor.

And better still to do it after his boldest triumph, the attainment —soon—of his holy grail.

6

Gillian Hart was telling the truth. Bonnie was almost sure of it. But if Gillian hadn't talked, who had?

There was nobody—nobody who was still alive.

She lounged in the parked Jeep, her eyes half closed, hat tilted back, a lazy stream of smoke curling from her cigarette. The night was fully dark and the wind was picking up. The surf sounded rough. She tried to think of anybody who would know the things her phantom phone caller knew. Business associate of the Harts? Friend of Kurt Land? A hunter in the Pine Barrens who'd witnessed the shooting and put things together?

None of those options seemed likely. But she couldn't come up with anything else.

She finished her cigarette and headed home. At her front door she punched a six-digit code into a control panel to disarm the security system. The system covered every access point. High-end locks on the doors and decorative bars on the windows completed her defenses. The half-duplex she called her own might not look like much, but it was a fortress. Nobody was getting in without her say-so.

Paranoid? You bet. But she'd learned early that eternal vigilance wasn't just the price of liberty; it was the price of staying alive. The world was a rough, unforgiving place, and it made you scratch and claw for every morsel, and it never let you drop your guard.

The house was quiet now; Mrs. Biggs generally retired early, which was a good thing, since while she was up she tended to engage in her hobby, which, as best Bonnie could tell, was banging things against the wall. The bad thing was that she also rose early, the better to get a head start on the day's wall-banging.

In a way Bonnie preferred the morning's racket to the dead silence that settled over the house at night. The silence had the texture and weight of loneliness. It wasn't so bad, though. She was accustomed to loneliness. Loneliness—and darkness. That was her life.

Kill or be killed, that was how she rationalized her way of doing business, but part of her couldn't help wondering why she'd chosen a profession that pretty consistently placed her in that position to begin with.

Sure, she filled a need. There were holes in the justice system, and it was her job to fill those holes. She was sort of like caulk, except she spent less time in the bathroom.

But she had no illusions. What she was, ultimately, was a killer for money. It didn't exactly put her in the same category as Mother Teresa.

And when she told herself she was different from other killers because she tipped Lizbeth the waitress, or because she got a kick out of playing dress-up and wearing hats, or because she set boundaries for what she would and wouldn't do, she knew it might be only so much smoke. Yeah, she had standards. But everybody had standards. The prisons were crammed with guys who drew the line at executing a child, a woman, a cop, a priest. Standards like that were no proof of humanity. They said nothing about the heart.

The heart. That was the real issue. Did she have a heart? Or was she a sociopath, like Dan Maguire said?

She didn't like that question, because she feared the answer.

Briskly she undressed and tossed on pj's and a robe, then went into her dining room, which she had converted into a home office by the simple expedient of setting her laptop on the dining table. She took out the thumb drive she'd retrieved from the knothole and popped it into the computer, then opened the audio files. The transmitter and recorder were voice-activated, so she didn't have to wade through a week's worth of ambient sound from an empty room. Roughly eight hours of content had been recorded, most of which was the girl's TV or stereo. She fast-forwarded through hours of junk, pausing to sample any conversations the bug had captured. Talks with mom and dad didn't interest her, but phone conversations with Sienna's friends were worth hearing. The chats were gossipy and silly and mostly innocent, with only a few allusions to a particularly hot make-out session with a senior in a McDonald's parking lot. That was okay. Bonnie wasn't trying to fit the kid for a chastity belt.

An hour of listening convinced her that things were still cool. She spent some more time on her computer, not buying anything, just window shopping. If she'd had the bucks, she would've sprung for a new speed-loader, a shoulder harness, maybe a Taser. You know, girly stuff.

A few minutes after nine, her phone rang. It was her cell, the only phone she had; as an economy measure she'd dispensed with her landline. It was either that or give up pizza, and she loved pizza.

Her phone was a Samsung Galaxy, and it was named Sammy. It had a shocking pink case and a ring tone that was the opening bars of "A Hard Day's Night." She'd equipped it with a Caller ID app that displayed names and addresses, even for callers using cell phones. Tonight's call was from Alan Kirby of 133 Old Road, Farmdell. She didn't know him.

"Parker," she said into the handset.

"Bonnie Parker? The private detective?" His voice was hushed and urgent.

"That's what it says on my business card."

"I need your help."

"You can see me in my office tomorrow—"

"You don't understand. I need your help *now*."

"It's getting kinda late. Can't this wait till morning?"

"By morning, Miss Parker, my whole family could be dead."

7

Bonnie made good time to Union Avenue, replaying the phone conversation in her mind. It hadn't lasted long. Alan Kirby had to meet with her, but not at his house. His wife and kid, gender unspecified, were asleep, apparently unaware of their impending demise.

She'd arranged a rendezvous at the little gazebo on the boardwalk near the Union Avenue entrance, then tossed on the first clothes she found in the hamper, unsure offhand if they had been washed or not—a pair of black denim jeans and a pullover shirt with tiny print across the breasts that spelled out *If you can read this, you're too damn close*. She'd stuck her feet into a pair of white Nikes, grabbed her handbag, and picked out a hat, settling on a powder blue bucket cloche. It never hurt to be stylish.

When she arrived, he was already there, sitting in the gazebo. Only one vehicle was parked nearby, a Honda minivan, just right for a family man.

The boardwalk and beach were nearly empty. Way down the beach, one of those big sweepers was combing the sand, the driver working late.

She settled onto the bench opposite Alan Kirby, keeping her purse on her lap. In a special compartment of the purse was a sweet little Walther P99. Just knowing it was there made her feel all warm and fuzzy inside.

She looked him over. He was about forty, nervous and chinless, with darting eyes and a tongue that flicked at the corner of his mouth. Sort of like a lizard.

"So," she said, "what's the deal, Neil?"

He looked confused. "My name's not Neil."

"It's a rhyming thing. Like, what's the plan, Stan? Or, what's the story, Maury?"

"Oh. Okay."

"Besides, nothing rhymes with Alan. Or Kirby. Except maybe furby, but I don't know how I'd work that in."

"I don't think I told you my name."

"My phone did. Told me where you live, too. Farmdell. Nice area. No ocean breezes out there, but the property values are way more reasonable."

He nodded, but she wasn't sure he was taking it in. He seemed distracted, looking past her, staring at shadows.

The wind was stronger now, but the rain was holding off. On the far horizon, silent flashes of blue and white lit up a stack of fat thunderheads. The moon was up, but playing peek-a-boo behind scudding clouds. The breakers thrashed themselves against the jetties, sending up cascades of foam that sparkled on the rocks.

"I think we're alone here," he said after a long pause.

"Why wouldn't we be?"

"I was afraid of being followed."

"We're alone. Relax, okay?"

He focused on her for the first time. "You're prettier than I expected."

"Aw, you're sweet. But I'll bet you say that to all the gumshoes."

"Sorry. I didn't mean any offense. It's just that I was expecting somebody, you know, tough."

"You wanna call the whole thing off, just say the word."

"No. No, of course not. I'm just wondering ... Well, I've been told you offer certain special services."

She liked the sound of that. "Maybe."

"And somehow, you don't look like the type."

"What type is that?"

He licked his lips. "I don't know. Forget it."

"I can get the job done, Alan. If that's what you're worried about."

"How long have you been a detective?"

"Six years."

"Not exactly an obvious career path. Why'd you choose it?"

"It was more interesting than joining the steno pool. Also, I don't think they have steno pools anymore."

"What's the real reason?"

"The real reason is I didn't have a college degree, or even a high school diploma, so what the hell was I gonna do? I had street smarts. I played to my strength. Or did you want me to say I got into detective work so I could help people?"

"Didn't you?"

"Shit, no. I hate people."

Alan laughed. She liked him a little better for that.

"And how long have you been doing ... this other thing?"

"Three years." She lit a cigarette, ignoring his disapproving wince.

"So you've got, um, experience?"

"Enough."

"Right." He rocked back and forth in his seat like a child.

A couple of joggers in annoyingly good condition chuffed past. She waited until the pair had gone before asking, "Something bothering you, Alan? What's on your mind?"

"I just can't see ... How can you, you know, *do* it?"

"Just pull the trigger."

"I meant, does it bother you?"

"No."

"Why not?"

"Because some people are asking for it."

"I see." But he didn't.

She wasn't sure just how to explain it to him. A person who needed killing was a lot like pornography—hard to define, but you knew it when you saw it.

"I have rules," she said, aware that the rules, like a lot of basic truths, were hard to put into words. "Lines I won't cross. Like, if you said you needed your daddy out of the way so you could inherit the family business, I'd tell you to take a hike. If you said you were bored with your wife and wanted her gone, I'd tell you to go fuck yourself. But if you said someone was out to get you and the law couldn't help—I'd be interested."

"That's the situation here."

"Okey-doke. If the biographical portion of the interview is over, I'd like to get down to business."

Alan nodded.

"So what's the dealio? Why do you think you and yours could be dead by daylight?"

He looked toward the beach, where the surf hissed on the sand. "A man is after me."

"After you, how?"

"Following me. Showing up at odd times in odd places. A stranger."

"When was the first time you laid eyes on this man of mystery?"

"Two days ago. But I think he's connected to something else. It's complicated. I'm not sure where to begin."

"Try the beginning. Keep going till the end. Then stop."

He breathed a sigh. "I'm an attorney. Six months ago I started a law practice in McKendree Park. My idea was to serve the low-income population. I guess I thought there would be a certain glamor in it. But the truth is, my clients are mainly, well ..."

McKendree Park had been a burned-out slum since the race riots of 1970. "Meth heads, hookers, and bangers?"

"I wouldn't go that far. A lot of them are just confused kids—"

"Yeah, whatever." She didn't care about his client list. Scum deserved legal representation just like anybody else. "Stay on point. You think your anonymous admirer is connected to your job?"

He nodded. "Back in April, a woman—girl, really—came to my office complaining about her boyfriend. She'd broken it off with him, but he wouldn't leave her alone. He was abusive, threatening. You know how it is."

"Yeah. I know."

"I got a restraining order, which naturally the boyfriend ignored. I went to the judge and reported the violation. Multiple violations, actually. The judge, a no-nonsense type—Kittridge, maybe you've heard of him—sentenced the kid to two hundred hours of community service. Specifically, picking up trash on the shoulder of Route 35."

"Okay."

"It seemed to work out, except there was something I didn't know. The kid in question—well, he's not a gang member himself, but he's got this cousin, Darius." He pronounced it Da-rye-us. "And Darius is a honcho in the G-Rocs. You know about them?"

She blew a jet of smoke at the gazebo's hexagonal roof. "Drug crew operating out of McKendree and Maritime, with some franchises farther south."

"That's them. Darius doesn't like having his cousin out there on the side of the highway in an orange vest. Thinks it's embarrassing for the family, or for the G-Rocs, or whatever. He's ... displeased."

"How displeased?"

"My client, the ex-girlfriend, saw me again two weeks ago. She said there was a rumor Darius wanted to come after me and my family."

"Come after as in terminate?"

"Of course. These people don't fool around."

"The G-Rocs are pretty hard-core, but I don't know if they're wacko enough to put out a hit on a civilian over something this minor. Maybe they're jerking your chain."

"That's what I thought at first. But a few days later she's on the phone with me, saying they've definitely hired somebody to get it done."

"Hired somebody? You mean like an outsider working a contract?"

"Apparently."

"Why would they outsource? If they're nutty enough to go through with the idea, they can handle it with a drive-by, keep it all in-house."

"According to her, word was it couldn't be anyone local. Had to be somebody from out of town, who can't be traced to the G-Rocs. She said they brought in someone from Colombia."

"Colombia?" This was getting weird.

"The gang is reputed to work with the Medellin cartel."

"You sure your client isn't using some of the G-Rocs' product? This is turning into a Steven Segal flick."

"I know it sounds far-fetched. But a couple of days ago I spotted a guy hanging out by my office. Yesterday he's sitting a few tables away from me at the Surfside Cafe. I heard him place his order. He has a foreign accent. Could be Latin American."

"There are a million Latin Americans around here."

"This guy was following me. I'm sure of it. I took his picture."

She lifted an eyebrow. "Considerate of him to pose for you."

"I snapped it with my phone."

He fumbled in his shirt pocket and took out his cell, then navigated to his photos. Framed in the screen was a shot of a man in a leather jacket sitting at a window table, a coffee cup in his hand. The street scene outside was a haze of glare.

"You said this was the Surfside Cafe? In Algonquin?"

"Yes."

She didn't think so. The view through the window might be only a white blur, but somehow it didn't have the feel of anyplace local. Alan was probably lying about that. It didn't faze her. Most people lied most of time.

The man in the photo was entirely bald, his scalp so polished it nearly gleamed. He was in his forties or older. His face was pale and oddly batlike, with its pushed-up nose and looming triangular nostrils.

And he was wearing gloves. Black leather gloves. That was kind of kooky. Nobody wore gloves in summertime. Maybe the guy was a germophobe. Or a fingerprintophobe.

"What do you think?" Alan asked.

She sucked down a long stream of smoke. "He's ugly as ass."

"And ...?"

"Definitely not local. I would've noticed a kisser like that."

"And the café is miles from my office. It can't be a coincidence."

"Anything could be a coincidence."

"He had to be tailing me."

"If so, it was sloppy of him to get made that easily."

"Maybe he wants to be identified. Maybe he likes to put a scare in his target before he makes his move."

"Maybe." It wasn't the way she'd do it. "And all this because Darius doesn't like his cousin picking up soda cans and fast food containers?"

"I'm just telling you what I know," he said, his voice rising.

"Okay, Alan. Settle down. Stay cool."

"I am cool."

"Sure you are. Like a squirrel on the turnpike. Mind if I send this pic to my phone for future reference?"

"Go ahead."

She transferred the photo, then gave him back his cell. "So, you're afraid this guy you spotted is the hitter, and he's getting ready to take you out."

"And my family too. Maybe. All three of us. That's how the G-Rocs roll."

"But you haven't told your wife?"

"I didn't want to worry her."

"Yeah, a hit man on her tail just might give her the heebie-jeebies. I'm a little surprised you left them home alone."

"They're asleep already. And our house has a security system, a good one. No one can get in."

She didn't argue. The customer was always right, even when he was wrong. "So tell me something. Where's your friendly neighborhood police department in all this?"

"Nowhere. I haven't talked to them."

"Why not?"

"Because they can't protect me. You know that. There's been no actual crime—not yet. Only a rumor and a couple of sightings of a guy who's not local. They'd tell me I'm paranoid. Especially given who I am."

"Yeah? Who are you?"

"A guy who represents the people they're trying to put in jail."

"So the cops don't like you because you help the bad guys get away? They're still obliged to come to your assistance."

"If you're naive enough to believe that, you haven't lived in Jersey very long."

"Long enough."

"So you know it's bullshit."

"Yeah. But it felt like something I should say."

A tribe of kids on bikes flashed by, ignoring the signs that banned bicycles on the boardwalk.

"The police aren't going to help me." He shrugged. It seemed to be less an expressive gesture than a nervous tic. "To them, I'm the enemy."

"I know the feeling," Bonnie said, taking another drag off her cig.

His story made a certain amount of sense, but she wasn't quite buying it, and not just because the photo was sketchy. She decided to change tacks. "You said you opened your law firm six months ago. What were you doing before that?"

"How is that relevant?"

"It probably isn't. Tell me anyway."

"We were living in Manhattan. I worked for an international charitable organization. People Against Poverty. They feed hungry people in underdeveloped—"

"Got it. You were a professional slacktivist."

"I take it you disapprove of charitable activity."

"I just think it's pointless. You spend your life trying to save a bunch of strangers. What for?"

"To make a difference."

"But you never do. You save one, and up pops another one. Nothing ever changes."

"So we shouldn't even try?"

"That's what I'm getting at."

"How about you? Why do you do your job?"

"I get paid."

"Are you always so cynical?"

"Pretty much. I don't have that high an opinion of my fellow man. If you're so gung-ho on do-goodery, why aren't you still polishing your halo?"

"We weren't accomplishing enough. There were too many bureaucratic and diplomatic obstacles. Too much politics. We needed to get things done, but really we were just spinning our wheels." His frustration sounded genuine.

"And there were no problems with this charity, no issues?"

"What kind of issues?"

"You didn't discover they were funneling donations into private bank accounts in the Caymans?"

"Of course not. There never was anything like that. It's a totally legitimate organization."

In her experience, there were no totally legitimate operations, but she let it slide. "Terrific. So you left on friendly terms. You had a good job there? Good salary?"

"Yes ..."

"Which means you could have parlayed that position into some other Manhattan gig, right? Corner office, personal secretary, key to the executive washroom, three-martini lunches on the company expense account?"

"If I were applying for a job in the 1960s, maybe."

"Funny. You know what I mean. You could've kept living *la vida loca*. But instead you're living *la dolce vita*. You ditched your high-paying job and your big-city life, and plopped yourself down in Mayberry RFD to be a low-rent lawyer for incorrigibles."

"I wanted to do some good. To accomplish something for once."

"You can take the boy out of charity work, but you can't take the charity work out of the boy?"

"Something like that. I still don't see why you need to know this."

"I'm just wondering if this stalker—assuming he really is a stalker—could be connected with your past, and not with the G-Rocs at all."

"That's ridiculous. I already told you—"

"I know what you told me. But there are holes in your story. I can't see the G-Rocs flying in a shooter from Colombia to take care of something this small-time. It doesn't add up."

"So you won't help me?"

"Didn't say that. The fact that all the pieces don't fit is a feature, not a bug. Makes it interesting. But if there's anything you're not telling me, anything you don't want me to know—either spill it now or walk away. Because I need to know it all, and I will find out. I have a way of getting to the bottom of things."

"There's nothing I'm hiding."

"All-righty, then. I don't suppose you've got any idea where to find this freak?"

"I know exactly where to find him. Room thirty-two of the Coach House. You know, the motel—"

"On the highway. I call it the Roach House. Nice place to crash if you don't mind spunk on your sheets."

"Evidently he's not too particular."

"And just how do you know your chum is holed up there?"

"The motel manager is a client of mine. He has his share of legal problems."

She didn't doubt it, inasmuch as the Roach House was a rendezvous point for half the hookers and johns in Millstone County, not to mention assorted drug dealers and their clients. "How'd the manager know you'd be interested?"

"I showed him the picture and asked him if the guy had a room there. As of yesterday he didn't. Tonight around six the manager called and said the man in the photo had just checked in."

This was starting to look a little too easy. It worried her. "He just happens to take a room in the one motel where you gave the manager a heads-up?"

"It's the only motel in town. Well, except for a couple of bed-and-breakfasts, but they're booked months in advance. The Coach House always has vacancies."

"Yeah, that's what happens when you rent rooms by the hour." She supposed it was a fairly high-percentage bet the hitter would go there. He would want someplace anonymous and close. But ... "If he's been shadowing you for two days, why is he just checking into the Roach House tonight?"

"How should I know? Maybe he moves around a lot. When the manager called me, I figured it was my chance. I know where he's staying. But there's nothing to arrest him on. I need to use ... other methods."

"And you thought of me."

"You came recommended."

"By who?" she asked, testing him.

"Someone I trust."

She liked the fact that he didn't spill the name. "All right."

"So what happens now?"

"You're going home to your wife and kid. And I'm going to the Roach House to pay a call on our mutual friend."

"And ... you'll take care of him? It's just that simple?"

"Nothing's just that simple. It's not that kind of deal."

"But I thought ..."

"I know what you thought. But I don't go to extremes unless the guy has it coming. For all I know, you could be putting two and two together and getting seventeen. Maybe this mook's an innocent tourist slumming it on the Jersey shore. Or you could have a hard-on to get him for some totally different reason than the one you gave me. You could be playing me."

"How can I prove I'm not?"

"You can't. But *he* probably can. I'll find out what he's up to."

"How?"

"I told you, I'm good at prying out secrets. I always find out what I need to know."

"But if you do have to, um ..."

"We'll cross that bridge when we come to it. Right now there's just one small but all-important detail to take care of."

Alan looked at her blankly.

"Cash on the barrelhead. Payment up front."

"Oh. Yes."

"My standard retainer ..."

"Twenty-five hundred. I know."

"And if my special services are required ..."

"Then there's a follow-up payment of twenty-five thousand. In cash."

"You came well informed."

He tried to hit a jocular note. "Hey, it's all about the Benjamins, am I right?"

"Way to keep current with the lingo."

She waited while he counted out hundred-dollar bills, placing them one by one into her palm. He seemed embarrassed by the transaction. She wasn't.

"I hope this'll be okay," he said as she stuffed the $2500 into the wallet in her purse.

"It's legal tender, isn't it?"

"I don't mean that. I mean, I hope you won't have to take any unnecessary risks."

"Taking unnecessary risks is my job description."

"I just don't want you to get hurt. All I want is for this to be over."

"I won't get hurt. And neither will you and your loved ones. I won't let that happen. Okay?"

"Okay."

"So chill already. I got your back, Jack." She smiled. "And yeah, I know your name isn't Jack."

8

Pascal, alone in the dark, nursing his tender hands.

The motel room was quiet. The sun was long gone, and with the curtains drawn over the front windows, no light bled in from the parking lot. The bed was comfortable enough, and though he was not tempted to sleep, he could close his eyes and watch the images that appeared and vanished behind his eyelids like splinters of dreams.

He saw his life, or snatches of it, moments plucked from memory—his boyhood in Chile, his life as a world traveler, the chances he had taken, the opportunities missed. So much of it was defined by his face and hands, the face that set him apart, the hands sheathed in protective gloves. His face had marked him as an outsider, denying him the pleasures of companionship, and his hands had made him wary of contact. He could not touch others or the world around him, a world that had never wished to know him anyway.

He had been forever cut off. And lonely. He could admit this to himself. He was lonely. He yearned.

He never spoke of it. To complain was not in his nature. Life was hard and unjust. So it had ever been. So it was meant to be.

Still, he sometimes caught himself wishing that things had been other than the way they were. If he had been blessed with better hands ... and another face ...

His face had not been so unnatural in early childhood, but by adolescence it had acquired its peculiar cast. The saturnine cheekbones, the razor-thin nose and prominent nostrils, the hollows of his eyes under black brows.

El Diablo.

Mephistopheles.

Lucifer.

Satan.

This diabolic quality had been accentuated by age. His receding hairline had progressively emphasized the high, smooth cliff of his forehead, until finally he had shaved off his remaining hair. His gums had receded also, giving his teeth an elongated, vampiric appearance when he smiled. And as he shed his last vestiges of youthful subcutaneous fat, his face became thinner, his chin more pointed, his bone structure more pronounced.

He had frightened a priest once. This was in Buenos Aires. He had taken refuge in a desolate slum church to escape the relentless sun. Inside, he was alone except for the priest, who saw him standing near the altar. The priest was about to say something when Pascal turned to him, and the man—a young man, younger than Pascal himself had been—gave a little gasp and shrank back. He did not make the sign of the cross or whisper a prayer or do any of the things a priest in a movie would do. There was only that sharp inhalation, that shuffling backward step.

Pascal wondered what the priest said of the encounter later. Did he speak about it to his friends, his fellow clerics, his congregation? Did he tell them he had met the devil?

Children, too, were afraid of him, except for the youngest, who stared with undisguised curiosity and sometimes even smiled. He liked children. He liked dogs, tolerated cats, enjoyed the company of horses. He read books of good quality—Cervantes, Dante, Shakespeare. He gave handouts to the poor. He was never rude, he was considerate of the elderly and the infirm, and he tipped generously. He was not the devil. He was only a man with a peculiar face and a profession that required the spilling of blood.

His employers—the ones who called him El Diablo and other such names—were hypocrites. He was their instrument. He acted on their behalf. They hired him, gave him his instructions, and then tried to shirk the blame. He, at least, was unafraid to confront the fact of what he did and who he was.

In his forty-six years he had learned many things. Hate and fear he knew. Love—yes, he knew love also. Knew it not quite so familiarly, not on the basis of such long and close acquaintance. Yet he did know. That was a secret he kept from his employers, from anyone who knew him.

The devil knew love. What a story that would be. Why had no one written it? The devil in love ...

He smiled in the dark, remembering.

They had been like children in some ways. They had pet names for each other. He was her Lancelot, she his Guinevere. He bought her jewelry and other trinkets. She wrote him poetry. In the darkness, close against his body, she whispered hungrily of obscene delights. She made him appreciate the pure pleasure of carnality for the first and only time in his life. She saw in him the soul of an artist, a soul uniquely made for her. She promised they would always be together, not only in this life, but in all their lives to come.

And then she left him. She gave no explanation. One morning she was simply gone, leaving behind a few handwritten verses as a parting gift.

He thought he knew the reason. She loved him, but she feared what he was and what they did together. She had been by his side as he practiced his dark trade. She had watched his victim die, and she had felt what he felt—the same forbidden joy. Taking a life could be a thing of beauty and sensual arousal. It frightened her. She ran from him to escape the shadow side of herself.

Perhaps she too had come to think of him as the devil. But the devil she feared was only the unadmitted desire of her own heart. The heart was not made only for love. It could conjure cruelties worthy of any imps of hell. He knew those cruelties. He had inflicted them himself, had taken pleasure in them.

Now there was no pleasure, only the dullness of an automated routine. He thought of the woman in Manhattan. At one time he would have received a thrill of uncomplicated sexual gratification from the successful completion of that act. Yesterday it had aroused him not at all.

He was tired. Tired of this life. A life well spent or misspent, he could not say. A life spent. That was all. A job done, or a long series of jobs, and now the last.

And then a new beginning.

He was not normally an optimist—in fact, he despised optimism as a weakness—but on this occasion he permitted himself a rare indulgence in hope.

He could be made new. He could be reborn.

9

Bonnie was behind the wheel of the Wrangler again, heading away from the boardwalk in the general direction of the highway, and thinking about her client's story. She wondered what was really going on.

She didn't like being played, and she was pretty sure Alan was playing her. But she couldn't see how or why. It intrigued her. The mystery was one reason she'd taken the case. The other was the $2500 folded into her wallet. Okay, that was the main reason, but the mystery didn't hurt.

A tinny rendition of "A Hard Day's Night" played in her handbag. Sammy was ringing. She fished out the phone, figuring Alan was calling with more info. Nope. The display read Unknown Caller. Which was weird, because her Caller ID app was pretty tough to defeat. Somebody must really want to be anonymous.

In New Jersey it was illegal to talk on a cell while driving. She answered anyway. It wasn't the first law she'd broken. "Parker," she said.

The voice that came back at her was a furious whisper. "You're dead, you little bitch. You're fucking dead."

She leaned back in the driver's seat, smiling. "Nice Freddy Krueger impression. Now do Bela Lugosi."

"Fuck you. You're a dirty whore, and I'm going to put you down."

"Is this the part where you ask me if I like scary movies?"

"God damn you to hell."

"Okay. Not a member of my fan club. So I'm guessing you're

my telephone stalker?"

"Put you down like a dog in the street—"

Bonnie chuckled. "You talked to Mrs. B. again, didn't you? And you didn't take it so good when she told you to fuck off."

"Go to hell."

"At least now we get a chance to chat." She cut her speed and eased over to the curb to hear him better. "So ... what's your sign?"

"Shut up."

"Mine's Gemini. The twins." She pressed the handset close to her ear, listening hard. The voice was familiar. It stirred a memory, one she couldn't quite grab hold of. "Which is funny, 'cause I'm an only child. It suits me, though. Geminis can be either very good or very bad. We're remote and distant, and some of us lead a double life—"

"Shut your goddamn mouth. Didn't you hear what I said?"

"Put me down, dog in the street, yadda yadda. Jeepers, who raised you, the Manson family?"

"Make all the jokes you want. You're still going to die."

"What'd I ever do to you?"

"It doesn't matter now."

The hoarse, crazed whisper was maddening. She almost recognized it. Almost. "Clue me in anyway. Just so I know what I'm getting killed for."

"You'll never know, Bonnie. And you'll never see it coming. I can get you any time. You could be taking a sip of coffee or reading the newspaper. Then—lights out."

"You're a freak with too much time on your hands. Move out of your mom's basement and get a life."

"I know you killed Jacob Hart. I even know why. You wanted to protect the girl. But you can't protect her. You can't even protect yourself."

"I'm hanging up now."

"Sienna Wright," he said.

A chill moved through her. He really did know. He knew everything.

"Who's that?" she asked as casually as possible.

"Sienna Wright of 44 Atlantic Avenue. She goes to Holy Cross High School in Miramar. Has a summer job at the Donut Shack on Route 71. Six thirty AM to one PM, Monday through Friday. She rides her bike to work."

"Are you stalking her, you asshole?"

"She's not the one I'm after. You are. And I know a hell of a lot more about your daily routine than I know about hers."

"Swell. At least you're thorough."

"It's not so much fun, is it? When you're the one being hunted?"

Being hunted ...

Then she had it.

The drifts of snow, the pale sky, the frozen pines.

He had whispered then too, his voice a wheezy rasp.

"Kurt," she said, "is that you?"

She heard a sharp intake of breath.

"Never mind. You just answered my question."

Kurt Land, Jacob Hart's blackmailer. A man who should be dead. Had to be dead. But wasn't.

"I'm going to kill you, Bonnie," he said after a long moment. A body speaking from the grave.

"Yeah, I got that."

"You took everything away from me."

She remembered the fallen man in the snow, his useless crossbow discarded nearby. The fear in his face, and the blood soaking through his trouser leg and his coat. "Not quite everything, I guess."

"You mean because I'm still breathing? That's nothing. I'm alive only because I have to kill you. That's my mission on earth. That's what keeps me going."

"Everybody needs a hobby," she said distantly.

"You think this is a joke?"

She shook off her shock and rallied. "No, buddy boy. I think *you're* a joke. Making threats over the phone—big whoop. Hell, until tonight you wouldn't even talk to me directly. I guess scaring grandma's more your speed."

"Fuck you, bitch. You're not getting it. You're a corpse."

"Funny, I thought that was you." People sure were in a hurry to put her in a cemetery plot lately. It was enough to make a girl feel unpopular.

"You didn't kill me as dead as you thought."

"Good to know."

"And now I get to take you out."

"Uh-huh. Tell you what, bub. When you grow the plums to look me in the face, we'll talk. Till then, I got places to go, and I really don't have time for this crap."

She ended the call and slipped Sammy back into her purse. Her hand, she noticed, was shaking just a little. Not from fear. It took more than a phantom phone call to put a scare in her. But knowing she'd left a loose end that big—it unnerved her. She was supposed to be better than that.

Well, live and learn. So it turned out Gillian Hart hadn't been altogether wrong. Kurt Land was alive. Bonnie didn't know how he'd managed it. She intended to ask him when they got together.

And they would.

Soon.

10

The Roach House was still her final destination, but after the phone call she had a stop to make first. She detoured down a side street on Brighton Cove's less fashionable south end, flicking her high beams on. The town was curiously low on street lights, and the few that worked seemed about as powerful as her keychain flashlight.

She parked outside a one-story bungalow. The house looked like all the others on the block, except for the ramp that had replaced the front steps.

Bonnie climbed the ramp and rang the doorbell, not worried about waking the occupant. He was a night owl. One of those up-till-two and sleep-till-noon types.

"Who is it?" Desmond called from inside.

"Parker."

"It's open."

Nice. No snooty housekeeper to contend with here.

She stepped into the living room. Moments later he appeared from the side hallway, moving fast, his hands spinning the chair's wheels. She had once asked him why he didn't treat himself to a motorized chair. He said he liked the exercise. Rolling himself by hand kept his upper body in shape.

It was no joke. From the waist down Desmond Harris might be a blighted and atrophied version of the man he had been, but above the waist he was a block of marbled muscle. "The Belvedere Torso," he called himself—an artistic reference that had meant nothing to her until she Googled it.

He was an artist, had been for years, and the car wreck that cut his spine hadn't changed that. Hadn't changed much of anything about him, actually. He still drove, using a handicap van. He had family money and ran a gallery in town, selling his own artworks and other people's. He had lots of friends, but Bonnie didn't know them. She liked keeping him to herself. They didn't go out. Their relationship wasn't exactly a secret; they weren't hiding it; but it was private. An emotional relationship, not sexual. She wasn't even sure it could be sexual, what with his injury. Maybe that was why she felt comfortable around him.

"Yo." Bonnie sketched a wave.

"Yo yourself. Restless legs again?"

"Say what?"

"When your feet start to itch, you come here."

"It's the only way I can see you. You never come to my place."

"That's because my feet don't itch." He shrugged. "Crip humor. So what's got you feeling antsy tonight?"

"Bunch of stuff. I don't want to talk about it."

"Fair enough. Hey, I just found *Wings* on streaming video. Want to watch?"

She looked at him blankly.

"You know, *Wings*? Clara Bow, William Wellman, World War One?"

"I've heard of World War One. The rest is just noise."

"It's a classic. From the silent era."

"A silent movie? Snooze."

"I'll take that as a no. How about some cocoa?"

"Cocoa would be good. I can make it."

"No one messes around my kitchen except me. Besides, I've tasted your cooking."

She nodded. "Fair point. Just let me freshen up. I'll be with you in a jif."

He headed for the kitchen, and she detoured down the hall. But she wasn't looking for the bathroom. Halfway along the corridor there was a ventilation duct in the ceiling, covered by a grill. She took a stool from the guest room, stood on it, and undid the screws holding the grill in place.

"What exactly are you doing?"

She glanced down and saw that he'd snuck up on her, the hum of his wheels inaudible. Damn. She was kind of hoping she wouldn't get caught.

"Only take a second," she said.

"That's not what I asked."

The grill popped free, flapping down on its hinges. She groped in the duct until her fingers closed over a Ziploc bag. She pulled it out and held the bag in her teeth while she pushed the grill back into place and replaced the screws.

"Is that a gun?"

She assumed the question was rhetorical, since the plastic bag was transparent, its contents clearly visible. She climbed down and returned the stool to the guest quarters.

"Parker," Des said again, "is that a *gun?*"

"It ain't a blow dryer."

She checked the bag without opening it. Inside was a matte black Smith & Wesson Bodyguard .38, five-round capacity. Four +P hollow-point rounds were still loaded in the cylinder. She had needed only one shot to kill Jacob Hart.

The bag was dirty, but the gun sealed in it looked no worse than it had in March, when she'd stowed it here during one of Des's bathroom breaks.

"You hid a gun in my *house?*" he said, outrage competing with disbelief. "Without even *telling* me?"

She bypassed his chair and retraced her route down the hall. "If I'd told you, you would've been an accessory after the fact."

"Accessory to what?"

"Let's just drop it, okay?"

"It's the Hart case, isn't it?"

Sometimes she forgot how small this town was, how much everybody knew. She'd never told Des about her extracurricular activities. How much he'd guessed, she couldn't say.

She turned. "I said, drop it."

"Why the hell would you stash it here?"

"Duh. Because nobody would look here."

She started walking again. When the hallway ended, she veered into the kitchen and poured herself a glass of water, stooping because all the sinks and counters had been lowered to wheelchair height. She didn't think he'd be fixing cocoa for her, after all.

"And if they did?" he asked, pulling into the kitchen behind her. "Wouldn't I be in a world of trouble if someone found it on the premises?"

"They didn't find it. No harm, no foul." She gulped the water, then felt his stare. "What?"

"You never thought about the consequences to me, did you? And you're not even sorry."

"What's there to be sorry about?"

He looked at her for a long moment, his face pale in the fluorescent glow. Slowly he shook his head. "You're a good person, Parker. I mean that. But damn, you can be cold around the heart."

She set down the glass. "Can I?"

He rolled forward, still watching her. He was no longer angry. He looked puzzled, pensive. "I think about you sometimes, you know. You're an interesting puzzle. An enigma wrapped in a mystery, locked away inside a hard shell."

"A shell, huh? You make me sound like a turtle." She considered it. "Or a bullet."

"I like turtles. Bullets, not so much."

"You should have better things to do than think about me."

"I have better things to do, but I think about you while I'm doing them. I multitask."

"And where has all this deep thinking gotten you?"

"You're angry."

"No, I'm just asking."

He shook his head. "That's my answer to your question. My

thinking has led me to the conclusion that you're angry."

"At what?"

"I don't know. Some injustice, maybe. Or ... something you lost."

"Everybody loses things."

"What you lost mattered."

"Care to take a stab at what it was?"

"I have a working hypothesis."

"Let's hear it."

"Your folks died when you were young, didn't they?"

She was surprised. "Did I tell you that?"

"You let it slip once. A rare moment of self-disclosure."

"So you think I'm pissed off at the world for taking my mommy and daddy away?" She laughed. "Yeah, Des, I'm all torn up inside."

"You must have felt something for them."

"No more than what they felt for me."

"Were they so awful?"

"Not awful. Just not—not parents. I mean, they raised me, sort of, but I was basically just an inconvenience." She stepped away from the counter. "Forget it. I'm not having this conversation."

He didn't move. His chair blocked the kitchen doorway. "You never open up, do you? Never let anybody in."

"Works for me."

"Does it? You're self-sufficient, I know. But you're also hard."

"Like a turtle. I got that."

"I'm serious."

She shrugged. "It's a hard world. As you ought to know."

"Why me? Because of this thing?" His fist smacked the armrest. "That's no big deal."

"It's all what you make of it, huh? Life gives you lemons ... Sorry, I don't buy that happy crap."

She moved decisively toward him, and he yielded, rotating the chair so she could get by.

"You'll tell me someday," he said, "when you feel you can."

She understood he was using psychology, offering her a challenge, and the really irritating part was that it worked. He knew she wouldn't back down from a fight.

"You want me to talk about my childhood? Okay, it won't take long. I didn't have a childhood. How's that?"

"Everybody has a childhood."

"Yeah? Well, I spent mine moving from one fleabag motel to another. My parents never raised me, never gave a shit about me. I was just one more item they had to remember to pack."

"Why'd they move around so much?"

"Because my dad was a crook. Not a very successful one. Strictly smalltime. He operated all over the Northeast, never stayed long in one place. He was always on the run from gambling debts and bad choices."

She had memories of her father, but not good ones. He stayed out all night drinking and playing cards, and sometimes he was gone for days, only to return with wads of cash that he doled out sparingly to her mom, keeping most of the money for himself. Bonnie didn't know where he got it, though she could guess it was nowhere good, and she didn't know what he did with it, but it never seemed to last.

"How about school?" Desmond asked.

"I went to a bunch of different schools, wherever we happened to land. There were long stretches when I didn't go at all."

"Friends?"

"Making friends is hard when you're always the new kid and you wear thrift-shop clothes. And when you cop an attitude, which I did."

"You had your reasons."

"Yeah, whatever. Anyway, when I was fourteen, I quit that life. I left a good-bye note for mom and dad, and went off on my own."

"And did what?"

"Bummed around the country, got a lot of mileage out of my thumb. Occasionally did some things that weren't strictly legal. Learned a healthy disrespect for authority."

"And you never saw your folks again?"

She shrugged. "My dad must've finally messed with the wrong people. Him and my mom turned up dead in a motel room in Pennsylvania. Shot execution-style. It was on the news. Pretty big story. Imagine that—my dad had finally made it big."

"How did you feel when you heard about it?"

"I felt—they're dead, and I'm not. Sucks for them, good for me."

"That's all?"

"A couple of outlaws on the run get whacked. Happens every day."

"Hmm."

"Hmm, what?"

"Outlaws on the run. Does that remind you of anybody in particular?"

She knew what he was saying. She didn't want to go there. "Give it a rest. Seriously, I don't have any depths."

"Maybe they're just unexplored."

"Let's leave them that way."

"You don't think it's significant that your parents—"

"Christ, Des. Just *drop* it. I don't give a shit about my mom and dad. You think I'd shed a tear over a couple of losers who never gave a damn about anybody but themselves?"

"I think losing them hurt you more than you're willing to admit."

"Well, I think you were right the first time. I'm hard and cold, like you said. And I like it that way. Okay?"

His eyes lowered. His voice was very soft. "Okay, Parker."

"Don't say it like you feel sorry for me." She brushed past him, flaunting her mobility, her legs. "You're a goddamn cripple, for Christ's sake. Feel sorry for yourself."

She left the house, pulling the front door shut behind her, not looking back.

11

Dan Maguire had spent an hour disinfecting his car after work, muttering curses the whole time. Dogshit all over the front seat, and a festival of flies. And it must have happened just after his little talk with a certain local PI.

Coincidence? Dan could just imagine himself raising that possibility with his old man, a longtime cop who knew the score. *Make like a shepherd*, Dan Maguire, Sr., would have told him, *and get the flock outta here.*

Then the old man would've busted out his big-bellied laugh, the same laugh Dan had heard from him right before his heart failed and he slumped over dead in their booth at the Lobster Pot.

Bonnie Parker was responsible for the pile of crap stinking up his Buick, but he couldn't prove it. He could never prove anything about her. He knew she was guilty—guilty of a whole lot more than vandalism. But as much as he wanted to pin that particular butterfly to his mounting board, she still fluttered maddeningly out of reach.

He reclined in the Barcalounger in his den, nursing a mug of Irish coffee, while some reality crap on Spike TV droned in the background. He wasn't watching. He stared at the motionless ceiling fan over his head, trying to figure out just how he could nail that blond bitch.

A sociopath. That was what she was.

Not long ago he'd read a book claiming that ten percent of the population were sociopaths. Since then, he'd been seeing sociopaths everywhere. The mayor was a sociopath. The mechanic at the Shell station. That asshole Gertz who was always being insubordinate at the morning meetings. All classic sociopaths. But Parker was the worst, because she was one of the minority of sociopaths who were actively violent. Not just a troublemaker, but a lawbreaker. And not just a lawbreaker, but a killer.

Her stunt with his car was typical sociopathic behavior. So was her blue-eyed innocent act. Even the hats she wore—they were probably a sign of a sociopathic tendency. You know, disguising her appearance, hiding her true self. What did the book call it? *Faking normal.* Right. She was doing her best to pass as normal, but he could see through her. He knew what she was.

"You're thinking about her again."

The voice was Bernice's. She stood in the doorway, arms folded, disapproval stamped on her face.

"Of course I am. I told you about the damn car."

"You don't know she did it."

He ignored her. "It was hardly out of the showroom. Still had that new-car smell. What you think it smells like now?"

"This will drive you crazy. It's eating away at you inside."

"It's my job," he said wearily.

"Oh, pish posh. It's your private obsession."

He thought about answering, but there was nothing to say. When he glanced at the doorway again, she was gone.

Bernice didn't get it. She didn't know how a problem like Bonnie Parker could work its way under your skin and fester and itch. And the more you scratched it, the more you made it bleed.

His wife was calm and practical. She knew how to let things go. Like when they had that row with the Dirksens. Bernice had patched things up with Molly right away, but Dan had held on to his grudge against Phil for months. Held on to it to this day, if truth be told.

Bernice liked to say she'd rather be happy than right. Dan didn't grasp that way of thinking. He couldn't be happy unless he was right. More to the point, he had to be proved right. He had to show the world. Had to show his old man, whose belly-laughing ghost still hovered around him, making him feel that even though he was chief of police, he hadn't measured up.

Sure, maybe he should just leave it alone. But he couldn't. It was like a puzzle where the answer was right in front of him, and he just had to *see*.

Their conversation in the diner hadn't given him much to work with. Parker played her cards close to the vest, he had to give her that. And he couldn't shake her, no matter how much he rattled her cage. She was cold, that one. Cold as fucking ice.

Still, there was one thing she'd said. When he'd brought up the subject of her name, she'd said her dad liked outlaws. And that was mildly interesting. Because among the many other mysteries surrounding Miss Bonnie Parker, there was the mystery of her past.

Dan had done his best to research her roots, but his efforts had come up empty. It was as if she had materialized in Brighton Cove at the age of twenty-two, with no history, no background, no family. He didn't know who her mom and dad might've been. There were candidates, though. A list of possible suspects.

Grunting, he heaved himself forward in the chair and leaned down to open the bottom drawer of the desk beside him. Inside was a manila folder, unlabeled. It contained everything he knew about Bonnie Parker, every scrap of information, innuendo, and speculation that he had acquired over the past six months. There wasn't much, but among the clippings were several news items, obituaries, and police reports pertaining to people who might have been her parents.

He riffled through the papers until he found the clipping he wanted. It was a newspaper story from the *Patriot-News*, dated fourteen years ago, and it reported the murders of Tom and Rebecca Parker in a motel in Conover, Pennsylvania, a rural area in the central part of the state.

The crime had never been solved. Dan knew that much from following up with the Conover authorities. And he knew something more. A teenage girl was with the pair when they checked in. This was confirmed by another guest and by the desk clerk, though neither witness could offer a decent description. It stood to reason that the girl in question was their daughter Bonnie, known to be traveling with them.

Their daughter was fourteen that year. And Bonnie Parker—his Bonnie Parker—was twenty-eight now. The timeline fit.

What's more, the girl hadn't been found in the motel with the bodies. Hadn't been found anywhere else, either. She had simply disappeared.

The newspaper story featured only a photo of the motel's exterior, which was of no interest of him. But the Conover Police Department had sent him a copy of their file on the case, which included a mug shot of Tom Parker from an arrest a year earlier. In the photo he regarded the camera with a quizzical, sly, half-amused expression. The arrest was a big joke to him. Maybe everything was a big joke.

Dan squinted at the photo, doing his best to see Bonnie Parker's face in Tom Parker's features. No luck. Tom Parker had been a scrawny, grizzled little guy, prematurely balding, rheumy eyed, snaggle-toothed. If Bonnie was his daughter, she got her looks from Rebecca, whose photo wasn't in the file.

But Tom sure looked like the kind of guy who admired outlaws. Hell, he had been an outlaw himself. Could have named his daughter after the most notorious female criminal in American history, the distaff half of Bonnie and Clyde, the white-trash matriarch of a gang that gunned down bank clerks and cops for fun? Dan thought so.

The authorities in Conover assumed the couple's daughter was long dead. Their hypothesis was that the killers, having finished with the mom and dad, took the kid and used her in unsavory ways until they got tired of her, then left her corpse to rot in the woods.

But suppose fourteen-year-old Bonnie hadn't died. Suppose she'd escaped somehow. Given that she'd never turned up anywhere, she must have gone off on her own, fending for herself. He pictured her, a feral wildcat of a girl, traumatized by whatever hell she'd been through, roaming the fields and the streets, learning to be cruel, to be indifferent to human life.

It was enough to almost make you feel sorry for her. But he was more interested in bringing her to justice. For the murder of Jacob Hart—and probably other crimes.

Once he'd figured out why Bonnie Parker's name was familiar, he'd taken the time to read up on her namesake at the library. He didn't care much about Clyde Barrow, a slick little dime-store crook, so gutless he'd hacked off his own damn toes to get out of chain-gang duty, a nobody in a pinstriped suit whose only skill was driving fast. Bonnie Parker was a more intriguing figure, famous for posing for her picture with a cigar clamped in her mouth, a waitress turned outlaw who shocked and titillated a nation. No one knew for sure if she had done any killing. Some said she murdered a state trooper, but the story was thin. Didn't matter anyway. She'd been Clyde's accomplice and a permanent, integral part of the ever-changing Barrow Gang. Any blood spilled by Clyde and his buddies—and there had been plenty—was on her hands. She had deserved no mercy.

And neither did Brighton Cove's Bonnie Parker. Dan was very damn sure about that. And he intended to show her none.

The show on Spike TV was ending. It made him aware of the time. No wonder he was tired. Bernice must have already gone up to bed, and he hadn't even noticed. All he'd been thinking of was Parker.

What the hell *did* happen in that motel room anyway? Dan Maguire pondered the problem as he replaced the folder in the desk drawer. Probably it didn't matter. Probably it wouldn't explain anything.

But the question still itched at him, itched like a bastard, and he still wanted to know.

12

Okay, she had been a stone cold bitch to Des. Bonnie admitted as much to herself as she cruised down Highway 35 on the way to the Roach House.

She hated being mean to him, because Des was pretty much the only person she knew who was worthy of admiration. Well, she might add Lizbeth the waitress, who cheerfully did her crappy job day in and day out without complaint. That was about it. People were basically animals. Few of them were as good as they pretended to be, and most were a whole lot worse. The world was a bleak and brutal place. There was a reason babies cried when they were born. Nobody wanted to be here, dealing with this shit.

And so what if she was hard, cold? Whatever her damage, it was her problem, not his. He had no business prying into her past. It wasn't like she was an oyster and all he had to do was claw her open and a goddamned pearl would drop out.

If she had open wounds, she'd earned them. And earned the right to keep them hidden.

"So fuck him," she muttered. "Fuck everybody."

She hooked left into the motel parking lot, checking the time on her phone, because she never wore a watch and the Jeep's clock was busted. It was 11:15. The sign outside announced VACANCY, a claim easily verified by counting the vehicles in the nearly empty lot. There were six, not including her own. One of them was an SUV with New York plates positioned head-out in front of room thirty-two.

She parked well away from the room and dug in her glove

compartment for the forty-dollar throwaway cell phone she'd purchased a few months ago. It was one of those items that could always come in handy. She'd installed a neat little app that uploaded the phone's GPS coordinates to a password-protected website. When the phone was turned on and in motion, its position was updated every five seconds and displayed as an icon on a map. Even if the phone wasn't moving, its position was updated every sixty seconds as long as it remained on.

Of course, the app's fine print made it very clear that it was not to be used for covert tracking. But she had this problem with rules. She tended to break them. It was something she really needed to work on.

She switched on the phone and approached the SUV. It was a Lexus RX, and it was black. No surprise. Bad guys always went for black. She planted the spare phone underneath the rear bumper, securing it with a lump of putty, then shined her keychain penlight on the interior of the vehicle, picking out a large satchel in the rear compartment and a map of the tri-state area on the front passenger seat.

Pocketing the keychain, she approached room thirty-two. The drapes were pulled shut, but one end of the drape was starting to fall off the rod, leaving a small triangle of glass uncovered. It glowed with yellow light from inside the room. If the guy was in there, he hadn't turned in yet, unless he was frightened of monsters under the bed.

Kneeling by the window, she peeked inside.

He was sitting on the bed, his bald head bent low, his thin shoulders hunched. It took her a moment to realize that he was cleaning a gun.

Apparently he expected to have a use for it.

She watched until he shifted his position, allowing her to get a glimpse of the firearm. It was a Beretta 9, just the thing she would expect a pro to carry.

He wore the black leather gloves she'd seen in the photo. She wondered if he ever took them off. The matching jacket was draped over a chair.

There was no sign that anyone shared the room. A single suitcase lay on the luggage rack. It was no surprise that he was traveling alone. Most killers weren't very sociable. She ought to know.

Silently she withdrew from the window. Back in the Jeep, she brought up Sammy's web browser and logged on to her GPS tracking account. The position of the throwaway phone was correctly displayed on the map.

She looked up the number of the Roach House and placed a call to the motel. Someone at the front desk answered, sounding sleepy.

"Can you connect me with the guy in thirty-two?" she asked.

A classier establishment would have made her give the guest's name, especially this close to midnight. The Roach House didn't adhere to such elevated standards. Calls came in at all hours, and names were seldom used.

"Hang on," the listless voice said.

The room phone rang five times before the occupant picked up. "Yes?"

A cultured voice, quiet and calm. And yes, there was an accent, possibly Latin American as Alan Kirby had claimed.

"I know why you're in Brighton Cove," she said.

"Who am I speaking to?"

"You don't need an introduction. All you need to know is that I'm on to you. And unless you meet me right now for a conversation, I'm going straight to the police."

"And what would be the substance of this conversation?"

"A financial arrangement. The amount won't be exorbitant. Just enough to make it worth my while to forget what I know."

"What exactly is it that you think you know?"

"Not over the phone. We need to meet. You know Alcatraz?"

"The island prison in California?"

"No, the bar on Cooper Avenue."

"I am unfamiliar with it."

"Well, you haven't missed much. Go south on 35, hook east on Cooper, and you'll run right into it."

"It is rather late for a meeting."

"Yeah, but we're both still up. Wait for me inside. I'll recognize you. If you don't show, you don't get a second chance."

"You are being most mysterious."

"Just be there. Or my next call is to the police."

She clicked off.

A couple of minutes passed, long enough for her to wonder if he'd taken the bait. Then the Lexus's headlights snapped on, spilling across the parking lot and erasing her view of the motel's doorway. She had an indistinct impression of a figure moving behind the glare, climbing quickly into the SUV.

Smart ploy. He'd used a remote starting function to switch on the lights, masking his exit from the room. It must have occurred to him that the phone call could be a ruse to draw him out into the open and gun him down.

She didn't think this man was stupid. That alone made him unusual, because in her experience most bad guys were stupid as hell.

Her Jeep remained out of the headlights' range as the Lexus eased out of the parking lot. She checked the map on her phone to be sure the GPS tracking worked. A blip on the screen traced the Lexus's progress down Highway 35.

She didn't know how much time she had—fifteen minutes, maybe. Long enough to get into the room and sniff around, get a feel for this guy, a better sense of what she was up against.

She walked to the motel room door, taking a key and screwdriver from her purse. The key was a bump key, filed down to fit a template she'd downloaded from an underground website. She inserted it in the lock and tapped it with the screwdriver's handle until a jar of impact popped the lock's pins into position, allowing the knob to turn under her hand. Easy.

It was called lock bumping, and all the cool kids were doing it.

She went inside, shutting the door behind her. He'd left the lights on, which was thoughtful of him. Her impulse was to toss the place at once, but she forced herself to take a quick overview first. It was your standard issue cheap-ass motel room, the kind she knew too well from her upbringing on the road. There was the smell of stale air, the mat of short-nap carpet, the play of distant headlights across the drapes.

The black leather jacket, she noticed, was gone. He'd put it on before going out. According to the GPS app, the Lexus was still on its way to Alcatraz.

She checked out the closet and bathroom to reassure herself she was alone. In the bathroom she noticed something odd. He'd taken down the vinyl shower curtain and draped it over the tub as a lining.

Now, why the hell would he do that? Maybe he'd been planning to take a bath, and he thought the tub was dirty. But the shower curtain wasn't any cleaner. She saw spots of gray mold in its creases.

An image flickered in her mind. Another shower curtain, this one likewise dappled with mold. And printed with pictures of baby ducks. Through the translucent screen, a dark figure, shadowy and huge, and coming closer ...

She shoved the memory aside and returned to the main room, making a beeline to the suitcase on the luggage rack. It was equipped with a small padlock but had been left open, a lucky break. She searched the contents: shirts, slacks, socks, underwear. The shirts were expertly folded, the pants perfectly creased. The sock pairs were clipped together. Neat freak.

Except for the underwear, most of the items were dark blue or black. And there were gloves, several pairs of black leather gloves. This guy definitely didn't like getting his hands dirty.

She looked in the pockets of the suitcase, hoping to find an airline ticket or an itinerary, even a sales receipt. All she discovered was a well-worn paperback of *Le Morte d'Arthur*. She'd never heard of it, which didn't mean much, since she hadn't read an actual book since she'd ditched high school. Reading just wasn't her thing. It seemed like there was always something more interesting on TV.

Skimming the back cover, she gathered that it was the story of King Arthur's knights. A long section on Lancelot and Guinevere, which looked boring as hell, was heavily marked up with careful underlining. A folded piece of paper served as a bookmark. It didn't look like just any piece of paper. The corners were dog-eared, and there was foxing on the edges. Like something that had been carried around for a while.

She opened it up and saw lines of flowing script in a looping ornamental hand. A poem, from the look of it. She wasn't sure, because it was in Spanish, and her *espanol* was limited to the Taco Bell drive-through menu. No title, and it was unsigned, but probably her guy had written it. She refolded it and stuck it into the back pocket of her jeans. Probably it was unimportant, but so far it was all she had.

Next to the suitcase was a duffel bag. Black, naturally. She unzipped it and allowed herself a little fist pump. It was his bag of goodies. Spare ammo, a couple of dark amber bottles with vaporizer nozzles, a roll of duct tape, a toolkit—wrench, pliers, screwdrivers.

And there was a strange little black box with no markings, obviously a custom-built job. The two metal prongs protruding from one end told her it was a stun gun. The little red button on the side must be the trigger. Commercial stun guns usually had two sets of prongs. One pair was mainly for show; the current passed between them, ionizing the air in a crackling blue threat display. This gadget had only the charge electrodes, the ones that did the real work. It was a serious weapon, probably packing a serious wallop.

He'd taken a few other items from the bag; there were empty pouches, the right size for a handgun, a spare clip, and maybe a suppressor tube.

She checked Sammy again. Her quarry's vehicle was now stationary in the vicinity of Alcatraz. He must have parked by the bar.

She went to the closet. A charcoal gray jacket was draped on one of those annoying motel room hangers that you couldn't remove from the rod. Nice jacket, fine quality, probably what they called bespoke, though she wasn't sure exactly what that word meant. The label was from a London shop on Savile Row. He was a world traveler, all right.

There had to be some kind of pocket litter. Everybody stuffed crap in their pockets, right? Not this guy. The jacket was infuriatingly pristine.

Next to the jacket was an immaculate and costly Turkish bathrobe, its pockets empty also. It was definitely not an item supplied by the Roach House. Her man must be accustomed to living the good life, even in a rat hole like this.

The GPS signal remained stationary. He was still hanging out at Alcatraz. She might have another few minutes before he gave up and headed back.

Her quarry was definitely a hired gun, but so far all she'd learned was that he dressed well, toted weapons, and was gaga for Camelot. It wasn't a lot to go on, and she was running out of time. The only places left to look were the bureau—empty—and the nightstand. She approached the nightstand without much hope. At best there might be a Gideon Bible inside, if the Gideons had bothered to canvass a dump like this.

She opened the drawer. Lying there was a nice shiny iPad and a rolled up power cord.

"Yachtze," she whispered, then felt stupid for saying it.

She tossed her purse on the bed, picked up the computer, and pressed the power switch. A passcode-lock screen came up—a numeric keypad and four blank spaces. Ten thousand possible combinations. But there might be a way to narrow it down.

She tilted the tablet so the light from the desk lamp illuminated it at an angle. The smudges of smooth glove prints showed up on the screen. The tablet's owner would enter and reenter the passcode more often than any other data. Smudges would cluster around the keypad buttons he used.

There were four large smudges, each corresponding to a different button. Suddenly the list of possibilities had been reduced to only twenty-four. Her fifth try was the charm. She was in.

The home screen was customized with a wallpaper image of the night sky, constellations like frozen pinwheels amid a freckling of stars. She looked over the folders. One was labeled *San Alfonso*. Inside there was a collection of photos—snow-capped mountains, glittering waterfalls, a luxury villa embraced by climbing ivy and fruit trees. His home? Where the heck was San Alfonso anyway?

Not important right now. Keep looking. She opened a word processing application, but the only files were blank templates. She checked the web browser—no bookmarks, no history, and the homepage was a general news site.

A glance at her phone again. The vehicle was still parked near Alcatraz. He hadn't started back.

Anything else on the iPad? Yeah, nested inside a folder labeled *Misc* was an app that saved webpages offline. She opened it and found a bunch of downloaded news items about various people— Amy Bernstein, Herb Sentner, Jeffrey Walker. The names meant nothing to her.

She brought up the most recent story about Amy Bernstein. It was a *New York Times* article reporting her murder. She'd been found with her throat cut in her Manhattan townhouse. Yesterday.

"Three guesses who did it," Bonnie muttered.

According to the article, Bernstein had worked for a human rights organization called Conscience Watch. Her death was viewed as a robbery gone wrong.

Next, Herb Sentner. The latest article about him, dated two weeks ago, was another death notice. This time homicide wasn't suspected. Supposedly he'd died in an accident up in Maine. And what do you know, he'd retired from Conscience Watch six months earlier.

That left Jeffrey Walker. The most recently downloaded file on him dated back three years. Not as sinister as the others. Cheerful, in fact. A press release. The headline read, "Conscience Watch

Welcomes Jeffrey Walker." The Manhattan-based group known for defending international prisoners of conscience was pleased to announce the arrival of Mr. Walker, who'd relocated from Chicago with his wife Caroline and their young son.

A photo of Jeffrey Walker accompanied the piece. It was a posed close-up, a professional portrait, and the smiling face belonged to her newest client, the man who called himself Alan Kirby.

So.

Alan Kirby, formerly Jeffrey Walker, had been shining her on about his identity and his past. Which meant he'd been lying about other stuff, also. That whole story about the client he'd gotten off, the rival gang—it had to be a crock. And the man who occupied this motel room wasn't some gangland hitter. He was somebody a lot more serious and probably a hell of a lot more expensive. A pro, sure, but not just any pro. There was some big-time intrigue going down here, and she'd been flying blind.

She and her client would need to have a conversation about that.

Alan had claimed he was with another do-gooder outfit, People Against Poverty. She clicked through other files on Jeffrey Walker, enough of them to know he'd been with Conscience Watch until about six months ago. He'd never been with the other organization at all.

She took another look at her phone. The blip hadn't budged. Back to the iPad. Maybe she could find an address book, a list of contacts. She clicked back to the home screen, but before she could check out other folders, she found herself looking at the night sky, the blaze of flickering stars.

Flickering.

But they couldn't be flickering. It was a static image.

There *was* flicker, though. A ripple of movement reflected on the glass.

Movement at her back.

According to Sammy, the guy with the Nosferatu face was still at Alcatraz.

Sammy was lying.

The son of a bitch was in the room, closing on her from behind.

She spun, dropping the phone, bending in a crouch.

He was three feet away, blocking her in against the nightstand and bed. Over his shoulder the door to the room hung ajar, framing the night. He'd opened the door and crept in without a sound. Distantly she thought it was a pretty slick move.

So he'd known her phone call was a ruse. He'd known she wasn't going to meet him at Alcatraz. Known she was just trying to get him out of the room.

But he'd left anyway. Because he'd wanted her in the room, wanted to trap her here.

And the bathtub lined with the shower curtain—it was meant for her somehow.

She twisted toward the bed, grabbing for the purse with the gun inside, but he was quicker. He batted the purse away. It flew off the bed and disappeared somewhere on the floor.

He reached under the sleeve of his jacket and unsheathed a knife. It looked like one of those silicon carbide jobs, the kind with no metal parts, made to pass through metal detectors.

The knife came at her fast. She dodged it, and the blade sank into the nightstand, embedded there.

She grabbed the motel phone off the nightstand and swung it at him. He brushed it away almost casually, the phone vanishing into a corner. She picked up the lamp and whickered it at his face. The bulb went out as the cord was ripped free, and the room was thrown into sudden half light, with only the ceiling lights in the entryway and bathroom for illumination. He threw a punch at the lamp, shredding the lampshade, then wrenched it away from her and cast it aside.

He was right up against her now, and smiling.

That smile pissed her off. She launched a knuckle strike at his throat. He parried, blocking the blow with one arm. The move left his midsection exposed. She tried delivering a punch to his abdomen, but his arm was there again, warding off the strike, then brushing her fist aside to jab her quick and hard in the right breast.

Okay. The guy had skills.

In the movies, the ninety-eight-pound girl was always beating the crap out of guys twice her size. Bonnie weighed more than ninety-eight pounds, but it was a simple fact, unadmitted by Hollywood, that men had greater upper body strength than women. In a match between two equally well-trained opponents, one male and one female, the smart money was on the testosterone.

Her best shot was to throw him off balance, break free of containment, and run like hell.

She hooked her left foot around his right ankle and angled her leg sidewise, pistoning out both arms to shove him in the chest. He fell backward onto the bed. She whipped past him, heading for the door ...

He seized the comet tail of her hair, jerking her head back.

The ceiling blurred, the bed creaked under her, and then his face filled her field of vision, a grinning death mask. She was on the bed, flat on her back, and he was on top of her.

She grabbed a pillow, pushed it into his face, squeezing hard, shutting off his breath.

He withdrew, clawing it free, and she was on her feet again, but not fast enough. He grabbed her from behind, his arm around her neck.

Blood choke. Crap.

It would put her under in ten seconds or less.

Panic flashed through her. She thrust out both legs, bracing her feet against the nightstand, trying to push back against him. No good. The nightstand shifted away from the wall, wobbling at a crazy angle, and she lost her leverage.

She threw an elbow at his face. Couldn't connect. Already her vision was graying. Running out of time.

The guy was a killer. If she lost consciousness, she would never wake up.

Scrabbling at his arm, trying to find purchase, tearing the

sleeve of his jacket, but he still didn't let go.

A high tuneless hum rose in her ears. Fading fast. She didn't want to die this way, gasping for air, thrashing helplessly.

Her fingers, bent like claws, stabbed blindly at his face, seeking an eye.

Then all her strength went away, just like that, and she knew it was over, really over for her. Elvis had left the building.

She had no time to feel sorry or scared. No time for anything now.

Plunge of vertigo, sudden darkness, and she was out.

13

The girl had fought well, Pascal decided. Though hardly his equal, she had made things interesting.

Now he would make things interesting for her.

Her swoon would last only fifteen or twenty seconds unless artificially prolonged. Briskly he removed one of the amber bottles from his duffel and gave her a good long whiff of halothane. It was a powerful inhalational anesthetic, and it would keep her under for ten minutes or so.

He was careful not to give her too much. An overdose might stop her heart. That would be a shame. They had much to talk about.

For the same reason he had not wanted to use his gun on her. He could have vanquished her with a silenced shot—it would have taken only a moment to remove the suppressor tube from his pocket and screw it into place—but he did not want her dead. Had he not lost the use of his knife, he could have incapacitated her with a nonlethal wound. As it was, he had rendered her immobile by other means.

The struggle had made some noise, but there were no neighbors on either side of his room, no one to hear or call for help. He was not sure the habitués of this establishment would be too quick to contact the authorities in any event. Brawls must be common here.

On the floor was the girl's phone, which she had used to track his vehicle, a predictable gambit. It had been easy to find the throwaway mobile phone secured to the SUV's bumper. He had discarded it in the vicinity of the bar, then doubled back, taking her by surprise.

He picked up the phone. The screen had cracked when it fell, but the phone was still on, not yet having timed out. The index fingers and thumbs of his gloves were threaded with carbon fibers, allowing him to operate the touchscreen. He checked the settings and found that the phone was set up with a four-digit passcode that would lock him out the next time the device shut off. He could not disable the code, but he knew a simple workaround. He navigated to Google Accounts, established a new account for himself, and logged in. Now he could bypass the screen lock whenever he wished.

Later he would take a look at the call log. For now he left the phone on the bed and set to work securing the girl. With duct tape from his duffel, he lashed her wrists behind her back, then ripped open a pillow, tore off a hunk of foam rubber, and wedged it in her mouth, taping it in place.

Lifting her in his arms, he carried her to the bathroom. On the way he nearly tripped over her absurd hat, lost in the struggle. Irritated, he kicked it under the bed.

He deposited her fully clothed in the tub, amid the improvised vinyl lining. The shock of movement roused her briefly to blinking half consciousness, but the sedative overpowered her and she stayed under. She lay on her back, her head against the tiled wall, facing the spout. He had to bend her knees to make her fit; the tub was short. Earlier he taped down the drain-control lever so that her kicking feet would not unstop the bath. Her footwear, he noticed, had rubber soles. That was good.

He ran the bath, dialing the temperature warm.

In his luggage he found his stun gun, fully charged. The unit was small but powerful, delivering five milliamps. There was no automatic cutoff mechanism. He could keep the current flowing as long as the battery lasted, and it would last a long time.

He pried his knife free of the nightstand, then used the blade to cut the power cords of the bedside lamp and the TV set, stripping the insulation on both ends. He carried the wires and the stun gun into the bathroom, where he checked on her, lifting one of her eyelids. The pupil—deep blue, he observed—was still dilated. She would be out for a little longer. The bath was more than half full.

With duct tape he attached the wires to the vinyl lining on both sides of the tub, letting the frayed ends dangle in the water, the girl's hips between them. He tied the other ends of the wires to the stun gun's dual prongs, equivalent to the positive and negative posts of a battery. When the trigger was depressed, current would flow from the positive post, taking the path of least resistance—through the first wire, into the tub, then into the ground wire on the opposite side. To reach the ground wire it would pass through the water and the girl's body. Her skin resistance would be dramatically lower when wet, making her a better conductor than the bathwater. She would take the bulk of the charge.

The tub was full now. He turned off the water and returned to the main room. Her handbag lay on the floor. He rummaged through it.

Her name was Bonnie Elizabeth Parker. She was a licensed private investigator with an office in Brighton Cove. She carried a Walther nine, a reliable weapon, well maintained. The serial number had been filed off. Interesting.

What else? An unusual amount of cash in her wallet, though he did not trouble to count it. Breath mints, cigarettes, and a lighter. The mints and the cigarettes seemed to be at cross purposes, but the logic of the female mind had always eluded him.

He examined the phone. It was possible, though unlikely, that the girl had been tailing him. If so, she might have taken photos. He found the photo gallery and frowned, feeling his first twinge of genuine curiosity.

There was indeed a photo of him, seated in a cafe by a window, but surely this girl had not taken it. He knew the time and place, though he had had no suspicion of being photographed.

Someone had sent it to her. She must know about New York, then. He wondered how much else she knew.

He put her phone into the purse, and stashed the purse in the nightstand. Later he would go over the phone in more detail before disposing of it, along with her ID and other belongings. The gun, however, he would keep. An untraceable firearm was always useful. He was something of a scavenger, anyway. He had no compunctions about picking Bonnie Parker's bones.

He heard the slap of water on the tiles of the bathroom floor. She was awake, struggling, trying to escape.

She wanted to live now. But by the time he finished with her, she would be more than ready to die.

14

Desmond was watching the last ten minutes of *Wings* when an alert popped up at the bottom of his TV. Jo wanted to Skype with him.

He froze the movie and connected with her, putting the video stream on the big-screen TV. His kid sister was sitting by a grove of palm trees in a flood of tropical sun, a floppy straw hat framing her face. A tall glass of something with alcohol rested in front of her, slightly out of focus. If she was trying to make him jealous, she'd succeeded.

"G'day, mate," she said.

"Hey, Jo." Desmond smiled into his netbook's webcam. "How are things Down Under?"

"Depends on who I'm down under, if you get my drift."

"I got it. As drift goes, it wasn't subtle. More like continental drift."

"We Aussies don't go for subtlety." She actually seemed to be developing an Australian accent. Going native, big time. "Hey, I'm not calling too late, am I?"

"You know me. Up till all hours. Project coming along okay?" Her company had sent her to Sydney to consult on beach erosion. She was an environmental engineer—a whiz kid, super-smart and more studious than he had ever been.

"It's great. I could be stuck here another few months, which is fine by me."

"Get in any surfing?"

"A little. Saw a shark the other day."

"I'm more worried about the land sharks. The ones in the local bars. They're harder to fight off."

"Who said anything about fighting?" She sipped her drink. There was a tiny parasol sticking out of it. "How about you? Getting any action?"

"Not at the moment."

"You need *some* contact with the opposite sex, you know. If only to stimulate the right cerebral hemisphere. That's your feminine side."

"I'm plenty stimulated on both sides. And I do see girls sometimes. Bonnie came by a little while ago."

"Ah, the woman of mystery."

"Is she?"

"You're always mysterious when you talk about her. Which you do, a lot."

"It's not like I'm in love with her," he said a little too quickly.

"No, of course not. Love is for suckers." She gave him a look. "You know, if you're holding back with her on account of that chair—"

"I'm not."

"Sure about that?"

"The chair isn't an issue. The issue is—forget it."

"Don't tease me, bro. If there's an issue, I want to know what it is."

"The issue is, I don't really know her."

"What's that supposed to mean? You see her all the time."

"Oh, sure, she's a friend. Probably my best friend. But I don't *know* her." He sighed. "It's complicated."

"Some complications can be good for you."

"True. But these particular complications might be a little too ... complicated."

"Well, there's nothing mysterious about that."

He caught the edge in her voice. "You really want to know?" he said slowly. "I think she's a killer."

"You mean she has a killer bod, or—"

"No. I mean, I think she's a hit man. Or hit woman. A paid assassin."

"Big brother, you've been hitting the bong again."

"She's a private eye. There are rumors that this guy in town who got murdered back in March was a client of hers."

"Doesn't mean she did it."

"I have reasons to think she might have. And I don't think it was an isolated case."

"Killing your clients is no way to get repeat business."

"I'm not saying she goes after her clients ordinarily. I think she's like a—a cleaner, you know? A fixer. Whatever."

"People hire her to put the kibosh on somebody?"

"That's what I think."

"Either you're crazy, or she is."

"Neither of us is crazy. But she can be ... hard."

"Have you ever asked her about these suspicions of yours?"

"It's kind of a tough thing to work into a conversation. 'Hey, Parker, killed anyone lately?' I don't know how to segue into that one."

"Good point." Jo bit her lip. "Plus, if she thinks you know too much ..."

"It's not like that."

"How do you know? She could be psychotic."

"She's not psychotic. Neurotic, maybe. Quirky ..."

"Nuh-uh, bro." She wagged her finger at the camera. "Quirky is changing your hair color every two months. Quirky is joining the *My Little Pony* fan club as an adult. What quirky definitely is *not*, is putting people on ice for fun and profit."

"If it's any defense, I think she does it mostly for profit."

"You're not helping her cause."

"Look, I don't know that any of this is actually true. It could all be empty gossip." Except for the gun in the air duct, he thought. "Sound and fury, signifying nothing."

"Don't be Shakespearean. It doesn't suit you."

"I'm just saying, maybe there's no there there."

"Don't do Gertrude Stein either. Are you really serious, or is this some kind of goof?"

"Do I look like I'm joking?"

Even from ten thousand miles away, she could see he wasn't.

"Okay, big bro. In that case I revise and extend my previous remarks. Stay away from this woman. Stay very far the fuck away."

"It's not like I'm scared of her."

"Maybe you should be."

"She's no threat to me. To other people, yeah. But probably only people who deserve it."

"Deserve it? What is this, a Charles Bronson movie? Your gal pal doesn't get to decide who lives and who dies."

"That's where you're wrong, Jo. I'm pretty sure she does."

They talked some more before she signed off, claiming she had to get back to work. He could tell she was a little rattled.

He hadn't told her the whole truth, though. He *was* scared. Not scared of Bonnie. Scared *for* her.

Whatever she was doing, it was dangerous business. Life-and-death stuff. Not the boring crap most PIs did. Not snapping photos of a husband and a hooker, or running a background check on your daughter's boyfriend.

She was into things a lot dicier than that. Things that could get her killed. She knew it, too, and she liked the thrill. Pushing the envelope, beating the odds.

He knew how that was. And how it ended. He used to take risks in his car. One night he took a blind curve and flipped over, and he'd been in a wheelchair ever since.

That was what scared him, and kept him from getting too close. He could see down the road a little farther than she could. And he saw where that road ended.

He only hoped it wouldn't end too soon.

15

Okay, she was officially in trouble.

Bonnie awoke in a tub of warm water, her hands taped behind her back, more tape over her mouth, and a maniac in the next room. Her knees were awkwardly bent, the soles of her sneakers resting against the vinyl shower curtain bunched up under the spout. The water rose to her breastbone, nearly as high as the lip of the tub. Her shirt stuck to her skin, and her black denim jeans were waterlogged and dripping.

A bathtub in a cheap motel. She had trouble letting go of that thought.

Resting on the closed lid of the toilet was the stun gun, with wires attached to the terminals. She saw where the wires ended.

Her breathing became a little faster, and the gag in her mouth felt bigger than before.

Oh sure, she was scared. No way around it. Her heart was running like a rabbit, and she tasted sour panic at the back of her throat.

But more than that, she was pissed. She wasn't a newbie at this game, but she'd let him get the jump on her. It was bad enough to die, worse when you knew it was your own damn fault.

She didn't have any illusions about the way this was going to play out. The freak with the gloved hands had every advantage. The only thing she couldn't figure was why he'd bothered to fill the tub when he could have simply taped the wires to her skin.

She had sometimes wondered how she would react in a situation like this—well, not exactly like this, not tied up in an electroshock tub by a psycho. Her imagination wasn't that good. But facing the end, how would she handle it? She was about to find out.

She couldn't stop staring at the stun gun, that tiny black box filled with pain and death. The worst electric shock she'd had in her life was one she received when unscrewing the cover of a wall outlet in her duplex. Some idiot had glued the plate to the wall, and the glue conducted current to her hand, zapping her fingers. It smarted a little, and scared the panties off her, but that was all.

This would be worse.

Dead in the bathtub of a cheap motel ...

She felt the pressure of tears in her eyes and hated herself for it. She wasn't a goddamned baby. She'd known what she was getting into when she chose this life, and there was no point getting all misty about it now.

Anyway, she wasn't dead yet. Her wrists twisted behind her, but the tape was heavy and tough, and she wasn't going to pull free. Still, if she could flip on her side and use an elbow for leverage, she might be able to push herself up and get her legs over the side ...

She didn't think she was making much noise, but even the faint slosh of water must have alerted him. She heard his approaching footsteps and sank back into the tub.

He entered the bathroom, still wearing the jacket and the damn gloves. The guy was into leather, that was for sure. The left side of the jacket showed the subtle print of his firearm in a shoulder holster. He must have been armed when he fought her, but he hadn't drawn his weapon. He'd wanted her alive.

"Awake," he said with a nod. "Good."

She didn't see what was so good about it.

He sat on the lip of the bathtub and smiled. "You look so much better without your silly hat. A cloche, I believe it is called?" He shook his head. "Hideous."

Hey, she would put her fashion sense up against his any day. Black leather gloves in August? Please.

Leaning down, he reached for the tape on her mouth, then hesitated.

"You see how it is, do you not?" he said. "If you scream for help, I will shock you."

She nodded. She didn't think screaming would help anyway. The rooms nearby had looked unoccupied, and the Roach House wasn't the sort of establishment where a cry of distress would necessarily draw much attention.

He stripped the tape from her lips. She coughed up a wad of foam stuffing, feeling spittle slide down her chin into the water.

"Hello, Bonnie Parker," he said.

It surprised her that he knew her name, until she remembered her purse in the other room.

"Pleased to meet you," she said, summoning all her willpower to look him in the eye.

"I'm glad you showed the self-discipline to remain quiet. It speaks well of you."

"I'm not screaming now. But I can't promise what'll happen when you start going all *Cuckoo's Nest* on me."

He frowned, not getting the reference. "The bathtub," he said, "is fiberglass, a poor conductor of electricity. Still, the metal drain and plumbing pipes would have drawn off some of the current. Hence the layer of insulation." He indicated the shower curtain. "It will contain most of the electricity within the water. It will also serve as a convenient carrying case for your remains."

"Terrific."

"The interior of your body is an excellent natural conductor, owing to the dissolved salts in your tissues and veins. Every part of you is sensitive to electric shock, but the heart most of all."

"So you're saying you can sizzle my bacon pretty good?"

"Then, of course, there is the matter of pain. As it happens, the threshold for perception of shocks is significantly lower for women than for men."

"There's not gonna be a pop quiz on this later, is there? 'Cause I don't test well."

He gave her a long stare. "Bonnie Parker, what do I look like to you?"

"An insane clown who's lost his posse?"

"I am a serious man. A professional, like yourself. A man who will brook no insouciance. A man"—he paused for emphasis —"who will get what he wants."

He retreated a couple of feet and sat on the lid of the toilet with the stun gun resting on his lap. She waited, her heart hammering, while fear burned like fever on her face.

But he didn't get started right away. He was good. He knew just how to play her. He let her wait for the moment when he would close the circuit and fry her in the tub.

How powerful was the damn stun gun, anyway? What would it feel like to be zapped with that much juice? And why did her mind persist in asking stupid questions she couldn't answer?

"Penny for your thoughts," he said.

"Just going over my plans for the weekend. Hot date. Though maybe not as hot as this one."

"According to the license in your wallet, you are a private investigator. I wish to know who hired you, how you found me, and what you have learned."

She tried out a flippant smile. "And if I tell you all that, you'll let me go?"

"If you tell me all that, I will let you die."

"Gotta say, you're not giving me a lot of incentive to cooperate."

"You will have all the incentive you need. The incentive of making it stop."

"You got issues, pal. You should get help. And hair plugs. Bald and crazy is no way to go through life."

He leaned forward, quick as the lash of a whip, and picked up the foam wedge, jamming it back into her mouth. She uttered a surprised grunt, and then his hand flexed, touching the trigger.

Her stomach clenched like a fist. Her midsection was on fire. The current jabbed like needles, a million miniature spearheads digging into her belly, her groin, her thighs. Rhythmic thumping echoed hollowly around her—the drumbeat of her Nikes against the wall as her legs kicked.

Then it was over. For now. He pulled out the foam gag and waited patiently while she coughed and gasped.

She was disappointed to find herself still alive. So the stun gun's battery wasn't enough to snuff her. Too bad.

"You think you are tough bitch, Bonnie Parker, but I will break you." He said it without boasting, as a simple factual statement.

She fought for breath. She couldn't have screamed now if she wanted to. "I don't suppose ... you could fetch me ... a cigarette from my purse?"

He smiled. "I like you, Miss Parker. It is Miss, is it not? I see no wedding band."

"Tough bitches don't get married."

"Pity."

He said it as if he saw every lonely night, every empty hour spent staring into the dark. She could almost believe he felt sorry for her. That made it worse somehow. Cruelty she had steeled herself for. Against compassion she had no defense.

"You gonna interrogate me or what?" she snapped.

He ignored the question. "I am intrigued. A woman like you could surely find romance if she sought it. Which leads me to conclude that you do not seek it. Why not?"

"For all you know, I got three studs on speed dial."

"I do not think so. You have a lonely look about you. The look of a solitary predator."

"If this is gonna be a therapy session, I should probably be on the couch."

"I think it is because you have acquired the habit of solitude. But that habit can become a prison. There is something to be said for sharing your life with another."

"You playing matchmaker, or just coming on to me?"

"Merely offering an observation."

"Glass houses, buddy. I doubt a guy in your line of work has too many soul mates."

"I have, in fact, none—at present. That is how I know the truth of what I say. You are throwing your life away."

"Under the circumstances, isn't that kind of a moot point?"

"It is true. Any advice I offer now would seem to have come too late." He shifted his weight on the toilet lid, assuming a more adversarial posture. "Who hired you?"

"Fuck off."

"At the very least you could offer up some clever repartee."

"Eat shit. How's that for repartee?"

"Your intransigence is futile. You can see that, surely?"

"I see it. And don't call me Shirley."

"You will make this unnecessarily hard on yourself. Nothing can save you. You are never getting out of that tub alive. I will wrap you in the shower curtain and drive you to the beach, where you will go into the ocean, to be swept out with the tide. Your body will feed the hungry things of the sea."

"Circle of life, huh?"

"Yes, the natural order. We are all born to die."

"I was hoping to buck the trend. So it's gonna look like a moonlight swim?"

"Your remains will be found once they have washed up on shore. The obvious conclusion will be that you swam out to deep water and suffered cardiac arrest. Given the deteriorating weather conditions, the authorities will not think you swam for recreation. They will rule it an act of suicide on the part of a lonely young woman."

"The autopsy—"

"Will show simply that your heart stopped. The only telltale signs of electrocution would be burn marks. You will have none."

So that was why he hadn't attached the wires to her skin. "I can still get burn marks from the juice in the water."

"Not at this voltage."

"I won't have seawater in my lungs."

"A sudden, massive coronary arrest would give you no time to aspirate a significant quantity of water."

"Yeah, but even with that gag in my mouth, I might still swallow some bathwater. It's a giveaway. They'll know I drowned in a tub."

"An electric shock produces an exhale reflex, so there will be no bathwater. Any further objections?"

"Nope." She let her head fall back against the tiles. "I guess you're pretty good at this."

"It is what they pay me for."

"Who pays you?"

He placed a finger to his lips. "Hush, Bonnie Parker."

"You're a pro, that's obvious."

"Hush, I said. I ask the questions. Who hired you?"

"I could make up a name. Fred Flintstone, maybe?"

"Who hired you?"

"Elmer Fudd."

"Who hired you?"

"Would you believe Big Bird?"

He picked up the gag, holding it daintily between two gloved fingers.

Oh hell, she was no hero, and he was going to get it out of her eventually. But there was a chance he didn't know her client's new name. She could protect him that much, at least.

"Jeffrey Walker," she said. "That's his name."

"Very good." He didn't seem the least bit surprised. "How did he get in touch with you?"

"Called my phone. My landline," she added, though she didn't have a landline. She was hoping he might not check the call log on her cell.

"And what was your assignment?"

"Just do some snooping, find out why you're in town."

"That is a lie."

"I'm telling the truth."

"Not yet. But you will. You merely require additional encouragement."

He reached over her and repositioned the wire leads higher in the tub, aligning them with the lower edge of her rib cage.

"This placement will allow the current to pass a little nearer to your heart. I do not expect the shock to bring on a fatal arrhythmia, but I cannot entirely rule it out."

Then let it happen, she thought.

"The pain, however, will be more intense than before. The worst pain you have ever known, very nearly the worst pain a human being can endure. And yet, when properly employed, this particular method leaves no marks. If the grand inquisitors had possessed such technology, think what confessions they could have extracted."

"Sounds like you missed your calling."

"No, I could never abide being a priest. I lack the necessary zeal. And like you, I prefer to be self-employed."

"We should swap notes on tax deductions."

He stepped back. "Once again, what were you hired to do?"

"I'm a PI, like you said. I spy on people. I find out things—"

He reached toward her again. Too late, she realized the gag was coming. He shoved it between her teeth and pressed the trigger.

A *whump* of impact, her belly heaving as fireworks exploded in her gut. She gritted her teeth so hard she thought they would break off in her mouth. Colored lights flashed across her field of vision, and a high hum filled her ears.

Then—silence.

She spat out the foam wedge. It floated on the water like a bath toy.

It hurts. The words repeated themselves pointlessly at the back of her mind, plaintive words in a child's voice. *It hurts, it hurts ...*

"Do you enjoy pain, Bonnie Parker?" he asked gently.

"Hey, who doesn't?" She almost laughed, found she couldn't. Her chest shuddered, her lungs straining for air. Her voice was hoarse and throaty, as if she'd been shouting.

"There are those who do. I once knew a woman who was a

connoisseur of physical pain."

"You must've made a cute couple." She coughed, tasting vomit. "You know, I'm at sort of a conversational disadvantage."

"I'd say you are at a disadvantage in more ways than that."

"I mean, you know my name, and I don't know yours."

"You do not need to know it."

"How do you expect us to be friends if you won't share?"

"Friendship is not on my agenda. What were you hired to do?"

She gave up. "Aw, fuck it. I was supposed to snuff you."

"To kill me, you mean?"

"Yeah. Ironic, huh?"

"I guessed as much from the firearm in your handbag. An untraceable weapon."

"Yup."

"Did you remember to wear gloves when loading the gun?"

"Always do."

"Good for you. No prints on the shell casings."

"I'm a licensed PI. My prints are on file with the cops. So I take precautions."

"You have done this kind of work before?"

"A few times. You?"

"More than a few. How much do you know?"

"About what?"

"About me. What did Mr. Walker tell you, and what have you learned on your own?"

"He told me a bunch of bullshit. What I learned myself— zilch."

"And still you lie to me. Disappointing."

She was sure he was going to shock her again. She squeezed her eyes shut, waiting for the gag and the pain.

There were many things she could have thought about— memories, regrets—but none of that mattered. The rest of her life was a daydream. Only the tub and the wires and the man holding the stun gun were real. This moment, nothing else. This interval between bouts of agony.

"Pascal," he said.

Her eyes opened. "What?"

"My name is Pascal. There, you see. I have shared."

"Mr. Pascal or Pascal somebody?"

"You need call me only Pascal."

"Great. A one-name wonder. You're not from around here, right?"

"My father moved to Chile from France. I grew up in Santiago, hearing both French and Spanish in the house. My parents were wealthy. They disowned me. But on my own I have become wealthier still. I have a luxury apartment in Santiago and a villa in the foothills of the Andes."

"San Alfonso?"

"Indeed."

"I saw the pics on your iPad. Looks nice. I'll have to go there someday."

"You should."

"Maybe I'll look you up. We can chat about old times. Like, remember the night you tortured me in a bathtub?"

"You have spirit, Bonnie Parker. It is refreshing. But my time is limited. I must insist that you tell me what you know."

"You've been pretty insistent already."

"I can be much more so."

"Okay, okay. What Walker told me is that a drug cartel sicced you on him."

"A cartel?" He found this humorous.

"That was the story."

"Perhaps it was. But he must have told you more than that, or you would not know his true identity. The name Jeffrey Walker is not the name he uses now."

"It's the only name I know."

"I do not believe you."

"So kill me then. Just fucking kill me."

"Your death is not the point. Even your suffering is not the point. Only your cooperation is the point."

"I am cooperating. Think I'd hold out, after this?"

"You might, if you were very stubborn—or very stupid. Or if you happen to have an unusually high tolerance for pain."

"I don't."

"How unfortunate." He reached for the foam wedge, drifting near her.

"Wait. *Wait!* Don't zap me again. Just give me a second to think, okay?"

She hated the pleading hysteria in her voice. She wasn't playing this as calmly as she might have hoped. Hell, he'd only shocked her twice so far, and already he was breaking her. How long could she manage to stall? One more shock? Two? Three? She would talk eventually. She would tell him everything. So what was the point in dragging it out? Tell him, and die. Just die.

She stared into the water, the ripples glinting in the fluorescent light, and saw a sharper glint.

On the floor of the tub, amid the pleats of the shower curtain— a gleam of metal. Her key ring.

She'd stuck it in the side pocket of her jeans. He must not have checked her pockets. In the violence of the shock treatment the keys had been shaken free.

He hadn't seen them. They were blocked from his view by her body.

The keys had serrated edges. They could saw through the tape binding her wrists.

She slumped to one side, reaching for the keys without being obvious about it. He was watching her, but from his perspective she was only twisting her sore body in the tub.

Her fingers touched metal.

"Will you say his name for me?" Pascal asked. "Think about it, Miss Parker. Think about how much pain you are willing to endure, when you do not have to."

She needed to keep him from immobilizing her, at least long enough for her to get the keys into her hand. "You already know, don't you? You know the name he's using now?"

"I do."

She snagged the key ring with her index finger. "Then why do you need me to say it?"

"Only to prove that you hold nothing back."

Slowly she drew the keys toward her. "You expect me to buy that?"

"I am not selling. And you are not in a position to negotiate."

The keys were up against her body now.

"He called himself Jeffrey Walker," she said firmly.

Pascal sighed. "I will give you one more chance. Your client's name?"

She eased the keys behind her back, thinking hard. He must know the answer. Had to know. Otherwise why would he even be in town? Besides, Alan's stalker had been following him, he said. Which meant Pascal had already located his quarry. Already knew where he worked and where he lived and who he was.

That made sense, right? There was no hole in her logic. Right?

"I grow weary, Miss Parker. Talk."

It had to be right because she needed more time. She took a breath. "Alan Kirby."

She saw the narrowing of his eyes, and cold doubt clamped down. She had a feeling that she'd miscalculated. That her tormentor really hadn't known that crucial piece of information until this moment.

"I appreciate your honesty," he said. "What more did he tell you?"

She maneuvered the keys into position, pressing the serrated edges against the tape on her wrists. "You've been stalking him."

"Have I?"

"He snapped your picture in the Surfside Café."

"I have never been to such a place. And I have not been stalking Mr. Kirby."

"Bullshit. I saw the photo."

"As did I. I found it on your phone. But I arrived here only this evening. And that photograph was not taken by your client."

Crap.

If Alan had lied to her about the stalking, then Pascal really hadn't known his quarry's new identity. It might have taken him days to discover it on his own. She'd handed it to him in minutes.

Great going. Real slick. Way to get a family killed.

But she couldn't have known. Her goddamn client had lied to her.

Carefully she began to rub them against the tape, up and down, in a steady sawing motion, trying not to move her shoulders too much. "If he didn't take the pic, who did?"

"Again I remind you," he said with a smile, "that you do not ask the questions."

Damn, she wanted to knock that smile off his face. She sawed faster.

"What more did he tell you?" he asked again.

"Nothing."

"He knows about New York. That much is clear. But how much does he know?"

"I don't know what the fuck you're talking about."

"Perhaps you have merely forgotten. Let me refresh your memory."

He forced the gag on her again. She clamped her jaws, unwilling to let him use it. He pried at her mouth. She shook her head back and forth, fighting him.

Not this time, bastard. Not this time—

With a smile, he slapped her across the cheek, a sudden stinging slap that startled her into opening her mouth. Then he was pushing the gag inside, forcing it deeper, until it clogged her mouth like a thick, sopping sponge. The sour taste of her own acid reflux clung to the wet foam.

Her world lit up again. Her head snapped back, striking the tiles. Another storm blew through her body, a lightning storm that fried the nerve endings of her midsection, delivering wave after wave of crippling pain like a hernia.

And it didn't stop. Didn't ... stop. He was maintaining the

contact longer, testing how much punishment she could take.

Hate you, she thought. Hate you, hate you, hate you.

Finally it ended. She opened her mouth and the gag fell out in two pieces. She'd bitten clean through it.

She lay motionless, nearly submerged. Her legs were sprawled over the side of the tub, her body slumped lower, water cupping her chin. She thought she should lift her head out of the water, but the will to do it had gotten lost somewhere between her brain and the muscles of her body.

Weightlessly she sank underwater, eyes closed, her body a sightless knot of pain. And she remembered the keys.

Not in her hand anymore. She'd dropped them, lost them.

She pressed her palms to the tub's vinyl lining and groped blindly.

A gloved fist clutched her hair and pulled her head out of the water. Her eyes opened. She saw her tormentor backlit by fluorescent glare.

"Tell me what you know about New York."

"Jeez. Let a girl catch her breath, will you?"

Her palm touched metal. The keys—she'd found them. She lifted the key ring into position, praying he didn't notice the contortions of her wrists behind her back.

"Tell me," he said.

"About New York? It's the city that never sleeps. If you can make it there, you'll make it anywhere."

She started cutting the tape again. It was fraying. She was sure it was.

"No more witticisms. They grow tiresome."

She could free herself, given time. But Pascal wasn't going to sit still for more delaying tactics. And if he shocked her again, she might lose the keys for good.

"Okay," she said. "I give. I'll tell you everything I know. But it may not be enough."

"Allow me to be the judge of that."

"I met Kirby for the first time tonight. An hour ago. He told me a story about a local street gang and a drug cartel and a Colombian hit man. He wanted me to look into it and, if necessary, use extreme measures. It's something I'm known to do on occasion. He paid me cash up front. It's in my purse, twenty-five hundred bucks. Check and see. You think I usually carry that much dough around?"

Keep talking. Keep doing anything as long as it kept his finger away from the stun gun's trigger and gave her more time to split the tape.

"And how did you know where to find me?" he asked, sounding interested for the first time.

"He told me you were staying here."

"How did he know?"

"He didn't say." She didn't want to get the motel manager killed.

"And you did not ask, of course."

"I assumed he tailed you. It's what I would've done."

"No one can tail me without being spotted."

"Want me to go back and ask him? I promise I'll come back so you can finish me off. Scout's honor."

"Were you ever a Girl Scout?"

"Nope."

"What is Mr. Kirby's home address?"

She wasn't going to give up that info, even though Pascal could obtain it easily enough. "I don't know. He called me, and we met on the boardwalk."

"Just the two of you?"

"Yeah, just us. Look, I know you don't believe me—"

"On the contrary, perhaps I do. There was a sizable sum of money in your wallet. I did not count it."

"Count it now. You'll see. Twenty-five hundred bucks is what he paid me. I didn't even stop to make a deposit at an ATM." She was making progress with the tape, but it was slow, too slow. "Just count it," she said again.

"So I shall." He rose, smiling down on her. "I would tell you not to go anywhere, but it hardly seems necessary."

"Good one. By the way, I'm gonna need that money back. Bills to pay."

"You do amuse me, Bonnie Parker. You truly do."

He walked out, and she worked the tape harder. If she could get free, she'd amuse him, all right.

She'd amuse the crap out of him.

16

Pascal was certain he had broken the girl. She was telling the truth. The money would confirm it.

He opened her purse and riffled through the bills, counting quickly. The amount was twenty-five hundred forty-one dollars. She claimed her client paid twenty-five hundred tonight, which would account for the bigger bills, leaving forty-one dollars she had left home with. It added up.

Of course, Walker had lied to her when he said he was being stalked. And Walker could not have followed him to this motel. That part of her story did not make sense.

But he was untroubled by a few loose ends. As he knew, Walker had been in contact with Amy Bernstein in New York. Bernstein had snapped the photo; the eatery was one he had visited when shadowing her just hours before her death. After dispatching her, he had found the photo on her phone. He had deleted it, of course; but evidently she had sent it to Walker soon after it was taken.

So Walker had known Pascal was coming. And he could have learned of Pascal's arrival at this motel in many ways. In a provincial backwater such as this, people gossiped about strangers with unknown accents and continental manners. And the motel manager had looked at him queerly when he checked in.

It did not matter. He would not remain long at the motel anyway.

He replaced the purse in the nightstand drawer, then switched on his iPad. Using a cellular connection, he ran an Internet search for the terms *Alan Kirby* and *Millstone County, New Jersey*. He found an Alan Kirby who practiced law in McKendree Park. His office address had been the home of an accounting firm only eight months ago, suggesting that the law practice was new. And this man Kirby had kept a low profile; there were no photos of him online.

A new arrival, with a law degree, lying low—almost certainly the man he sought.

Kirby's home address was unlisted, but perhaps the girl's phone would be of help. She had claimed he called her landline, but she could have been lying. He switched on her cell. The most recent call in the log was from Mr. Alan Kirby, and his address was conveniently provided.

Well, then. All the pieces had come together. He could reasonably plan on concluding things within the next few hours. He would dump the girl in the ocean, then proceed to his target's home.

He took out his cell phone and called a memorized number. The man who answered said, "Sunrise Transport."

"I require a pickup," Pascal said. "Before dawn, at Millstone Airport in southern New Jersey. It was a public airport at one time, but it is no longer in operation." He had passed the closed-down county airfield on his way from the city.

"Okay, we have someone available for that. Can you narrow down the timeframe?"

"The departure window is two o'clock AM to six o'clock AM."

"And will you be requiring transportation out of the country?"

"Yes. To South America."

"You know our policy regarding payment?"

"Remittance in the amount of ten thousand dollars will be transferred to your account within five minutes."

"Very good. Look for a Beechcraft turbojet, tail number N219LK. Our pilot will arrive at two. If you're not there by six, you lose your ride and your money."

"I will be there."

"Any complications, and he takes off. Flight's canceled, and your deposit is nonrefundable."

"There will be no complications."

He went online and made the transfer, moving the cash into a Cayman Islands account. The service he was buying wasn't cheap, but it was dependable. Within six hours he would be in the air, en route to a new life.

He returned to the bathroom and found the girl struggling pitiably in the tub, her shoulders twisting with effort as she strained at the tape on her wrists.

"Very well, Miss Parker," he said. "I believe you. You have indeed been on the case just long enough to get paid. You have learned next to nothing and accomplished less. You are, in fact, precisely what you appear to be—a small-town rube in over your head, kept in the dark by Jeffrey Walker, with absolutely no conception of whom you were up against."

Her shoulders continued to twist. "You're kind of a dick, did you know that?"

"I can safely assume there is nothing more you can tell me. And that brings us, I am afraid, to our denouement. That is a cultured way of saying the end, my dear."

He bent over her again, moving the leads, placing them alongside her heart. She stared up at him, her blue eyes big in her face.

He would not gag her this time. It no longer mattered if she bit off her tongue or shattered her teeth. Any such damage to her body would be ascribed to an impact with the jetty or to the actions of ocean predators.

He had felt no carnal thrill when taking Amy Bernstein's life. But with this one, he did feel something. A stir of the old passion, the primal pleasure of indulging this most atavistic and forbidden urge. It was only a stir, nothing more, but it surprised him. He had thought he was past all that.

Watching the girl suffer had been pleasurable, he realized.

Watching her die would be more so.

"As I mentioned before," he said, pressing the tape into place, "the heart is the organ most sensitive to electric shock. The current will now pass directly through your chest cavity. It will initiate ventricular fibrillation, meaning that your heart muscle will begin to spasm. Death will follow—though not, I think, as quickly as you might hope."

She stopped struggling and lay still. "So this is it? Just like that? I don't get a cigarette or a blindfold?"

"You get nothing—not even my regrets. You were sent here to eliminate me. Instead, you are the one to be eliminated. It is simple justice." He smiled down on her. "Any last words?"

"Just three." Her eyes blazed. "Fuck you, asshole."

Then she was up, out of the water, her hands free, something shiny and metallic in her fist.

He had time to realize she had not been struggling helplessly— she had cut through the tape somehow—and now she was stabbing at him as he stumbled back and warded off the blow. He grabbed for the stun gun, hoping to immobilize her with another shock, but before he could reach it, she seized him around the legs and yanked him forward, halfway into the tub, shoving his head underwater as she climbed onto his back.

He reared up, throwing her off. She hit the floor. He spun to face her, and she kicked out with both legs, knocking him off balance, his shoes slipping on the wet floor. He plunged backward, submerged in the tub.

He thought of the stun gun. If she switched it on—

A slam of impact lit up his brain.

She had closed the circuit, and somewhere beyond the flood of pain that engulfed him, he heard her ragged, triumphal shout.

"You like that, jerkoff? *You fucking like that?*"

Pascal thrashed and writhed, his head whipsawing underwater, legs and arms jerking in random directions. Distantly he remembered reading that the worst pain a human being could experience was a nonlethal electric current coursing through the skull. He had trained himself to withstand pain, even torture, but nothing like this—nothing like this—

His neck strained as if fighting to pull free of his shoulders. Brightness blazed behind his eyes, and a screaming whine filled the echo chamber of his head. Pain shouted like a migraine in his forehead, invading his cheeks, his sinus cavities, his eye sockets. It was a pain too large for his head to contain, a pain that threatened to shatter his skull like ice.

And then it ended.

He gasped, going limp, amazed that she would spare him, until he saw that one of the wire leads lay on the bathroom floor. His flailing limbs must have dislodged it.

She saw it too, but before she could grab the wire, he surged upright, howling. She retreated through the bathroom door, her sneakers squishing like sponges, water streaming off her hair and clothes. He clambered out of the bath, sliding on the floor, steadying himself against the towel rack.

When he looked up, she was already gone from the motel room, the door swinging wide. He followed at a run, his legs shaky.

He could not catch her. But he could kill her. It was all he wanted to do.

He drew the Beretta from the shoulder holster under his jacket, and a new pain hit him.

His hands.

The bathtub water had cooled since he'd run it, cooled enough to trigger one of his attacks. A sudden, violent onset, one that made his hands shake with palsy.

He bit his lip and fought off the crippling pain as he lifted the gun. His target was halfway across the parking lot, arrowing toward a beat-up Jeep. She was moving fast, but the session in the tub had taken its toll, leaving her muscles weak, her actions uncoordinated. Twice she nearly fell.

The distance was not great. He should not miss. But his hands refused to hold steady. He could not draw a bead on her.

She reached the Jeep, unlocked the door, threw herself behind the wheel. The engine started. He had to fire. Had to will his goddamned hands not to betray him.

Teeth gritted, both hands on the pistol, he forced his seething wrists to lock in place. He pulled the trigger.

No good.

He knew it as soon as he fired. He had jerked the trigger too sharply, and the gun had tilted up, the shot going wild. He had missed the Jeep entirely.

Worse, he'd had no time or ability to screw on a silencer tube. The report echoed through the parking lot. Even in an establishment this seedy, it would probably attract the police.

Stupid. Careless.

There was no use shooting again, not with his hands on fire.

He watched the Jeep skid out of the parking lot, fishtailing onto the highway. Then he backed away from the open door, massaging his aching fingers.

He must pack his things and depart. Immediately, before the authorities arrived. Run, then make things right.

Despite this setback, he would still take care of business. Then somehow he would find Miss Bonnie Parker.

And when he did, he would not underestimate her again.

17

Spots of rain lashed the Jeep's windshield as Bonnie sped away from the motel. She drove straight home, checking the rearview mirror with paranoid frequency to be sure Pascal wasn't following. She didn't think he could be after her, not this soon, but getting cooked in a big pot of water like a poached egg had a way of putting her on edge.

Even if he wasn't following her now, he might head for her place before long. Her address was on her driver's license, and he had that, along with everything else in her purse. She wished like hell she'd retrieved the purse, but in the rush out the door she hadn't had time to look for it. It could have been in the nightstand or in his luggage or anywhere.

So, yeah, he could come after her. Realistically, though, she didn't think he'd play it that way. He was a pro, and Alan Kirby—formerly Jeffrey Walker—was his primary target. He would focus on Alan first. For the moment, she was probably safe.

More than that, she was still alive, which was amazing, even if she couldn't exactly enjoy it because she felt like a sack of garbage. Her abs ached as if she'd done a million crunches. Her stomach was kind of whoopsy too.

Dying wasn't so scary when it was impersonal and quick. What had happened in the tub was something different, something sadistic and crazy, and she kept flashing back to it in Dolby quadraphonic sound and Imax 3D.

All in all, she'd had better nights. And this one wasn't over yet.

Her house came up fast in the Jeep's headlights. She parked in front of the garage and took a moment to grab the Ziploc bag on the passenger seat, which contained the .38 from Des's house.

She had some trouble exiting the Jeep. The muscles of her legs still weren't working right. She stumbled to the front door, grateful that her house keys and car keys shared the same key ring, so she could let herself in. The only difficulty was disarming her security system. The tremors vibrating through her fingers made it hard to punch in the six digits on the keypad.

She didn't think Pascal could have beaten her here, but events had already proven how wrong she could be. She entered the house cautiously, checking for any sign of forced entry. She half expected the son of a bitch to jump up out of the dark and grab hold of her with his black-leather hands.

He didn't, though. He wasn't there.

She locked and bolted the door, then headed toward her bedroom. She'd lost her Walther, and she needed another weapon. Hell, she needed more than one.

She was halfway down the hall when abruptly she felt sick. Her stomach twisted. She bent double and threw up.

Get yourself under control, Bonnie. God damn it, you're not doing anybody any good puking like a damn baby.

The severe little scolding didn't help. Her legs were shaking, her knees threatening to fold. The room swam around her, its contents doubled, the air sparkly, the lights too bright. She could see the bedroom doorway—two doorways, actually. They were just a few strides away, those twin doors. Fighting for balance, she staggered nearly all the way to the bedroom before a high hum rose in her head and the room grayed out.

She came to with her face on the carpet. At first she didn't understand what had happened. She'd forgotten everything except the tub and the pain. And now the pain was gone. Maybe she was dead. Maybe this was what death was—this numbness, blankness, this bright fog everywhere, and no sound, no feeling. It could be worse.

Then she remembered. She'd escaped.

So get moving already.

She was on her feet again, stumbling into the bedroom.

Next to her bed was a small fireproof safe. The lock was keyed to her fingerprint. She opened the safe and put in the plastic bag containing the .38. She would need the gun soon, but for now it had to be kept in storage.

There were other guns in the safe, backup weapons. All of them were unregistered. Over the years she had acquired them through black market channels. None except the .38 had been used in anything criminal; she made it a point to dispose of any weapon that could tie her to a crime.

She chose a Glock 17 with an Osprey silencer, and a Ruger 10/22 carbine. The Glock shot 9mm Luger ammo. The Ruger fired .22 Long Rifle rounds. Ordinarily she wanted more stopping power than a .22, but the Ruger had a surprise or two up its sleeve.

She felt stronger now. Sharper.

She heeled fresh magazines into each weapon and gathered up all the extra mags she had. When both guns were loaded, she allowed herself a moment of rest.

Son of a bitch had tortured her. Had come damn close to frying her good. Without the keys and the extra time she'd bought by getting him to count her money ...

She shuddered, not just from cold, although she *was* cold—soaked to the skin.

In her bathroom she grabbed a towel and dried her hair. She tried not to look at the bathtub.

Her clothes were a sopping mess. She kicked off her shoes and wriggled out of everything else. While pulling off her jeans, she found a scrap of paper in the back pocket. The poem from his motel room. Waterlogged but still readable, if she could find someone who knew Spanish.

She grabbed a dark blouse and a pair of navy blue pants out of a laundry hamper, not knowing if they were dirty or clean, and put them on, angry at every small delay, even the time it took to snap a button or tug on a zipper.

Come on, get it together. You've got a family to save.

She'd given Pascal his quarry's name. And Pascal had her phone. He would disable the lockout screen somehow, then check the call log and find the call from Alan. The Caller ID app listed his home address. After that, all he had to do was drive there and— well, a guy like Pascal wouldn't leave any witnesses. If he came for daddy at home, he'd put down mommy too, along with the kid.

Bonnie wasn't the type to get all sentimental about children. She didn't think they were precious angels. Most of them were noisy, snot-nosed little monsters who belonged in a damn zoo. Still, all things being equal, she didn't especially want some rug rat knocked off just because papa got himself involved in something crazy.

She thought of calling Alan to warn him. Nope, bad idea. The call would only freak him out, throw the whole family into chaos. Better to get over there and deal with the situation on the ground.

Before leaving the bedroom, she grabbed a fanny pack to replace her purse. It would hold the Glock and two spare magazines in a zippered breakaway pocket, along with a pack of cigs, a lighter, her tool kit from the Jeep's glove box, and the spare cell phone she kept in her bureau. On her way out of the room, she grabbed a smart little beret. Never go hatless, that was her motto.

At the dining table she opened up her laptop and navigated to her cell account. If her phone was still on, she should be able to track Pascal with it. Knowing she was ditzy enough to misplace it, she'd made sure to activate the unit's find-my-phone feature.

She searched for the GPS signal. A moving blip appeared on an onscreen map at the intersection of Highway 35 and Jefferson Boulevard.

She had an insane urge to call her own number and see if Pascal answered. She wanted to rage at him. She wanted to swear she would hunt him down and get revenge.

Pascal had left the motel, but he wasn't heading toward Farmdell, not yet. He must have just fled the scene, worried that his gunshot would draw the cops. What with packing up his gear and clearing out, he might not have had time to check the call log yet.

She could wipe the phone remotely, turn it into a brick. Her account had an emergency feature—

Even as she had that thought, the blip disappeared.

Crap.

He'd either turned off the phone or deactivated the app that allowed remote access. Hardly surprising. He knew she'd tracked him via a cell phone once before.

Okay, she couldn't keep tabs on him, and she couldn't erase the call log. All she could do was speed to 133 Old Road. The house was only a few miles inland, not a long run from here. With any luck she would beat him to it.

And then ...

As dispassionately as possible she calculated the odds. She knew the territory better than Pascal did. She was a good shot, and she reacted quickly in an ambush, as she'd proven with Jacob Hart. She'd killed before, and she had no doubt she could kill Pascal if she got the drop on him. And she was sure as hell motivated.

Balanced against all that was Pascal's undoubted competence and experience. It was safe to assume that a globetrotting assassin had gone up against tougher and more seasoned adversaries than Bonnie Parker of Brighton Cove.

So what were her chances? Maybe one in two. Oh hell, be realistic: one in three.

Which meant there was a high probability she would end up dead tonight, defending a client who'd lied to her, fighting a battle she didn't even understand.

Well, she wasn't in it for the glory. She was in it for the money —except she'd lost that.

Okay, then. She was just in it. That's all.

She was in it, and there was no getting out.

18

A mile north of the motel there was a Kmart, closed for the night. Pascal pulled the SUV around back, out of sight of the highway. He got out of the car and found a stack of moldering corrugated boxes by the dump bins. Though he never smoked, he did carry a lighter, and he used it to set the cardboard on fire. He stood before the flaming pyre, warming his hands in a soft mist of rain.

The spasticity of his fingers had hampered him as he threw his possessions into his suitcase. The pain had quickly progressed from a dull ache to an electric burn. Fortunately there had been very little to pack. He had taken the girl's purse, his iPad, and the jacket and robe he had hung in the closet, and he had retrieved the stun gun after tugging off the wires.

The first squad car had entered the motel's parking lot only seconds after he had pulled out. It had been a close-run thing.

The girl had outmaneuvered him. He respected her for that. She was not his equal, but she was better than she had any right to be. In her own way she was a knight errant like himself, a fellow combatant on the field of battle, an almost worthy adversary.

She was also a corpse. Oh, she might not know it yet. But she had bought herself only a little time. The small-town detective had cost him trouble and pain, and soon he would put her in the morgue.

First he needed to find her client, the newly minted Mr. Kirby. Parker would get to the Kirbys first, of course, and perhaps move them to a new location—send them out of town, even out of state, and advise them to lie low. Conceal them and cover their scent so the bloodhound could not follow. That would be the smart, safe play.

Or she might set a trap for him and lie in wait. That was the more reckless move. A less foolhardy individual would not risk it. But it was what he would expect of her.

When his hands had recovered and the fire was mostly out, he returned to the Lexus and took out his iPad, pinpointing Alan Kirby's address on a map. It was four and one half miles from his present location.

The rain, he noticed, was falling harder now. He disliked rain. He had to exercise caution to prevent trickles and rivulets from leaking under the cuffs of his gloves, freezing the skin of his wrists and palms and fingers, incapacitating him. But the weather, like the girl's escape, was only a minor setback. Nothing could truly impede him now, not when he was so close.

His hands were trembling suddenly, and not from pain. He was so near to his quarry. In another ten or fifteen minutes he could conclude this business. True, he would have to deal with Bonnie Parker, but she was an inconsequential detail.

He found himself whistling. This was quite extraordinary. He never whistled. Yet there it was, a series of high, clear notes decorating the air around him. The tune was an aria, "Le veau d'or." One of his favorites.

As a boy he had been known for his fine full-throated voice. His family had thought he might sing professionally. This would not have been scandalous. His parents were affluent, cosmopolitan, and quite open-minded about such things. They were patrons and connoisseurs of the arts, always encouraging him in his piano lessons and watercolor classes.

But he had known, even then, that he would never be a singer. Even as a child, he lacked the necessary lightness of heart. And half the time, when his parents believed him to be attending theater rehearsals or choir practice, he was prowling the streets of Santiago, making his acquaintance with the whores and pimps, the bootleggers and black marketeers, and the more powerful men who profited by them.

Eventually he disgraced his family once too often, and even his broad-minded parents were compelled to disown him. He was sixteen, living on the streets of Santiago, carrying out kills for petty drug dealers and gang leaders at a few thousand pesos a head —sometimes literally, when delivery of the victim's head was required for final payment.

His skills brought him to the attention of bigger men, men who paid more than a few thousand pesos. He acquired a passport. He began to travel, expanding his knowledge of the world one cadaver of the time. He learned craft and cunning. He learned patience, and the inner calm born of the mastery of emotion. His reputation grew. He was offered permanent positions, which he politely declined. He styled himself as a consultant. No longer was he paid in rapidly depreciating pesos; he insisted on American dollars. He invested his money in Krugerrands and Credit Suisse notes and his mountain hideaway in San Alfonso. He had grown wealthy. He had earned respect. More than respect—he inspired fear.

But he never whistled anymore. Until tonight. Now he was a child again, making birdsong, and happy. Happy.

The phone rang.

He did not recognize the ring tone. It startled him, because it was not his. Then he realized Bonnie Parker's phone was ringing.

Might she be calling her own number, trying to get through to him? To work out some sort of deal? He checked the display but it disappointed him, reading Caller Unknown.

Curious, he pressed the screen to answer the call, but said nothing, merely listened.

"Hope I didn't wake you, Bonnie."

A man's voice.

"Hear me, bitch? You think you can hang up on me and not get a return call?"

The words slurred. Drunk. Angry.

"Not gonna talk? Who's scared now, huh? Who's the fucking

coward now?"

Pascal cleared his throat. "I am afraid Miss Parker has become estranged from her phone, my friend."

"Who the hell are you?"

"A recent acquaintance of hers. I am beginning to suspect that our Miss Parker is not very popular."

"You could say that," the man said warily.

"You hold some grudge against her, I take it."

"She tried to fucking kill me."

"Ah."

"Now I'm going to return the favor."

Pascal laughed.

"What's so funny?"

"I merely find it amusing that so many people want to eliminate this one girl."

"What other people? You tell them to lay off. She's mine."

"Of course she is. Have you killed before?"

"None of your goddamned business."

Pascal was sure the man was a novice at killing. More than that, he was a drunken fool.

"If you have not," he said quietly, "I would advise you to set your sights on a different target. Miss Parker is a professional, and she is not without skills."

"What are you, her bodyguard?"

Pascal smiled. "Hardly that."

"She's no threat to me. Not the way I got it worked out. Next time you see her, you let her know I'm going to take her down."

"Next time I see her, my friend," Pascal said, "she will already be dead."

19

Speeding west, Bonnie groped in her fanny pack and took out a pack of Parliament Whites and a lighter. She tamped out a cig and fired it up. Her hands were still shaking, and the first hungry inhalation made her cough.

Damn, she'd needed that. She hadn't been completely kidding when she'd asked Pascal for a smoke.

She switched on her wipers. The rain was coming harder—not yet a downpour, but more than a drizzle. It was a good thing Pascal's shot had gone so far wide. If he'd blown out one of her windows, she might be getting wet right now, and she'd had enough water for one night.

It occurred to her that this was the second time she'd been shot at in the Jeep within the past six months. First Jacob Hart, now Pascal. Did that make the Jeep lucky or unlucky? Hard to say.

The circumstances had been totally different, of course. Pascal had been acting on pure adrenaline and rage, while Jacob had planned his move and lain in wait. Maybe she could have avoided the confrontation with Jacob if she'd played things smarter. She couldn't see how, though. If she could have done it over, she would probably have done it the same way.

She had taken care of Kurt Land in the woods—well, she thought she'd taken care of him, anyway—then returned to his townhouse to search it. She'd turned up a safe deposit key. No surprise. He would have needed a secure place to stash the blackmail documents, not to mention his loot; dumping a big pile of cash into a checking account would raise too many questions.

Retrieving the money for her client wasn't strictly part of her job, but she was a full-service PI.

She went to the bank, opened the safe deposit box, and found herself looking at bricks of thousand-dollar bills in neat bundles. The money went into her backpack. At the bottom of the box she discovered an envelope. The financial documents, she assumed. Wrong. Photo printouts. Night shots taken with a camera phone. They were vague and indistinct, but she could make out enough detail to see Jacob Hart's profile and the slim figure of a girl.

On a January evening she again met Mr. and Mrs. Hart in her office. She handed over the money—all of it. She might be a killer, but she wasn't a thief. Then she dealt out the photos like a hand of poker, only these cards were face up, and she watched Jacob's face as she said, "You lied to me."

She expected a denial, but there was none. He nonchalantly admitted the truth. He really had dismissed Kurt Land for embezzlement, as he'd said. But the blackmail attempt had nothing to do with Hart & Hawthorn's business practices. It involved a personal matter.

"This girl." Bonnie tapped the nearest photo.

"Yes," Jacob said, while his wife closed her eyes and looked away.

It seemed Kurt Land had become obsessed with Jacob after his dismissal and had staked out his house. One night when Jacob left, Kurt followed him. He saw Jacob pick up a girl in Brighton Cove and drive her to an apartment in Maritime. Later he saw Jacob drop her off a block from her home. He followed her to her house and got her address. Using a reverse directory, he identified her as the only daughter of Mr. and Mrs. Andrew Wright. Her name was Sienna, and she was fifteen years old.

"Fifteen?" It was the first time Bonnie had heard Gillian Hart speak above a whisper. "My God, she's still a child."

"There are no children in this town," Jacob said complacently. "They grow up fast. The girls, especially."

"I've overlooked a lot ..." Gillian said in a warning tone.

Jacob gave her a hard stare. "And you'll overlook this."

Bonnie figured he was right. His wife wouldn't leave him. She would do anything to avoid a scandal that would wreck her image and her perfect life.

"There's nothing you can do, Miss Parker," Jacob said in his unruffled way. "Yes, I misled you about the details of my blackmail problem, but you are the one who removed Mr. Land. You're in it with me. If you bring me to justice for abusing a minor, I'll tell the authorities about the work you've done for me. With my reputation ruined, I would not care about saving my own skin."

"I'm not real big on working through the system," Bonnie said.

He leaned forward, his eyes glittering and cold. "Perhaps you're thinking you can dispatch me, as you dispatched Mr. Land. I wouldn't do that. The details of our arrangement will come out postmortem in the event of my demise."

"That's probably bullshit."

"Don't test me, Miss Parker. One way or the other, if I go down, you go down. You may count on that."

Bonnie figured he had her pretty much by the balls, metaphorically speaking. There were a lot of nasty things she would have enjoyed doing to him, but she couldn't risk the repercussions. And yet she had to do something. Though Jacob had promised his wife that the affair was over, Bonnie assumed it was only a matter of time until he resumed seeing the girl. She bugged Sienna's room and started keeping tabs on her. A month passed. Nothing happened. She was beginning to think Jacob might keep his word.

But evidently he'd never had any intention of doing that. He had held off from seeing Sienna only because he knew that Bonnie was sure to find out about it. He didn't want word getting back to his wife. His course of action was clear: eliminate Bonnie Parker, and then there would be no obstacle to his love match.

Jacob could not have killed Kurt Land, because their known acrimony would have made him an obvious suspect. But he had no known connection with Brighton Cove's only PI. Their relationship was completely off the books.

He lay in ambush in the alley behind her office. When she left late one night, he took his best shot. It wasn't good enough.

There had been no postmortem exposure of their arrangement, though the prospect had cost her a few sleepless nights at the time.

She hit Highway 35 and turned north. Within a mile she saw the Roach House coming up on her left. Couple of cop cars in the lot. Some lookie-loos standing around. She cruised past without slowing. In another mile she would hit Branch Avenue and head inland. Away from the highway, away from the motel. That was good. She didn't like being near it, didn't like the feelings it brought up.

The camper in front of her was obeying the speed limit, which meant it was going way too slow. She was thinking about passing on the shoulder when red and blue lights flared in her rearview.

Crap.

She pulled over, worrying about the carbine in the rear storage compartment of the Jeep. She'd tossed a blanket over it, but she wasn't sure it was fully concealed. The unregistered Glock in her fanny pack could be trouble too. Luckily she'd pulled on a rain poncho before leaving her house. It was a big floppy sheet of black vinyl with an attached hood and snaps at the sides, and it was loose enough to conceal the bulge around her waist.

She took a closer look at the car in the mirror and recognized it as Dan Maguire's Buick, his personal ride—the one she'd trashed a few hours ago. He'd stuck a portable light bar on the roof. This was getting better and better.

She adjusted the mirror to see if Dan was alone in the car. He was. Then she noticed a ragged strip of duct tape on her wrist.

Hell. She'd never removed the tape. Bits of it clung to both arms. If Dan saw it, she'd have some 'splaining to do.

In the mirror, he climbed out on the driver's side, wearing civilian clothes.

She clawed at the tape on her right wrist, tearing it free, and tossed the scraps on the floor.

Dan approached the car, moving quickly in the rain.

There was still tape on her left wrist. No time to get rid of it. She lowered her arm, wedging it between herself and the car door. With any luck he wouldn't see it.

He rapped on the window. With her right hand she rolled it down. Glancing down, she saw the discarded tape on the floor mat and nudged it under the seat with her foot.

"Surprised you're doing traffic stops, Dan. They bust you down to patrolman?"

He wiped a smear of raindrops off his face. "That's funny, Parker. You're a riot."

"Whoa, what's with the attitude? You seem more constipated than usual. Getting enough fiber in your diet?"

"Maybe I just don't like it when people mess with my personal property."

"Somebody TP your house?"

"An unidentified party dumped a pile of dogshit in my car."

"Kids these days."

"I'm not so sure it was kids."

"Mischievous raccoons?"

"I'm thinking it was you."

"Jeepers, Dan. What do you think I am, some kind of sociopath? Oh, right, you do."

She didn't know why he was wasting her time. Pascal must have determined the Kirbys' address by now. He could get to them at any moment.

"So tell me," Dan said, hunching his shoulders against the rain, "why exactly are you tooling around at midnight?"

"Got a yen for some Taco Bell."

"Where were you before this?"

"On the beach."

"In the rain?"

"It hasn't been raining long."

"What were you doing on the beach at night?"

"Meditating."

He lifted an eyebrow. "You?"

"What, I can't be spiritual? I was opening my friggin' chakras."

She was glad she had the cigarette. It steadied her, gave her something to do with her hand. Her right hand, anyway. The left was still wedged out of sight.

"No witnesses?" Dan pressed.

"Why would I need witnesses? I'm not a suspect in anything, am I?"

"It seems like you're always out and about when there's trouble."

"No more than you, Dan. What kind of trouble are we talking about?"

"You don't need to know."

"Must be something big, to bring out the chief of police at this hour."

"We received an anonymous shots-fired call from the Coach House. And you just happen to be in the vicinity."

"It's a small town. I'm in the vicinity of pretty much everything."

"I just think it's interesting. The coincidence, you know."

"You think I fired the shot, Dan? Is that it?"

"It's not the gunshot that got me out of bed. It's what's inside the motel room."

"Dead body?"

"The officers at the scene report a bathtub rigged with wires. Like something was hooked up to the wires. A car battery, maybe. Any idea what that's about?"

"Either the world's worst high school science experiment or a torture setup."

"It's summer. High school's not in session."

"So, torture."

"That's what we're thinking." The rain fell harder. "And that's why I was headed over there. We don't get too many torture cases in Brighton Cove."

"Maybe that should be our slogan."

"They tell me whoever was in the room cleared out in a hurry."

She wondered how far she could press him for info. "Any ID on the guest?"

"Some foreigner. That's all the manager remembers. Latin American, he says."

"That covers a lot of ground." Alan's friend must have kept his mouth shut about a local attorney's interest in that particular guest. "Any way to narrow it down? Credit card, license plate, vehicle description?"

"I'm told the guy paid cash. Manager didn't see the car. And the Coach House isn't the kind of place where you sign the register."

"Guess not."

He leaned in through the window, squinting at her. "When was the last time you were in the Coach House?"

She blew smoke in his face. "I don't frequent dives like that."

"So you're saying we won't find your prints in there?"

This was a bluff. Any motel room would have thousands of prints, too many to process. "I haven't been inside, so how could I leave prints?"

"Yeah. How could you?"

He was staring at her from inches away. In the close confines of the car, she was reminded of Pascal's penetrating gaze. A tremor threatened to zigzag through her body.

"You okay, Parker?"

Apparently she hadn't suppressed the tremor well enough. "Torture kind of freaks me out. Good thing I wasn't around during the Spanish Inquisition."

"If you had been, you'd've found a way to beat the system. Unless you came up against me."

"Wanna put me on the rack, Dan?"

"It would be one way to get answers. I know you're involved somehow. Like before, I'm smelling your stink all over this thing."

"I'm smelling your stink, too, buddy boy. Maybe you didn't clean out your car as good as you thought."

He squinted harder. "You think you're smart, smarter than me."

"That's not setting the bar very high."

"But it's the smart ones who always trip up."

"Sounds like somebody's been watching *Columbo*."

He stared off into the night, then turned his head to face her. "Tom and Rebecca," he said.

She was sure she hadn't heard him correctly. "What?"

"They were your parents, right? Tom and Rebecca Parker."

"You're into genealogy now?"

"They were crooks. They got murdered in a motel. Probably not much different from the Coach House."

"You sure you haven't been sampling the illegal substances in the evidence room?"

"Are you saying Tom and Rebecca weren't your folks?"

"I'm saying it's none of your damn business who's in my family tree."

"Everything about you is my business. I've made it my business. You're a bad seed."

She thought about giving him the finger, but her right hand was occupied with the cigarette, and her left had to stay out of view. "Look, am I getting a ticket or what?"

"No ticket. I just stopped for a chat."

"Great. Nice talking to you. Now if you'll excuse me, there's a Burrito Grande with my name on it."

"Got my eye on you, Parker. I'm watching. Always watching."

"With all the great stuff on TV, I'm surprised you can find the time."

He started to walk off. She peeled off the tape on her left wrist, then thought of something. She stuck her head out the window into the rain.

"Hey, Dan? What got lifted from the sporting goods shop?"

"Why do you want to know?"

"I might have a lead on some hot merchandise."

"Well, unless it's a PSE Mach-twelve, you're on the wrong track. That's a—"

"I know what it is."

"Is that your hot merch?"

"Nope. Guess I'm wasting your time."

"Tell me something I don't know."

And fuck you, too, she thought.

She drove off, maintaining the posted speed limit until she turned onto Branch and was out of his sight. Then she floored the gas pedal, accelerating down the two-lane rural road at sixty, hoping she didn't hit a damn deer.

She'd lucked out, anyway. If Dan had noticed the carbine in the rear or the tape on her wrist, she would be cooling her heels in the station house. She could have talked her way out of it eventually, but by then it would have been too late to save Alan Kirby and his family.

She only hoped it wasn't too late now.

20

The Kirbys lived in an old farmhouse on a half acre, with a rickety fence marking off their property's perimeter, and piney woods on three sides. An isolated location, well away from the neighbors. Bonnie didn't like it. It meant Pascal could break in and take care of business with little risk of attracting attention. For all she knew, he might be inside already.

Right now the house was dark, with only the porch lights aglow. She pulled off the road into a wooded grove across the way and parked the Jeep out of sight, hoping the rain wouldn't come down too hard and leave her tires stuck in a slop of mud. She left her hat in the car, not wanting to lose it like her last one, but she took everything else—the fanny pack with the Glock, and the Ruger carbine, which she strapped to her shoulder. She packed her pants pockets with extra twenty-five-round banana clips for the Ruger, and slipped the tool kit from her glove box into one of the poncho's two front pockets.

Some houses in Millstone County dated back to the Revolutionary War, and the Kirby place was probably one of them. It was a three-story whitewashed pile with a rickety front porch and two tiers of dark windows. The top floor was a windowless loft or attic. Despite the rain, a couple of heavy-duty AC compressors hummed at the rear of the house. The summer night this far inland was humid and stifling, and the steady downpour had done nothing to lower the temperature.

She circled the house, examining every ground-floor entrance for signs of forced entry. She saw no tamper marks on the door locks and window latches, no footprints on the window sills to disturb the settled dust, and no footprints that preceded hers.

Unless her adversary had chosen to enter via an upstairs window—improbable—he wasn't here yet. But he could arrive at any time.

On her second circuit of the house's perimeter, she noticed a small item mounted on a three-foot pole about twenty feet from the driveway. She approached it from behind and carefully inspected the device. It was the sensor-transmitter of a driveway alert system. It sent a pulsed infrared beam across the driveway to a reflector aligned directly opposite. If a car interrupted the beam, a warning would chime inside the house. A solar panel on top allowed it to store power throughout the day.

She disabled the unit and unscrewed it from its mounting, then stuffed it and the reflector into the other front pocket of her poncho. She had a use for both items. But first she had to get into the house.

On most of the windows, her keychain flashlight—yeah, it still worked, despite immersion in the tub—had revealed wire sensors that would trigger an alarm if the window was raised or broken. Well, Alan had told her he had a security system. But a couple of windows at the rear were unprotected. She chose one that looked in on a utility room.

With a glass cutter, she carved along the edges of a window pane, removing it from the sash, then reached in and opened the latch. After that, it was easy to raise the window and climb through. She kicked wet dirt off her shoes and scattered it on the sill to conceal any scuff marks left by her entry, shut the window, and pressed the pane back in place. She didn't want Pascal to know she'd beaten him there.

The only way to get from the utility room to the rest of the house was through a hall doorway. She figured there would be a pressure-sensitive mat under the carpet at that spot. It was a cost-cutting measure. A mat at the bottleneck was cheaper than sensors on two windows.

Kneeling, she peeled up part of the carpet and confirmed her guess. She stepped around the mat to avoid triggering it.

Quickly she explored the downstairs. Dining room, kitchen, half bath, den. In a living room cozy enough to be called a parlor, she found the battery-operated receiver for the driveway alert system. She concealed the sensor-transmitter under a table in the parlor at the foot of the stairs, taping the reflector to the wall directly opposite. When the unit was switched on, it sent a continuous invisible beam across the stairway.

She was careful not to break the beam and trip the alarm as she headed up the stairs to the second floor, where the staircase took a dogleg behind a wall and continued to the loft. Rain drummed on the roof. In the stillness of the sleeping house, she looked in on the bedrooms. One of them was a child's room, with a small sleeping shape under a mound of bedcovers. Nearby was the master bedroom—two shapes.

She saw no need to wake the Kirbys. Better to keep the house silent so she could listen for any sound of intrusion.

Down the hall from the master bedroom was an office. In it was a file cabinet. Her penlight played over tabbed folders marked Finances, Taxes, Real Estate, Insurance. Most of the folders were thin, which was no surprise, since the Kirbys' history didn't extend very far.

She wanted to take a better look at some of those folders, especially the unmarked ones at the back of the cabinet, but not now. Her spider sense was tingling. She had the unsettling feeling that her bathroom buddy was about to make his move.

She returned to the stairs and set down the receiver on the second flight, dialing the volume low. She could wait there, screened from view by the wall, with the chime to alert her when Pascal started up the staircase.

She removed the poncho and took up her position on the stairway to the loft, the Glock in her hands, the Osprey silencer screwed on tight. With the windows shut and the neighbors far away, she wasn't worried about the sound of gunfire, but the silencer would minimize her muzzle flashes and give Pascal less of a target in the dark.

Not that she intended to give him time to aim and shoot. When the chime sounded, she couldn't hesitate. It was all about speed. Shoot first and ask questions never.

She had no problem with that. After what he'd done to her, pulling the trigger on that fucker would be a pure pleasure.

Was she scared? Nah, not really. On edge. But not scared. Fear was for those times when you were helpless, and she wasn't helpless now, not with two guns and plenty of spare ammo and a workable plan of action.

In the tub she'd been helpless—and plenty scared. She really had thought it was over for her. Somehow her life had come full circle, and she was in another bathtub in another cheap motel, only this time she wasn't hiding ...

She shook her head. Bad memory. Bad enough that she hadn't owned up about it to Des. She'd told him she ran off on her own, and her parents were killed. Both things had happened—but not in that order.

The motel in Conover, Pennsylvania, could have been a motel anywhere. Always there were the same faded bath towels, the same balky TV set that got only some of the channels, the same hairs of unknown origin in the shower drain, the same noisy neighbors who could be heard through the walls, laughing or fighting or screwing. There was the bed where her parents slept, and the cot—if the motel supplied one—where Bonnie slept. When there was no cot, she slept on the sofa; when there was no sofa, she slept on the floor. In this particular motel, there was a sofa, at least.

They hadn't been at the motel long, not even long enough for Bonnie to find a local school where she could play the role of outcast. And that night it became clear they would be moving on soon, probably the next morning.

Bonnie was only fourteen, but she knew the signs. Her dad was acting worried, the way he always did before they hit the road. He was talking about things going south, about a deal that hadn't worked out as planned.

Her mom nodded and mumbled noises signifying concern, sympathy, agreement—noises that could have signified anything, actually.

Neither of them paid any attention to their daughter. They never did. Her father seldom addressed her directly, and when he spoke of her, he didn't use her name. She was "the girl." "Tell the girl to stop moping around ... Let the girl do it ... Don't talk about that in front of the girl ..."

Two things saved Bonnie that night. The first was that her mom had done the laundry in the afternoon, using some coin-operated machines at the rear of the motel, and she hadn't laid Bonnie's freshly washed blankets on the sofa yet. Without the blankets, no one could tell that a child would be sleeping there, or that a child was staying in the room at all.

The second was that she was in the bathroom with the door half closed. Not open, so anyone in the main room could see her, and not closed entirely, signaling that someone was inside. Half closed—just enough to conceal her, but not enough to draw attention. Such a little thing, but it made the difference.

She was in her underwear—her parents had never sprung for pj's—and she'd just finished brushing her teeth when there was a pounding on the motel room door, then harsh whispers and hurried footsteps. Visitors, three of them at least, crowding into the room. Her dad uttered some kind of protest, and she heard a smack, then a thud. Her mom started to cry out but fell silent. Too silent.

Bonnie knew something bad was going down. Her dad had been on the run for years, running from everybody, and this time it appeared he had not run fast enough.

The bathroom was small and not very clean, but it did have a nice big bathtub with a vinyl shower curtain. The curtain was yellow and printed with images of baby ducks. Bonnie climbed into the tub and hid behind the curtain, smelling shampoo, seeing the mildew in the grout between the shower tiles, and listening to the sounds of torture from the next room. Fierce whispers, groans of denial, cries of pain or protest immediately stifled. The mirror over the sink offered a partial view, and by craning her neck Bonnie could see her father in the room's one straight-back chair, his hands bloody. Her mother lay on her stomach on the bed, one arm jerking feebly as she made low whimpering noises.

From the questions it was obvious that some money had gone missing and the men thought her father had taken it. He denied he had, and Bonnie believed him, but the men didn't, or maybe they just didn't care. *He's telling the truth,* she thought furiously, *just leave him alone, he's telling the truth.*

And then the strangers began to search the motel room.

That was the scariest part. The bathroom door opened fully and someone came in, a man, breathing hard, his footsteps heavy. She balled up behind the pleated curtain among the baby ducks, squeezing herself as small as possible, knowing all he had to do was glance into the tub and he would see her huddled there, and then ... and then ...

She was a witness, and she knew what happened to witnesses.

But he didn't look in the shower. He was interested in the medicine cabinet, the storage space under the sink, even the inside of the toilet tank. If he saw the toothbrush drying on the lip of the sink, he ignored it.

Then he swore luridly and stomped out of the bathroom, leaving her unseen and untouched.

The other searchers had no better luck. There was a brief, muttered exchange. She caught only a few words. One man said they didn't need to do it, and another man said, *No loose ends.*

Just before they left, Bonnie heard two noises, muffled, like a distant door slamming twice. She knew what it was. She'd watched her dad practicing in the woods with a silenced gun.

She emerged from her hiding place and found her parents in the other room. Her dad was missing several fingers, and her mom's skirt and undies had been pulled down, and there was blood on her thighs.

Both of them had been shot in the temple—clean shots,

efficient and professional.

She understood what had happened. Her dad hadn't taken the money. One of the others had stolen it and let him take the blame. Maybe it was the one who'd raped her mother, or the one who'd snipped off her father's fingers one at a time.

A man who could do a thing like that, Bonnie often thought, was a man who deserved to die.

Outside, the rain fell harder, banging its fists on the farmhouse's roof. She heard a distant roll of thunder. She hoped the storm didn't wake one of the Kirbys. It would be awkward if wifey or kiddo were to wander out into the hall for a drink of water and come across her.

She wondered how much the wife really knew, and what the hell her client had gotten himself into. Most of all, she wondered what was taking Pascal so goddamned long.

By this time he had to know the location of the house. He could easily get in. It was his only logical move.

So what was he waiting for?

Beside her, the chime sounded.

He wasn't waiting.

He was here.

She sprang to her feet, pivoting out from behind the wall to stand at the top of the staircase, ready to open fire.

But there was no target. No Pascal. The stairway was empty.

False alarm?

No.

Centered on her chest, the red dot of a laser sighting system.

He was hidden somewhere in the shadows of the prrlor, and he had her dead in his sights.

But he didn't fire.

Not for a half second—long enough for her to duck behind the wall. As she was in motion she heard a distant pop—silenced shot, subsonic round—and felt a burning stripe lash her left arm.

Then she was back on the higher staircase, hearing thumps of impact as he fired at the wall.

Dimly she was aware of blood on her arm, a stinging tear in her left biceps, but she could still move the arm, it wasn't broken, so it didn't matter.

And how he'd tricked her—that didn't matter either, not right now.

Even silenced gunfire was loud enough to wake people, especially when the shots were punching into a wall. Down the hallway, the kid cried out in confusion, and from the master bedroom came the stir of the parents, then Alan's voice. "Who's there? What's going on?"

"Don't sweat it, Alan!" she yelled back. "I got it under control!"

Like fun she did.

She leaned out and fired two wild shots into the parlor, just to get Pascal's attention. Three bullets answered her, landing perilously close even as she retreated, and then there was a blast of noise, a deafening clamor all around her.

The alarm system. Alan or his wife had hit the panic button.

It wouldn't faze Pascal. He knew the response time was measured in minutes, not seconds. He still had plenty of time. She, on the other hand, needed to end this standoff pronto. Bullets flying around was not a good situation for anybody.

She jammed the Glock into her waistband and unshouldered the carbine.

Pascal thought he had her trapped. "Well, asshole," she hissed, "say hello to my little friend."

She pulled back the bolt and put her finger lightly on the trigger, then spun out from cover and opened fire.

The carbine was another of her black-market toys, one she'd modified, removing the trigger assembly to grind down the bolt catch with a diamond bit. What had been a semi-auto rifle had been converted into a full automatic. Easy peasy.

Holding down the trigger, she spat all twenty-five rounds into the parlor in a continuous burst. It might have been noisy if the scream of the burglar alarm hadn't swallowed all other sound.

When the gun was empty, she retreated behind the wall and pulled out the magazine, then slapped in a fresh one and retracted the bolt again.

Back to work. Another spray of gunfire lit up the parlor. She swiveled on her hips, tracing a semicircle across the room as expended shell casings flew out of the gun.

It took only a couple of seconds to empty the magazine. She took cover and heeled in a third one. The gun was already getting hot, the barrel smoking.

One more fusillade. In the flickering light of the muzzle flashes, she glimpsed Pascal on the run, darting toward the front door. Then she was out of ammo again, shoving in a fourth mag.

But she held her fire. From the top of the stairs she could see that the front door was open. He'd fled.

She came down fast, nearly stumbling over something at the foot of the staircase, and ran to the door. Raindrops beaded on her face as she risked looking out, just in time to see a black SUV explode out of a stand of pines and swing onto Old Road, speeding east.

He hadn't been expecting a machine gun. He'd been in a bad tactical position, outgunned and occupying lower ground. Retreat was the only option.

And he was wounded. She felt the tackiness of fresh blood on the door frame at shoulder height.

She'd fleshed him, at least. She had drawn blood, and she felt good about that.

21

The alarm was still howling throughout the house. She returned to the stairs and shouted up to the second floor. "Turn that goddamn thing off! He's gone!"

A moment later—silence. But it was a loud silence, because her ears were still ringing.

She knew the drill. The security company would call to see if a police presence was required. "Tell the alarm guys you set it off by accident," she yelled. "Alan, you hear me?"

"I hear you."

The phone rang. She let him deal with it as she switched on some lights and surveyed the parlor.

A lot of holes in the walls. A lot of broken glass and splintered furniture. Amazing how much damage seventy-five rounds could do. The slugs themselves littered the floor, a sea of misshapen pellets.

The wall by the sofa was spattered with blood. Pascal had been crouching there when she'd hit him. Not a bad hit, she thought; not enough blood for a head wound or a spurting artery.

She tracked the trail of droplets across the carpet. His strides were long and even. He seemed mobile enough. Probably she had nicked him in the upper body or an arm.

Her own arm hurt like a bastard, but she would handle that little problem in a minute.

She returned to the staircase and took a closer look. By the bottom step lay a throw pillow from the sofa. Pascal had pitched it at the stairs to trigger her early-warning system and lure her out of hiding.

But how the hell had he known about the infrared beam in the first place? She could only assume he'd realized the staircase was the best place for an ambush, and a likely spot for her to rig a booby trap.

Earlier he'd seen through her attempt to track his vehicle with a cell phone. Now he'd anticipated her strategy inside the house.

He was good, this guy. Always one step ahead.

She recalled him saying, *It is what they pay me for.* She had a feeling he was worth every penny.

Still, he could have taken her out on the landing if he'd been a hair quicker. Which was weird, because it wasn't like a pro to hesitate. She knew she wouldn't have.

By now the phone call was over, Alan having given some explanation and recited the necessary security code. She started up the stairs, taking her time, because she was feeling a whole lot of different things right now and she was afraid that any sudden, violent action might set her off like a hand grenade.

Some of the second-story lights were on. She saw the wife comforting the kid in his bedroom. Little boy, maybe six, looking more confused and sleepy than scared. Wifey, on the other hand, looked positively distraught.

Alan was still in the master bedroom. When she entered, he was pulling on his trousers. He stopped when he saw her, leaving his fly unzipped.

"What in Christ's name just happened here?" he breathed in a fierce whisper. "You come into my house—"

She knew he was only flipping out from stress, but she didn't care. She closed the distance between them and grabbed him by his collar and shoved him up against the closet door.

"You fucking asshole," she hissed.

He stared at her, sudden fear in his eyes. She didn't understand the fear at first, until she saw herself as he did—the Glock snugged in her waistband, the machine gun riding on her shoulder. Like her namesake, maybe. Had bank tellers and state troopers stared at Clyde's Bonnie that way when her blood was up?

Slowly she released him. "You sold me a load of bullshit. What's the point of hiring me if you feed me a bunch of lies?"

"I didn't. I—"

"Shut up, Alan, or should I say Jeffrey? Yeah, that's right, I'm on to you. You've been running a game on me. Everything you told me was a big fat shit sandwich."

He almost denied it, then took another look at her face, and nodded.

"Okay," she said. "You and me—we're gonna have a serious conversation about this."

"Yes, sure, of course." He was being very agreeable all of a sudden.

"But not now. First things first. We need to get you, the missus, and the rug rat outta here. Have 'em get dressed, and don't let 'em take all day about it. I don't know how long we can stay in this house."

"You think the neighbors heard the shooting?"

"Nah, the alarm covered it. It's not the neighbors I'm worried about."

He got it. "It's him. You're thinking he may come back."

"That's exactly what I'm thinking."

"Cynthia." Alan held his voice steady. "You and A.J. need to get dressed right away."

Bonnie smiled. "A.J., huh?"

"Alan Junior."

"Cute. What's his real name?"

"Christopher." Alan rubbed his forehead. "How'd you get past the alarm system?"

"Buddy boy, I hate to break it to you, but your security measures are strictly open-mic night at the Improv."

"What?"

"They're amateur hour. Didn't stop me. Didn't stop him."

"Oh." He looked away, his face troubled. "I never thought he'd find us this soon."

"Yeah, company always drops by at the most inconvenient

time." She had no intention of telling him she'd helped Pascal track him down.

She was saved from further conversation by the arrival of Cynthia with A.J. in her arms. The lady of the house was blond—it looked like a dye job—and unnaturally thin, like one of those starved waifs in the fashion pages. She stopped in the bedroom doorway and gave Bonnie a hard stare. "Was that a machine gun you were firing?"

"It wasn't a water pistol."

"Alan, who is this woman?"

And I love you too, Bonnie thought. "I'm a PI, name of Parker. Your hubby hired me, and I just saved your ass."

"You hired her?" She spoke in the clipped dialect of fancy-pants private school kids. Came from money, probably.

Alan nodded glumly. "I didn't think I had any choice. There was someone after us."

"And he's still after you. So throw on some clothes, toss a coat over the tyke, and grab a couple of overnight bags. We gotta amscray."

The woman stood her ground. "I'm not going anywhere until I know what this is about."

"It's about Jeffrey and Caroline Walker. *Capisce?*"

"You told her about that?" Cynthia asked her husband.

"She found out."

"How much do you know about her? How do you know we can trust her?"

"She was recommended by a friend."

"Hey," Bonnie interrupted, "in case you haven't noticed, *she* is right here in the room with you, and *she* is getting majorly pissed off. You two have your marching orders. Start doing the high-step."

Cynthia glared at her. "You're quite full of yourself, aren't you?"

"Yeah, I'm a freakin' spitfire."

"Well, you can't order me around. I demand to know what's going on."

"You want the background story? Here's the *USA Today* version. You guys got involved in something messy and had to change your names and hide out here. It didn't work. The boogeyman tracked you down and he's gunning for bear."

"What—what boogeyman?"

"A professional killer from Chile."

Cynthia hugged A.J. tighter. Bonnie was glad to see it. It meant she was taking this business seriously, though the bullet holes in the wall should have been enough to clue her in about that.

"Chile?" she asked, her voice low and uncertain.

"That's his base of operations. But he gets around. I'm guessing his frequent flyer miles pile up pretty fast. His name's Pascal, by the way. Or so he told me."

Alan glanced at her. "You talked to him?"

"Oh, yeah, we're best buds now. He gave me a nice little workout, free of charge. On second thought, there were a lot of charges. And he took Sammy."

"Oh my God, who's Sammy?"

"My phone. So can we get a move on, or what?"

Cynthia didn't seem to be listening. She set the boy down on the bed. "Pascal," she said quietly. She saw Bonnie's questioning gaze and added, "As in Pascal's Wager?"

"I don't follow."

"Blaise Pascal? The philosopher?"

"Sorry, I'm not too up on my philosophy."

"He's the one who said the heart has its reasons."

"Did he? I thought that was Woody Allen. Well, I don't think this sick son of a bitch has a heart. As for his reasons, he's in it for the pesos."

"A killer for hire," Cynthia uttered tonelessly.

"Don't sweat it. It's my job to see he doesn't earn his keep. Get dressed and packed. I'm gonna clean myself up." She plucked at her sleeve, and Alan jumped a little.

"You're wounded," he said, shocked.

"More like grazed. Kind of a rush when that happens. Like

winning the Powerball."

She went into the bathroom down the hall, stripped off her bloodied shirt, and tossed it into a wastebasket. She cleansed the wound with hot water. The bullet had shaved off a layer of skin, and some cotton fibers from her sleeve were embedded in the wound. In the cabinet under the sink she found first aid supplies. With tweezers she plucked out the trapped fibers before applying antiseptic and wrapping her biceps in a bandage. From a hamper in the hallway she stole a dark blue blouse. Dark blue was the preferred color for camouflage at night.

With the blouse on, she checked herself out in the bathroom mirror. The bandage was invisible under the sleeve. That was good. She didn't want Pascal to know he'd nicked her. It was never a good idea to reveal any weakness, no matter how minor. Let her adversary think she didn't have a scratch.

Back in the bedroom, she found Alan tossing prescription meds and other essentials into a small suitcase while A.J., a perfect replica of his dad in miniature, watched from the bed. The kid was surprisingly calm, all things considered. Apparently he interpreted this late-night ritual as just another of the incomprehensible things grown-ups did. Which was good, because a squalling child might have been more than she could take just now.

Cynthia emerged from the walk-in closet, suitably attired. She frowned at Bonnie. "Is that my blouse?"

"Looks good on me, huh? I'll try to get it back to you without any holes."

"You sure you're okay?" Alan asked, looking up from the suitcase.

She found his solicitude touching and irritating at the same time. "I told you, it was a pinprick. I've had manicures that did more damage. So, we ready to roll?"

"I'm not done packing."

"I'll give you five minutes. Think of it as a fire drill. Take only the stuff you can't live without. I'm gonna go grab my car. Meet me at the back door in"—she checked her watch—"four minutes thirty."

She retrieved her poncho and was about to go downstairs when she remembered the file cabinet. She detoured into the den and riffled through the folders. At the back of the top drawer she found a cache of documents from the Kirbys' previous life. Many related to Conscience Watch, the nonprofit outfit Alan Kirby joined when he was still Jeffrey Walker. Conscience Watch was an international human rights organization that put pressure on dictatorial regimes to release political prisoners. It seemed legit. A bunch of heavy hitters from politics and the entertainment industry were listed as honorary board members. One glossy brochure was devoted to thanking the biggest donors. She scanned the list, and right there, near the top, were two names she knew.

Jacob and Gillian Hart.

"How now, brown cow," she murmured for no good reason.

Things were starting to make just a little more sense. Ponying up the cash for new IDs and a replacement law degree would have been a stretch for a mid-level exec at a nonprofit firm, but no stretch at all for the Harts. Naturally the new-made Kirbys had ended up in the vicinity of Brighton Cove. They needed to stay close to their benefactors.

And there was another possibility, one that was a little more troubling. But she didn't have time to work it all out now. She would deal with it later.

If she was still alive.

22

Dan Maguire knew Bonnie Parker was dirty in all kinds of ways. Dirty in ways he couldn't even imagine, probably. And she had something to do with the crime scene at the Coach House, he was sure of that.

He had spent the past hour talking to the manager and to those guests who hadn't cleared out fast enough. Nobody knew anything. In a crap hole like this, nobody ever did.

Now he stood under the overhang by the parking lot, staring past the cycling light bars of parked cruisers and a sheet of steady rain. On the highway, post-midnight traffic blurred past, headlights and taillights making watercolor streaks. He watched the traffic and tried to figure out what the hell had gone down here.

"It's a puzzler, huh, Chief?" That was Phil Gaines, the only detective on the Brighton Cove force. "You know we're going to have to bring the Highway Patrol in on this, right?"

"I know." The state police had more expertise in these situations. They had a crime lab. They had—no offense to Phil—real detectives, not glorified beat cops who investigated the occasional bicycle theft or late-night break-in.

"Be nice if we had something to give 'em. Some theory of the case."

"Fire away," Dan said irritably.

"Sorry. I'm all out of ammo. I mean, it seems clear enough that someone was in that tub, getting shock treatment. And somehow they got away, and a shot was fired. But the who, what, and why is a mystery."

Dan surveyed the parking lot. "At least four vehicles left before the first officer got here. And naturally we have no description of any of them. It's enough to make you lose your faith in human nature."

"One was probably our victim, running away. Another was our perp, fleeing the scene. The other two, or however many more there were, had to be some of the Coach House's upstanding clientèle, heading for cover."

"They're the ones we really need to talk to. They might've seen something."

"Good luck finding them. Nobody wants to admit to checking in here."

"Then we squeeze the ones who didn't get away. The hookers and the johns. The manager too. We apply pressure until somebody's memory improves."

"If they saw anything in the first place. Most of them say they never even heard the gunshot."

"How can you not hear a gunshot?"

"Maybe they were preoccupied." Phil poked his index finger into the curled fingers of his other hand, in and out, in and out, accompanied by a creaking-bedspring noise. He liked illustrating his thoughts with gestures and sound effects. A comedian, Phil was.

"Yeah. Maybe." Dan turned toward the motel room, blinking in the spill of light from its open door. "What do you say we take one more walk-through, then call in the big boys."

"Fair enough."

They lifted the crime scene ribbon and stepped inside. The place was just as Dan had seen it when he arrived, fresh from his fruitless dialogue with Bonnie Parker on the side of the highway. The unmade bed, the nightstand out of place and scarred with a knife blade's thrust, the discarded phone and lamp. The carpet was damp, and water was pooled on the bathroom tiles near the half-full tub lined with a shower curtain. One wire floated in the cold water, while the other lay tangled on the floor.

"He cut the wires off the lamp and the TV," Phil said as they stood in the bathroom doorway, "and trimmed the insulation off the ends."

"Sounds like he wasn't planning to put on this little show. He had to improvise."

"Wonder what he used for juice."

"He couldn't have plugged the wires into the wall socket?"

"Not without tripping the breaker. No, had to be an independent power source. Something he had with him. A hair dryer, say."

"Would a hair dryer pack enough punch to torture somebody?"

"That, I don't know. They say you can fry somebody if you toss a hair dryer into a tub." His hands fluttered, and he made a sound like a bug zapper. "But it could be a, what do you call it, urban legend."

"How about that stuff floating in the water?" Dan pointed to two ragged chunks of foam.

"I'm thinking it was used as a gag. To silence the victim, and maybe to prevent him from biting his tongue off."

"Looks like there's some blood on it."

"Maybe he bit his tongue anyway."

"You keep saying *he*. What if it was a woman?"

Phil shrugged. "Could have been. Some sexual thing. Maybe consensual at first. Bondage play that got out of hand. Somebody didn't respect the safe word."

"Or maybe not like that. Maybe a revenge thing."

"You'd have to piss somebody off really good to drive them to this kind of revenge."

"Yeah," Dan said. "Yeah, you would."

Who was better at pissing off people than Bonnie Parker? Nobody, that's who.

He remembered how she'd shivered when the subject of torture came up. Her hand holding the cigarette had been a little shaky. And he sure as hell didn't believe she'd been meditating on the damn beach in the rain.

He turned away from the bathroom, and his eye picked out a hint of powder blue protruding from beneath the bed.

"What's that?" he asked.

"I dunno."

"You're telling me nobody looked under the bed?"

"I instructed our guys to do only a cursory search. Drawers and closets, that's it. Figured I'd leave the CSI stuff for the bag-and-tag brigade. Otherwise we'll just catch hell for doing it wrong."

"You have a rubber glove?"

Phil dug in his jacket pocket and produced one. Dan slipped it on, then got down on his knees and took hold of the item, drawing it into view.

A woman's hat.

"Now that's interesting," he muttered. "That's very interesting."

He turned it over, examining the label. The hat had been purchased at Evie's Consignment Shop in downtown Brighton Cove.

Parker shopped there. He had seen her.

"Think it's something, Chief?" Phil asked, crouching beside him.

"Could be. See the label? I need to know who bought this hat."

"We can talk to Evie in the morning."

"We can talk to her now."

"It's the middle of the night."

"Then we'll wake her up. Put some excitement in her life."

"I take it you have a suspicion who the hat belongs to."

"Not just a suspicion, Phil. I know. I *know*."

An unhealthy obsession, his wife had said. But she didn't know about the itch. How it kept him up nights.

And how good it would feel to scratch that itch at last.

23

The rain was falling harder as Bonnie retrieved her Jeep, and the wind was picking up, clutching with invisible fingers at the canvas roof. It looked like they were in for a genuine drenching.

Settled behind the wheel with her beret back on her head, she steered down the gravel track of the driveway and pulled around to idle alongside the back door. She was pretty sure she'd squashed some of Cynthia's flowers, but the main thing was to keep the family out of sight of the road in case Pascal came back.

It took the Kirby clan six minutes, not five, to appear at the door toting two small suitcases and a sleepy towheaded boy in a rain slicker and pj's. The kid was plugged into a pair of earbuds and gazed mesmerized at a smartphone's screen.

Bonnie leaned out the window and whistled. "Let's get a move on. Everybody into the car, chop-chop."

Alan slid into the front passenger seat while Cynthia and A.J. took up the rear, sharing the space with the suitcases. Bonnie pulled off before her passengers had finished fastening their seat belts.

She reversed onto Old Road and turned east. Wet asphalt blurred beneath her hood. Trees framed the road on both sides. In time with the beat of the wiper blades, her gaze kept flicking from the windshield to the rearview mirror and back. Pascal had left the farmhouse, but he might not have gone far.

"How much can Junior hear?" she asked.

"Nothing," Cynthia said from the backseat. "He's in his own world."

"Okay, here's the thing." She lit a cigarette. "Time for us to have a powwow. I need the truth, folks. And I need it now."

Cynthia coughed. "Must you smoke?"

"Just doing my part to keep Phillip Morris profitable. I'm a shareholder."

"Secondhand smoke isn't good for children."

"Neither are bullets. That oughtta be your priority right now."

"I don't think I like your attitude."

"Yeah, I need to work on that." She expelled a stream of smoke, hoping the bitch choked on it. "So before you two were Alan and Cynthia, you were Jeffrey and Caroline. I'm guessing there's a story that goes with that."

Alan looked at his hands. "It's complicated."

"Let's stop the dance. Was there anything you told me on the boardwalk that was actually, you know, *true*?"

"Parts of it."

"Which parts?"

"I did work for a nonprofit organization in New York—"

"Yeah, but it was a human rights deal, not a feed-the-hungry deal."

"Um ... yes."

"You'd been involved with that stuff for years, right? Going back to Chicago?"

"There I was mostly handling immigration and refugee cases."

"And then you moved to New York and joined, uh, what was it called? Bleeding Heart?"

"Conscience Watch," Alan said peevishly.

"Potato, po*tah*to."

"The abuse of political dissidents is no laughing matter," Cynthia said.

Bonnie glanced in the rearview mirror. "Who are you, Sally Struthers? Jeez." Then she caught sight of a distant flash of headlights behind Cynthia's head. "Uh-oh."

"What's the matter?" Alan asked.

"Someone's behind us."

"You mean ...?"

"Let's find out." She floored the gas pedal and watched the speedometer bend to sixty, sixty-five, seventy. The headlights shrank momentarily, then expanded as the vehicle accelerated to match her speed. "Aw, shit."

Cynthia was staring out the back window. "That's him? That's really *him*?"

"Sure looks that way. Hang on."

His strategy was bound to be pretty basic: pull alongside the Jeep and take out the driver—namely, her. She didn't intend to cooperate.

She watched the sides of the road. Trees, trees, more trees, a blurred wall of trees hemming her in. No good. She needed open space.

And the headlights behind her continued to brighten as the SUV closed the distance with the Jeep.

Still more trees, too goddamn many trees. Hadn't they ever heard of development around here?

The son of a bitch was close now. She couldn't outrun the Lexus on a straight stretch of road. In another few seconds Pascal would be right on her ass, and then he would swerve into the other lane and overtake her.

She reached for the fanny pack, preparing to pull out her Glock, and then the right side of the road opened up, the trees disappearing to reveal a flat stretch of open field.

Finally.

She flung the wheel hard to the right and swerved off the road, bumping up onto the grass. For a bad second her tires were caught in a drift of mud—she felt them spin helplessly—and then they tore loose and she barreled forward, cutting a path at a ninety-degree angle to the road. The Jeep rocked on the rutted ground, throwing up pinwheels of mud. On her left, rows of crops flickered past—corn stalks or some goddamn thing.

"Did we lose him?" Alan asked.

"Of course not." Even without looking, she knew the

headlights were still dogging them. Cynthia's low moan confirmed it.

She ground the gas pedal into the floor. The Jeep pulled away from the Lexus, maybe because it had better traction off-road, or maybe because Pascal wasn't accustomed to blowing through muddy meadows at night.

A lone oak tree came up fast out of nowhere. She skirted it, but just barely. One of the low branches whickered against the Jeep's side panel.

That'll leave a mark, she thought ruefully.

She kept going. A bevy of nesting birds exploded out of the grass directly in front of her, launched like buckshot into the night sky.

She had crossed at least a hundred yards of open field, and she was just about to run out of room. Dead ahead lay another street, one that ran parallel to Old Road.

"Hold on tight," she said, as much to herself as to her passengers.

She touched the brakes to prevent the Jeep from tipping over. She took a hard left, and took it fast.

Too fast. The muddy tires slipped on the rainswept pavement, and for a moment she was sure the Jeep would skid across the road into the utility poles along the far shoulder.

She spun the wheel, the Jeep straightened out, and she gunned the engine.

For the next few seconds they would be screened from their pursuer by the farmhouse and a high wall of crops. She raced east for half a block, then veered into a narrow clearing on the right-hand side of the road, nestling the Jeep amid a stand of tall evergreens. She killed the motor and lights.

"No one move or make a sound," she said quietly. She took a look in the backseat and observed that A.J. was asleep. Amazing. Little bastard could doze through anything.

Cynthia hunched low in her seat. "It won't work. He'll see us. He'll see us." The words repeated like a mantra.

"Shut up."

She did. Which was good, because otherwise Bonnie might have had to shoot her.

Alan whispered, "What if he does see us?"

"Then we're fucked, Chuck."

She eased the Glock out of her fanny pack. The carbine was stowed in the back of the vehicle, difficult to access. She hoped she wouldn't need it.

There were a lot of ways for this to go south. If she'd left tire tracks on the asphalt, they would point directly to her hiding place. If Pascal had glimpsed her maneuver from a distance ... or if he spotted the concealed Jeep as he was driving by ...

He was always one step ahead. Always outthinking her. Why would it be any different this time?

She waited. Pascal hadn't been that far behind. He had to be close, very close. He might have pulled to a stop already, headlights dark. He might be training his gun on her right now.

With a whoosh the SUV careened past, not even slowing. It hurtled around a blind curve, disappearing into the dark.

Gone.

"Score one for our side," Bonnie said, hoping her voice didn't sound as shaky as she felt.

24

Pascal had begun to respect Bonnie Parker.

She had shocked him in the tub, drawn blood in the farmhouse, and even, by some black magic, eluded him on the road. By all rights and all logic she should have been dead three times over, yet she persisted in staying alive. She was proving a worthy enemy.

This surprised him. His first impressions rarely led him astray. He had sized up Parker as a mere annoyance—a raw blister of a girl, uncouth and rash, a weed in a dunghill. And so she might be, but like a weed, she was tenacious, thorny, and frustratingly hard to pluck.

Still, he would get her eventually. He had to. For her to defeat him would go against all reason. It would violate the natural order of things.

He steered the Lexus onto Highway 35, using the wipers to flick away the ribbons of mud that festooned the vehicle. No purpose would be served by aimlessly cruising the streets in hope of spotting her. The ambush on Old Road had been his best chance of taking her. He had waited in a turnout, his left shoulder bleeding slowly under his jacket, the pain distant and unimportant. He had assumed she would escort the family to a new location now that their home was no longer safe. The Jeep, which he remembered from the motel parking lot, was a rusted, battered thing, and he had no doubt the new Lexus could outpace it on the road and outmaneuver it in the rain.

All odds had favored him. It should have been easy to intercept her from behind, kill her with a shot through the side window of the Jeep, then nudge the driverless vehicle off the road and finish things.

Yes. Easy. Except she had led him on a chase through a farmer's field, then vanished like a ghost. She must have cut down a side road or concealed herself behind a barn or in the woods. He had no hope of finding her. And his wound demanded attention.

First he needed to find a place to park his car. Leaving it on the street was not a good option. It was a possible that someone at the motel had seen the vehicle and given a description to the police. A parking garage would have been ideal, but there seemed to be no parking garages in the area.

He took an eastbound road off the highway and returned to Brighton Cove's beachfront. On Ocean Drive he found a massive three-story edifice that surely dated to the Victorian Era. A hotel, he assumed, as he could imagine no other purpose for the structure. At the rear was an ungated parking lot, crowded but not full. He parked the Lexus there. Camouflaged by other cars, it was less likely to draw notice.

He switched on the ceiling light and removed the first aid kit from his satchel. He shrugged off his jacket, wincing, and removed his shirt, then inspected the damage. It was not severe. The bullet was of small caliber—a .22, he believed—and it had passed cleanly through his shoulder, leaving a neat round hole in his deltoid muscle, but missing the thoracoacromial artery and cephalic vein. There was intense pain when he moved his left arm, but pain was of no consequence. He had long ago trained himself to tolerate pain.

With iodine and sewing thread, he set to work repairing the shoulder. He had been wounded many times. Of necessity he had learned of the rudiments of combat surgery. Every killer must be his own corpsman. On countless occasions he had tweezed bullets from his sinews, cauterized wounds, darned his own skin with needle and thread.

Now, at forty-six, he was seamed with scars, a patchwork thing. With every death he had dealt, he had surrendered a small part of himself.

It could not have been otherwise. He had the dharma of a warrior. To fight, to kill, was bred into his bones. Down a hundred lifetimes he had followed this path, and only now could he see its end. Respite from battle for the remainder of this life, and for every life to come. After endless soldiering, he was on the threshold of a new destiny.

There was only this girl still standing in his way, this one fascinating, damnable girl.

When the wound was closed, he applied a self-adhesive bandage, then tested his freedom of motion. Despite discomfort, he could work the arm freely. He was unimpaired. He was fortunate indeed that the shot had not caught him in the neck, severing his carotid or jugular, or cutting his spinal cord. The girl had surprised him with automatic-weapons fire. But she would not surprise him again.

The phone rang. Her phone, the stolen cell.

He dug it out of his pocket. He had expected her to call her own number, seeking some sort of parley, but not this soon.

He answered. "Yes?"

The voice that reached him was not the one he wanted to hear. "Did you do it? Is it done?"

Miss Parker's telephone harasser. The drunken lout who had called him earlier. Pascal almost ended the call, then thought better of it. "It is not," he said.

"She's still not out of the way?"

"She is still very much in the way."

"I thought you said she was as good as dead. Big man. Big fucking man."

"Like a stubborn stain, she is more difficult to eradicate than one might think."

"Then leave her to me. I'll get her. I'll put that bitch in the ground if it's the last thing I do."

That was good. That was what he wanted to hear. "Perhaps, my friend," Pascal said slowly, "there is another way."

"What way?"

"Perhaps the two of us can get it done ... together."

25

"This is where you're taking us?" Cynthia asked as Bonnie braked the Jeep. "A donut shop?"

"Chill, girlfriend." She shifted into park and killed the engine. "It's only a way station, okay? I need to hear the rest of what you've got to say, and I can't concentrate as long as I'm watching the road for another surprise appearance by Tall, Pale, and Ugly."

"But why here?"

"You know any other place that's open twenty-four hours around here? This ain't exactly Sin City."

She'd parked the Jeep at the side of the building, behind a trash bin, where it couldn't be seen from the road. If Pascal was circling the streets like a shark, he wouldn't expect them to be hanging out in a donut dive anyway. Probably. Although with this guy, you never knew.

"Okay," she said wearily, "wake the kid. Everybody out."

They trouped through the rain into the Donut Hutch. Usually the place was a magnet for cops, but Bonnie was betting all the local units were still occupied at the Roach House. She was right. There were a lot of empty seats and a distinct absence of customers. From the kitchen came the sizzle of lard. It didn't exactly make her salivate. Deep-fried dough wasn't one of her weaknesses.

She led the family to a booth in a corner, away from the windows, and slid onto the banquette next to Alan, across from Cynthia and A.J.

They were a bewildered, bedraggled group. Cynthia sat

silently, her face expressionless. The kid, still wearing earbuds, played a game on the cell phone, restlessly kicking his feet together. Alan swallowed way too often as he stared, hollow-eyed, at nothing at all.

"Come on, you guys, shake it off." She undid a couple of snaps on her poncho, then leaned back in her seat and lit a cigarette.

A waitress trudged up to the table, looking bored. "Can't smoke in here."

"Oh, right." Bonnie stubbed it out. "Force of habit. I'll just have coffee."

"Same for my wife and me," Alan said. "And a jelly donut for the boy."

"Sugar will keep him up," Cynthia warned as the waitress retreated.

"After what he's been through, he deserves something."

"You spoil him."

"Folks." Bonnie held up her hands. "Can we save the domestic drama for some other time? We need to finish up our talk and get where we're going."

"Just where are you taking us, anyway?" Cynthia asked.

"Never mind that. I got a plan."

"I hope it works out better than your other plans."

"Me too. I've already been shot at a couple times, not to mention our mutual friend tried to electrocute me in a bathtub."

"Electrocute?" Cynthia said, sounding more skeptical than horrified.

"Electrocute," Bonnie confirmed. "He also said unkind things about my hat."

"That hat?"

"No, a different one. Why, what's wrong with this hat?"

Cynthia looked away, a sour grimace riding her lips. It was pretty clear they weren't destined to be BFFs.

"So you really did talk to him face to face?" Alan asked. "And it was the same man? The one in the photo?"

"If it wasn't, it was another top prize winner in the Skeletor look-alike contest."

Cynthia didn't get it. "Skeletor?"

Her husband shrugged. "She's trying to be funny."

"Yeah, I'm a laugh riot. I work comedy clubs on weekends."

"What photo are you talking about?"

"On my cell," Alan said. He eased the phone away from his son with a smile. "Just need to borrow this, buddy."

He paused the kid's game and found the photo, showing it to Cynthia. She studied it intently, her face losing some of its color. Her hand was shaking when she handed it back.

Alan resumed the game and let A.J. have the phone. The boy was instantly lost again in his tiny electronic world.

The waitress returned with their orders, leaving a bill. Bonnie reached for her purse, then remembered she didn't have it. "Um, I'd cover this, except Pascal took my cash."

"I've got it." Alan dropped some money on the table, then registered what she'd said. "All of it?"

"Afraid so."

"Then—your retainer ..."

"Not your fault. My carelessness, my problem." She took a sip of coffee. "Let's get back on track. You were saying you moved from Chicago to take a job at Conscience Watch. Why the move?"

"The chance to do more. Which was a joke, because at Conscience Watch I hardly accomplished anything."

"You must have accomplished something, because you've got a hitter on your ass. At least, I'm assuming your current troubles are tied in with your previous do-goodery."

"Yes."

"How so?"

"I broke the law," Alan said quietly.

"Great. Dig through enough shit, and we find our pony. Was it just you, or were others involved?"

"There were others. Two of my colleagues—Amy Bernstein and Herb Sentner."

"The ones who croaked?" Bonnie said, remembering the news

stories on Pascal's iPad.

"Herb died two weeks ago. Amy died just yesterday."

"Amy is dead?" Cynthia whispered. Bonnie glanced at her and saw the woman's eyes widen. It didn't look like she was faking surprise.

Alan nodded soberly. "She was killed in her co-op. I saw it in today's paper."

"First things first," Bonnie said. "Tell me about Herb."

"He retired around the time I left the company. Moved to Maine with his wife. She found him in the lake by their house. The official verdict was that he slipped on the dock, fell into the water, and drowned. But there were no witnesses."

"You told me Muriel saw it happen," Cynthia said in a low, reproachful tone.

"I lied. I didn't want you worrying. You'd been through enough."

"For God's sake, Alan, you owed me the truth."

Bonnie grinned. "Seriously, Skeezix, you were trying to protect this shrinking violet? Newsflash—I don't think your wife is auditioning for the role of damsel in distress."

Alan looked abashed. He glanced at his wife. "From now on, no more secrets."

"Great." Bonnie took some more coffee, enjoying the caffeine hit. "We've had our Hallmark moment. Now how does this all hang together?"

"We're getting there," Alan said. "You have to understand, I wasn't sure what it meant. Herb's death could have been an accident. Amy talked to Herb's widow. Muriel didn't know anything."

"But you and Amy suspected foul play?"

"We did."

"Why? What were you so scared of?"

Alan hesitated, staring into his coffee. "A year ago, the three of us did something reckless. It involved Mariana Ortiz."

"Alan ..." Cynthia warned.

He waved off her objection. "She needs to know."

"Who's Mariana Ortiz?" Bonnie asked.

"An attorney in Colombia who made a name for herself handling legal issues for farm workers. A real idealist. She'd lived abroad, but returned to her native country to help the poor. She taught them about their rights. She helped them stand up to the government."

"And I'm guessing she paid for it."

"The authorities convicted her on trumped-up charges of collaborating with FARC, the insurgency group. She was sentenced to twenty years at the Buen Pastor Women's Prison in Bogotá. By the time Conscience Watch got the case, she'd been there for eight months—subjected to constant abuse, even physical torture."

"Okay ..." Bonnie said, not quite sure where this was going. Cynthia shook her head in disapproval. The little boy hummed to himself, playing with the phone.

"Conscience Watch works with foreign governments to secure the release of political prisoners. Mariana Ortiz became the top priority for our Latin American division, which I headed up. But the Colombian authorities wouldn't budge. They intended to make an example of her. They didn't want other lawyers helping the farmworkers. There was no way we could get her out. And we had to. We just *had* to. I guess—I guess I got a little bit obsessed about it."

"Alan's a romantic," Cynthia said dryly. "He has a chivalrous streak."

"I take it you're not so much on Team Mariana?"

"I had no objection to helping her. But it's pointless to idealize the woman."

"She risked her life—" Alan said.

"Yes, certainly, but who knows why? Maybe for ideals. Maybe just because she wanted adventure. She could have had a death wish. We can't know a stranger's motives."

"I knew everything I needed to know about her," Alan said

stiffly. "And I still do."

Cynthia looked at her hands. "I'm sure you believe that."

Bonnie thought wifey might be a little put out by her husband's evident fascination with another woman—and an exotic foreign freedom fighter, to boot. "Focus, people. What does Mariana Ortiz have to do with Amy and Herb getting snuffed?"

Alan took a breath. "As I said, we were getting nowhere with the Colombians. Then we learned something that made the situation even more urgent. Mariana had cancer. She wouldn't receive treatment in prison. The government was content to let her waste away. If she didn't get out soon, it would be too late. All legal options were exhausted. All conventional avenues ... So we thought outside the box. We threw a Hail Mary pass." He met Bonnie's eyes. "We hired a merc."

"A what?"

"A mercenary. A soldier of fortune."

"Holy shit." Bonnie let out a low whistle. "I really fell ass backward into something, didn't I?"

No one answered.

"Whose idea was it to go rogue?" she asked, already sure of the answer.

"Mine," Alan said.

"And how did you happen to get hold of a mercenary?"

"Herb had connections from his Army days. I don't know exactly how he did it. There were only three of us involved—him and Amy and me. It was a black op, so to speak. No one else at Conscience Watch knew anything about it."

"I take it the three of you met with this guy."

"Several times. We worked out the whole thing. Amy did some fancy accounting to divert funds to the project. We supplied our man with all the intel we had on Mariana. His job was to assemble a team, enter Colombia, penetrate the prison, and break her out."

"Who was your hired gun, anyway?"

"His name was Hector Bezos."

"So I take it Lee Marvin wasn't available."

"You can laugh, but we were trying to save a woman's life. You know how I said the frustration gets to you—the bureaucracy? Well, this was our chance to bypass the red tape and political obstacles and really make a difference."

"If it had worked."

"Yes."

"Which it didn't."

"Well ... no. How'd you know that?"

"These things never work, except in the movies."

Cynthia set her mouth in a frown. "At least they tried."

"That's what people always say when they've screwed up. By the way, Cindy, when exactly did you find out about all this?"

"Early on. We don't keep secrets from each other."

That was a laugh. Everybody kept secrets. "Okay, so let me guess how this played out. This guy you hired—what was his name? Bozo?"

"Bezos," Alan said irritably.

"Right. Bezos and his team got captured during their raid on the prison. Correct?"

Alan turned the coffee mug in his hands. "Um ... actually they never made it to the prison. Their arrival in-country apparently didn't go unnoticed. But only Hector was captured alive. Two others were killed. The remaining three escaped."

"And one of those three reported back to you."

"Yeah. We were devastated, of course. It didn't occur to us until later that we should also be afraid."

Bonnie understood. "Because the Colombians would make Bezos spill everything. His mission, and the people who hired him. I'm guessing he knew your identities or had some way of figuring them out."

"We made no secret of who we were." Alan coughed. "Guess that was a mistake."

"One of many. You guys were in so far over your head, you couldn't see daylight. You were like kids playing around, but the Colombians don't play games. You should've known that."

"This man, Hector Bezos—"

"—was probably more of a wannabe than the genuine article. For every real commando out there, you got a hundred dime-store Rambos who like dressing up in camo fatigues and firing AR-15s. Their only training in special ops comes from watching *The Expendables* on pay-per-view."

"Herb thought he was the real deal."

"Herb is dead," Bonnie said bluntly. "So is Amy. And the guy who killed them—*he's* the real deal."

Cynthia bristled. "If you're trying to scare us, you're wasting your time."

"If you're not scared already, you're not paying attention."

"Maybe your idea of taking action is to run and hide—"

"You were already on the run and hiding out, Cindy. Remember?"

"My name is Cynthia, not Cindy."

"Actually your name is Caroline. But I realize it's tough to keep track."

Alan raised a hand. "Please ..."

Bonnie yielded. "Right, gotta stay on point. So Bezos' Colombian jailers learned all about the people behind this paramilitary raid on their soil. They didn't take kindly to it. They could have lodged a formal complaint with the US government—"

"That's what we expected," Alan said.

"But they didn't."

"No."

"And that's when you got really scared."

"We knew they wouldn't just let it go. If they weren't coming after us legally ..."

"Then they were coming after you extralegally." She glanced at A.J. and was glad to see he was still ignoring the conversation. "They turned the tables and hired a freelancer to enter this country and take care of you."

"We didn't know for sure. We didn't know what Hector might have told them or what they might do. We each chose a different way of dealing with it. Herb was close to retirement anyway, so he left the organization and relocated to Maine. Amy stayed on at Conscience Watch. She wasn't going to be intimidated. And I—Caroline and I ..."

"You got the papers to establish new identities and started laying low at the beautiful Jersey shore."

"Yes. And time passed. Nothing happened. We started to think we were off the hook."

"Until Herb died."

Alan sighed. "As I said, it wasn't clear if it was an accident or ... something else. Amy and I exchanged emails about it. Yesterday she sent me that photo I showed you. It was a man she thought was following her. She snapped his picture in a coffee shop in Manhattan. Heard him place his order. A Spanish accent, she said. A cultivated voice. That's the last time I heard from her. Today I read a story in the *New York Times* saying she'd been murdered in her apartment last night. It must've happened very soon after she took the photo."

Bonnie nodded. Now she understood why the hitter had checked into the Coach House only hours ago. He hadn't been in town before that. He had been in New York, taking care of Amy Bernstein.

"Okay," she said. "So Pascal learned enough from Amy to trace you here."

"He must have. But I don't know how. I never told Amy our new names or where we'd relocated. She didn't even have my cell number. We only kept in touch by email."

"Did you send your emails through an anonymizer?"

"A what?"

"I'll take that as a no. An anonymizer is a service that conceals the origin of an email. Since you sent your messages directly, all Pascal had to do was go on Amy's computer, bring up the emails, and analyze the routing info. Then he would know roughly what town you're in."

"But not our new names, our address ..."

"Wouldn't take him long to track you down," she said, preferring to pass over that part of the story. "Anyhow, he zeroed in on you and made his move." She shrugged. "Dude works fast. You gotta admire that."

Alan reached across the table and squeezed his wife's hand. It was not clear if he was providing reassurance or requesting it.

"You said he's from Chile," he said quietly. "That doesn't make sense. Why would the Colombians contract out the job instead of sending one of their own people?"

"Deniability. They're conducting wet work on foreign soil."

"But if he's caught, he'll implicate them anyway."

"I don't think so. This guy won't break under pressure. And I doubt he would let himself be taken alive in the first place."

"You talk about him like he's some sort of supervillain," Cynthia said.

"He's a professional. That's all." Bonnie hoped this was true. At this point she wasn't so sure. "And it's my job to see he doesn't collect his fee. What I don't get is why you didn't go straight to the police after you saw the newspaper story."

"We can't. What we did was illegal. Hiring a mercenary, arranging a raid on a prison—we're responsible for an international incident."

"The authorities still would have to protect you."

"They also would have to charge us. Recruiting mercenaries for a military action against a foreign regime when we're not at war is a violation of the Neutrality Act. Then there's section 956 of Title 18, which prohibits conspiracy to commit mayhem or damage property in a foreign country. Those statutes are aggressively enforced. We're talking federal felonies with maximum penalties of twenty-five years to life."

"Spoken like a true attorney-at-law. All right, so you met with me—but you made up a bunch of crap about the G-Rocs because you didn't trust me not to go to the cops. That was a dumb-ass, chickenshit move, pal."

"Look"—his voice dropped to a whisper—"if you want off the

case, I wouldn't blame you."

"No can do, Stu. And yeah, I know your name isn't Stu. I do want off the case, but what I want doesn't matter. It's all about what the baldheaded hombre from south of the border wants. Pascal will be gunning for me, whether I'm on the case or not."

"You're not the one he's after."

"I am now. I'm on the hit list. And I can't just bail. He knows my name."

"I'm sorry, Bonnie. I didn't want ... I'm sorry."

He sounded so morose, she had to laugh. "Brighten up. Believe it or not, this is not the first person who's wanted me dead. Hell, he's not even the first person who's wanted me dead *today*. Now here's the plan. You guys need to go to ground for a day or two. I'm taking you someplace where he won't find you."

"To a safe house?" Cynthia asked.

"Well, it's my friend's house, which oughtta be pretty safe."

"And after we're ensconced at your friend's house," Cynthia pressed, "what are we supposed to do? Just wait for this man to leave town?"

"He won't leave town. It's not like they're gonna take off the hit. He'll nose around until he finds you—unless I find him first."

"You mean you're going after him?" For the first time Cynthia seemed at a loss for words. "You're going to hunt him down all by yourself?"

"Looks that way."

"But ... this man is a killer."

Bonnie finished her coffee and smiled. "I hate to break it to you, toots—but I'm a killer too."

26

Pascal sat on a bench on the Brighton Cove boardwalk, watching the rain come down. He had found a sheltered spot by a pavilion. The observation deck, supported by brick pillars, provided a roof over his head. From this vantage point he could watch the boardwalk in both directions as he waited for the arrival of the man named Kurt.

It had not been easy to persuade Kurt to join him. The fellow was as skittish as a kitten. Plainly he was terrified of Bonnie Parker, sure that having escaped death at her hands once, he could not risk a second encounter.

His fear competed with his hatred. He wanted her to die, and he wanted to see it happen, but he was afraid to be anywhere near her. Pascal had required all his diplomatic skills to seal the deal.

"Are you shitting me?" the man had asked more than once.

Pascal had kept his voice low and soothing. "We have a common interest, a common objective. And she will not be expecting a second man."

"I don't know ..."

"There will be no danger. I will do the actual killing. You will serve merely as a diversion."

"As bait?" The man's voice jumped with panic. "That what you mean?"

"Not as bait. There will be no risk to you. I have it all worked out."

This was true. He had worked it out in that moment, his mind accessing some stratagem perhaps tested in another incarnation.

"You're sure it's safe?" the wheedling voice pressed.

"Absolutely. You will come to no harm. And you will see Bonnie Parker die. That is worth something, is it not?"

"Yeah." Pascal could actually hear the man lick his lips like a starved animal. "Yeah, it's worth a lot."

They had said a few more rewords, making their introductions. The man was Kurt, just Kurt. Pascal considered using an alias but decided it was unnecessary. He had already taken a dislike to Kurt, and he expected to eliminate the man after his usefulness was exhausted. This was a point he prudently did not mention.

Kurt agreed to meet him by the pavilion, which lay across the street from the parking lot where Pascal had stashed his car.

Even so, he still could not be certain Kurt would come. The man was a coward, obviously, and he could easily back out.

He was also a fool. He had not learned the most elementary rule of the hunt, to keep one's emotions in check. It was perfectly all right to hate one's adversary, Pascal knew, but the hate must be cold, ice cold—as cold as his own hands.

To the north, lightning flared, seconded by a whipcrack of thunder. Spiderweb traceries of fire lit up the bellies of churning storm clouds, casting the earth in sharp relief. In the sudden unnatural glare, a figure stood revealed, far down the boardwalk, coming this way.

Pascal peered past the plunging curtains of rain. Dimly he made out a man in a tan raincoat and baseball cap. He walked slowly, stiffly, each stride an effort. His left leg was unnaturally stiff. But he was coming. Kurt had not failed him.

It took a long time for the man to cover the remaining distance. Pascal waited, patient as a trapdoor spider. Even when Kurt had crossed under the observation deck and stopped, staring at him, Pascal made no move to rise. To greet him, to show the slightest deference, would be a sign of weakness. With a man like this, it was necessary to establish dominance early. Once instituted, it would never be challenged.

"Is that you?" Kurt said finally. It was the same hoarse rasp

Pascal had heard on the phone.

Pascal nodded. He waited for Kurt to approach him. The man seated himself tentatively on the bench, choosing the spot farthest from Pascal, not making eye contact. Good. Very good.

"I am pleased you came, my friend," Pascal said.

"Still not sure this is such a great idea. I had my own plan for getting her."

"And yet you have not executed it."

"I was getting ready. It was all set up. But ... your way might be better. I can't be connected with it, if we do it your way."

"Indeed not. No one will ever know. Did you bring a gun?"

"Haven't got one."

"And you intended to kill Miss Parker on your own, without a firearm?"

He bristled. "Look, if you can't you use me, I'll just get going."

"I can use you."

Pascal studied the man. His pale face wore a thick fringe of uncombed beard. The beard looked new. Pascal suspected Kurt had grown it to disguise his appearance. He had been awake all night and must have been drinking earlier, but the rain seemed to have sobered him up, leaving him more alert, and also more nervous—a scared, trembling thing, huddled against the chill, wincing at distant thunder.

He was no knight errant. Of that, Pascal was certain. He was a weakling with no stomach for killing. A useless creature who had not earned the right to survive.

Yet somehow he had. The riddle of it intrigued Pascal. "You said Bonnie Parker tried to kill you. Why then are you still alive?"

Kurt flicked an angry glance at him. "You think she's so damn good she always gets her man?"

"I think she is more than good enough to get you, my friend."

For a moment Kurt seemed to think about challenging him. Then his head nodded in defeat, his eyes drifting away. "She had me, all right. I was just lying there. Couldn't move. Two slugs in me." Unconsciously he touched his leg, and Pascal understood his slow stiff-legged gait. "All she had to do was ..."

"Deliver the coup de grace," Pascal said.

"It sounds nice and civilized when you say it like that. When you're choking on your own blood, staring down the barrel of a gun, it doesn't feel civilized. It feels like you're a goddamn animal in a trap."

An animal, yes. But not one of the more heroic animals, those that qualified for inclusion on coats of arms. Not the lion, the wolf. Not even the wily fox. Rather, there was a rodent-like quality about this man, a quality stemming from his matted facial hair, his small pink hands, and his habit of chewing at his lower lip, like a rat obsessively gnawing, gnawing ...

"But she did not shoot," Pascal prompted.

"She nearly did. I saw her draw down. But she didn't go through with it. She just walked away." Kurt worked his lower lip. "She was scared, I think."

"Scared of you?" The words came out with just the lightest lilt of contempt.

"Not me. Scared of going through with it, face to face. Up close and personal, looking right into my eyes."

This was possible. And if so, it meant Bonnie Parker had a weakness. That was good to know.

"So she let you live," Pascal said thoughtfully.

"Fuck, no. I mean, she didn't intend to. She wasn't showing me any mercy. She thought I would bleed out in the snow."

"But she was wrong."

"She was wrong. I was stronger than she knew. Stronger than *I* knew. It was hate that did it. Hating her—that's what made me strong. You know how that is?"

"I do."

"Somehow I limped out of the woods, all the way to a gas station. Made up a story about how I'd been shot in an alley by a couple of kids. I tossed my ID, used a fake name, said I was homeless."

"Why the deception?"

"I couldn't have the police investigating what really happened. She was after me for a reason. I'd broken some laws."

Pascal thought the man had an additional motive. He had not wanted Parker to know her quarry was still alive. She would surely have targeted him again.

"They patched me up at the hospital," Kurt said. "Three surgeries. Then rehab. The whole nine yards. When I finally got out, I tracked her down and started making plans." He chewed his lip, drawing blood. "She cost me everything. I'm in pain every damn day. Can't show my face for fear of being recognized. I was on the way to having money, serious money, and now I'm living in a one-room apartment above a store. I cook canned beans on a fucking hot plate. That's my life. And the only reason I get up in the morning is to have the satisfaction of seeing that bitch dead."

Pascal smiled. "If circumstances proceed as I expect, my friend, you soon will have your chance. We need only wait for her call."

"What the hell makes you think she'll call you?"

"She is young and brash, and her blood is up." He gazed past the pillars of the pavilion, into the lightning-streaked sky. His gloved hands were steepled, his voice knowing and calm. "She will call."

27

Desmond, it seemed, knew her better than she realized. At least, he was a lot less surprised than Bonnie expected him to be when he opened his door at one AM and found her shepherding the Kirbys inside.

The doorbell had roused him from bed. He'd thrown on a flimsy summertime robe that did nothing to conceal the stark contrast between his sculpted torso and his shrunken legs. He rolled his chair backward and let the family file into the living room while Bonnie locked the door behind them.

"I didn't see your Jeep outside," he said. They were the first words out of his mouth.

"I parked in the alley behind the house."

He nodded, and she saw how much he'd learned from that brief exchange—that she was on the run, the family was hiding out, and somebody dangerous was after them.

"I hate to do this to you, Des, but we got a whole thing going on here, and these guys really need a place to crash."

"There's a guest room down the hall, on the right." He waved in that general direction.

Alan and Cynthia filed past, but A.J. stopped, staring with frank curiosity at the man in the wheelchair.

Desmond smiled. "Hey, little man."

"What happened to your legs?" the boy asked.

His parents winced, but Des was unfazed. "They went to sleep and didn't wake up. Bummer, huh?"

The boy nodded gravely.

Cynthia took the boy's hand. "Come along, A.J."

"Sorry about that." Alan said. "He just—he's not old enough to know ..."

Des shrugged. "Don't sweat it. Make yourselves at home."

"I'll be with you in a sec," Bonnie added as the trio tramped down the hall. She peeled off her poncho and turned to face him. "Des, I know this is a lot to ask, especially after the way we left things."

"Forget it. I shouldn't have been playing shrink. Although if I were, I'd say that trying to save a family is a highly symbolic act. What kind of trouble are they in?"

"Someone's out to kill the daddy. Maybe waste the whole crew."

"What kind of someone?"

"A sadist. A pro."

"Way to sugarcoat it."

"He's good, Des. I mean, he's bad, but he's really *good* at being bad. Hey, speaking of the bad guy, how's your Spanish?"

"Awesome. Why?"

"I lifted this thing he wrote. A poem, I guess." She dug it out of her pocket and unfolded the damp page. "Care to translate?"

He frowned at the close lines of script and recited slowly.

Farewell my dearest, my kiss of death, my grave.
When the moon rises, I will remember your lips,
A night-blooming flower with poison perfume.
The chill of your touch, the carrion cold ...

He looked up. "And more of the same. Creepy. Like a love poem to a corpse. But I guess that fits this guy, huh?"

"Oh yeah. Fits like a glove. No pun intended."

"Why is that a pun?"

"Never mind."

"Anyway, it goes on for a while. A whole lot of death imagery. And something about samsara."

"I told you, *no hablo espanol.*"

"Samsara isn't Spanish. It's Sanskrit. It means the cycle of life, death, and rebirth. You know, reincarnation and all that."

"Maybe he thinks he was Julius Caesar in a previous life."

"Actually, I don't think he wrote the poem. It looks like a woman's handwriting. And there's a line calling the loved one a *compañero de viaje*—fellow traveler. *Compañero* is the masculine form. Whoever wrote this was addressing a man."

"Huh. Well, he told me he had a girlfriend."

"They must've made a beautiful couple."

"Yeah. Like Dracula and the Bride of Frankenstein." She retrieved the poem and stuck it back in her pocket.

He looked her over. "You need some tea."

"I just had coffee."

"Not the same thing."

"I don't have a lot of time."

"There's always time for tea."

He wheeled himself into the kitchen. She followed with a shrug. Tea. She would have preferred a Jack and Coke, but getting liquored up probably wasn't the best idea right now.

She watched while he filled the teakettle and set it on the stove. As he rummaged in a box of tea bags, he asked, "So what happened to you tonight?"

"Lots of stuff, none of it good."

"What'd you do after you left my place?"

"Took a bath."

"Doesn't sound too stressful."

"Wanna bet?"

He selected valerian and draped the teabag over a porcelain mug. "This bad guy of yours—any chance he'll track your clients here?"

She didn't give him a direct answer. "The only way he could trace them to this location is through my phone. He's got it, and you're in my contact list, but so are a bunch of other people. He shouldn't have any way of narrowing down the search to just you."

The teapot began to whistle. Des ignored it. "But ..."

"But he's been ahead of me all along. It's got me kinda rattled. I'm starting to think he can beat me, no matter what I do."

"That doesn't sound like the Bonnie Parker I know."

"I'll get over it. Just keep them alive, Des. They got mixed up in something complicated and stupid, but they don't deserve to die for it."

He filled the mug with hot water. "I'll look after them. Somebody's got to, and the hubby doesn't seem quite up to the job. He strikes me as more of a beta male."

"Yeah. And the wife's an alpha bitch. I don't know what they see in each other."

"The heart has its reasons."

"Whoa, that's what *she* said to me. Different context—which she had to explain." Bonnie sipped her tea and wished it could soothe her. "Sometimes I think I should've stayed in high school. Then I might not be the least educated person in every room."

"This thing's really got you doubting yourself, huh?"

She said nothing. They lingered in silence. Then slowly he reached out and clasped her hand.

She'd lied when she told Dan Maguire she had no friends. She had one.

She had Des.

***

Bonnie caught up with the Kirbys in the guest bedroom, where Cynthia was bedding down the kid, and Alan was pacing like an inmate scheduled to walk the Green Mile.

She spent some time examining the attached bath. The sight of the tub triggered a twinge of nausea in the pit of her belly, but she powered through it.

"Okay," she said, emerging. "This could work."

Alan stopped pacing and looked at her. "As what?"

"A panic room."

"Picnic room," A.J. said sleepily from under a hill of blankets.

Cynthia was skeptical. "A lavatory is a far cry from a panic room."

"You make do with what's at hand. The bathroom has no windows. The walls are tiled; the floor is a concrete slab. Door is oak, solid-core. Lock's in good shape. If you hide in there, it'll buy you time. You brought in your cell phone, right?"

Alan nodded. "I always have it with me. It's the one I called you from, to set up our meeting."

"If there's trouble, hustle your loved ones into the bathroom and call nine-one-one. Police response time around here is maybe four minutes on a busy night. Two minutes if nothing else is going down, and usually nothing is. I know you don't want the authorities involved, but if it gets to that point, the boys in blue will be the least of your concerns."

"Right, right." Alan glanced past her into the bathroom, and she knew he was imagining himself and his wife and child huddled inside as a killer prowled the house.

"It's not gonna come to that," she said. "I'm just preparing for every contingency. It's what I do."

"What about, you know, weapons?"

"There are kitchen knives, maybe a couple hammers, and the toaster oven makes a nice blunt instrument."

"You know what I mean—firearms."

"There aren't any, and you don't need any. You'd just end up shooting yourself or someone you care about. Or me, most likely."

"I have a hard time believing your friend doesn't keep a spare piece in the house."

"Spare piece? Who are you, Bugsy Malone? When you got guns lying around, it just gives the bad guy more opportunities to get hold of one."

"Okay, okay. And your friend—he doesn't have a problem with us being here?"

"He's cool about it. He sort of rolls with the punches. Well, maybe *rolls* is a poor choice of words."

"How much does he know about your, uh ...?"

"My special services? I've never discussed it with him. I don't know what he's guessed."

Cynthia watched her closely. "So you really are a killer?"

"That's my stock in trade."

"And you're all right with that?"

She shrugged. "I've always believed it's not what you do, it's how you do it."

"Then your private investigator business is just a cover?"

"It's for real. I do regular PI work most of the time. I kinda stumbled into this other thing."

"Just like that?" Cynthia didn't sound judgmental. She seemed honestly curious.

"Yeah, pretty much. I'm one cold bitch, huh?"

"I don't know what you are," Cynthia said quietly.

"Well, I'm sure you'll give it some thought. Seems like someone pinned a sign to my butt that says 'Analyze Me.' Everybody wants to get in on the head-shrinking action tonight."

"You really think you can kill this man Pascal?"

"Or die trying." She frowned. "You know, usually that's just an expression."

"I suppose there's no hope of reasoning with him."

"You'd have more luck reasoning with a shark. Look, dealing with scum like Pascal is my job. Why don't you let me do it, okay?"

"I suppose we have no choice. But it seems there'll always be more killing. It never ends. Even if you get Pascal, they'll just send someone else, and it will start all over again."

"Don't think of it like that."

"It's the truth."

"Then try lying to yourself. Sometimes it's all that gets me through the night."

"You're an unhappy person, Bonnie," Cynthia said.

"Me? I'm Little Miss Sunshine. Okay, you guys hang out here. Stay safe. And don't open the door for any Candygrams."

She stepped into the hallway. Alan stopped her. "Bonnie. I just wanted you to know—I feel really stupid about the way I misled you."

"Everybody is stupid sometimes. Just try being smart for the next few hours."

"If we, uh, don't hear from you, what should we do?"

"If I'm dead, you mean? Go straight to the nearest FBI field office and tell them everything. No bullshit about the G-Rocs. You'll have to come clean and take your medicine." She turned to go, then looked back. "Hey, what ever happened to Mariana Ortiz?"

"She died in prison. Of cancer."

"Sorry."

He raised an eyebrow. "Are you?"

"Not really. I can't get too worked up about somebody I never knew."

"Even if you know she was doing good?"

"A lot of people try to do good. It doesn't make them immortal."

Alan looked at her sadly. "Have you always been so angry at the world?"

"Not always. Just since I was fourteen."

***

On the front porch she found Des in his chair, a shadow among shadows, watching the street. She didn't have to ask what he was watching for.

"There's no need to make yourself a target," she said.

"I could say the same to you."

"Yeah. Guess you could."

She stood next to him. Rain drummed the roof in a hard, steady rhythm. Puddles glistened on the street. The trees shook, and the utility lines strung among the branches swayed ominously.

"You're going after him, I take it," Des said quietly. "A guy who's a sadist and a pro. You're heading off for some kind of showdown."

"That's the plan. This is between he and I ... him and me ... whatever." She studied him. "You don't seem too surprised."

"I'm not entirely in the dark about what you do."

"Yeah, I guess the thirty-eight in your air duct was kind of the giveaway."

"I figured it out long before that."

"And you never said anything?"

He shrugged. "None of my business."

"When has that ever stopped you?"

"Touché."

"It's not like I do it for fun, Des."

"I know that."

"Or even for money. I mean, the money's part of it, but ..."

"It's about justice for you."

"I guess."

"That's what makes you different from that other Bonnie Parker, you know. She wasn't in it for justice. She was in it for kicks."

She nodded, hoping he was right.

There was no one else she could talk to like this. No other close friend or confidant. No family. No lover. Her death, she thought, would leave an awfully small hole in the world.

She wondered if it meant anything—her life, or anybody's. If there was any purpose to it all. She'd never considered it. Questions like that were best left to the deep thinkers, people who read books. She'd never been much of a reader, unless *Guns & Ammo* counted.

"I lied to you about one thing, Des," she said slowly.

"Just one?"

She smiled. "One thing tonight." The smile faded. "You know how I said my folks getting killed didn't faze me?"

"I had a feeling that might not be the whole truth."

"Yeah. The whole truth—well, I didn't think you'd want to hear it."

"Why not? You got upset that your parents had died. What's so terrible about that?"

"I didn't get upset. I got even."

"Oh."

"I was just a kid. But I tracked down the bastards that did it. Three of them, in Pennsylvania."

"How could you possibly find them?"

"It's a whole long story, and it doesn't matter now. I've always been good at finding things out. It took me half a year, but I learned who'd done it and I located them. And I made sure they wouldn't make any more orphans."

"How old were you?"

"Fourteen. But I grew up fast."

"Too fast."

"Maybe. Anyhow, I made things right. And now I need to make things right again."

"You don't have to go after him. We can call the police. Or grab the Kirby clan and go on the run till this thing blows over."

"I'm not running, and it won't blow over. And the police can't get involved." She folded her arms across her chest. "I'll take care of this guy."

"Or he'll take care of you."

"Right. That's how the game is played. It's what I signed up for."

"There's a fine line between courage and craziness, you know."

She found a smile for him. "Oh hell, Des. I crossed that line a long time ago."

28

In the alley at the rear of the house, Bonnie found her Jeep. She stood for a moment, looking it over in the hard downpour. She loved the old girl—somehow she was sure her Jeep was female—even if the vehicle had seen better days. The door hinges and the bolts on the side mirrors might be rusted, the radio might be broken, and the rearview mirror might be Krazy-Glued in place, but the duct tape liberally applied to the cracked and split upholstery gave it a certain charm.

The Jeep reminded her of when she had started out, scraping together sofa-cushion spare change to bankroll her venture as a PI, assembling yard-sale furniture in her low-rent office. She'd chosen Brighton Cove on the theory that if she didn't have money, the next best thing was to work for people who did. The theory proved correct. She had moved up in the world, but she'd kept the Jeep and the office, and even the furniture.

She wondered why she was feeling sentimental about her ride. Then she realized it wasn't just her ride. It was her life. There were a lot of things she'd taken for granted. A lot of things she'd miss.

Screw that. Moping around wasn't going to get the job done.

She needed to catch up with Pascal again, but she wasn't exactly privy to his itinerary. The one thing she knew, because she'd overheard his phone conversation in the motel room, was that he hoped to be picked up at Millstone Airport later tonight. She was betting he would go there only after the successful completion of his assignment. As long as Alan and his family were alive, the airport was irrelevant. If it ever became relevant, it meant she had failed.

In the meantime, she had no way to find the son of a bitch. So she would just have to arrange some other approach. She had an idea about how to play it, if she could get him to go along.

She climbed into the Jeep and took out her new cell, dialing the number of her stolen phone. She had to hope Pascal still had it, and that he'd left it on.

Two rings, three, and he picked up.

"Guess who," she said.

"Miss Bonnie Parker."

She sighed. "Sounds like you didn't bleed out after all."

"My injury was a mere scratch. I suppose it is too much to hope that you also were wounded."

"Not a nick on me," she lied. "You had your shot and you blew it. You're getting old, buddy boy."

"I may be old, Miss Parker, but the night is young."

"That's the spirit. Okay, here's the pitch, hotshot. We're getting no place fast. You zap me, I wing you. It's a zero sum game. Time for us to go another way."

"What other way?"

She lit a cigarette. "You and me in a cage match. Two desperadoes enter, and only one of us leaves. We pick a spot and both come packing. The winner is whoever's still breathing when the last shot is fired. You in?"

A tick of silence. "I think not."

"Come on, it's right up your alley. A couple knights of the Round Table challenging each other to a duel or a joust or whatever."

"Why would that be, as you say, up my alley?"

"I saw the book you were reading. King Arthur, Maid Marian, all that happy crap."

"Maid Marian is from the Robin Hood stories."

"Meh. Details. What's the appeal of that medieval booshwah, anyway?"

"The knight errant lived by his own code. As do I."

"You have a code? Does it involve torturing fair damsels with electric shocks?"

"It involves showing no mercy to an adversary. It is your code too, Bonnie Parker."

"So you're not just a hired gun. You're Sir Lancelot."

"Indeed I am." He sounded pleased.

"Well, I'll bet old Lance never turned down a challenge. The other knights would've made cluck-cluck noises at him. So what d'you say?"

"Your offer is tempting. But I have learned to resist temptation."

"And here I thought you were a true romantic. I even have something you wrote. You know, the moon's rising, kiss of death, yadda yadda. Very friggin' poetic."

"You took that from me?" She heard his first real emotion—an edge of anger.

"Yup." She patted her back pocket. "It's a little soggy, but still legible."

"You crude, illiterate, stupid little bitch."

"Been called worse. You want it back?"

"I will pin your scalp to it."

"Does that mean we're on?"

"I hold out only one condition. I choose the venue."

"Fair enough. Let's get this party started."

"Won't you assume I am leading you into a trap?"

"Sure. But I'm smart enough to improvise a workaround."

"Very well. Your boardwalk will do."

"The boardwalk is two miles long. Narrow it down."

"There is a spot just across the street from a large old hotel."

"That's not a hotel anymore. It's an old folks' home. But I know the place."

"You will find me there. Bring my poem."

"Will do. And you bring my twenty-five hundred bucks."

"Oh, I will pay you back, Bonnie Parker. Of that you may rest assured. I anticipate the outcome of our rendezvous with deep satisfaction."

"Anticipate a bullet in the noggin, friend. 'Cause that's what you're gonna get."

She ended the call and sat in the Jeep, finishing her cigarette. She intended to smoke it all the way down to the filter. She had a funny feeling it might be her last.

29

At the corner of Ocean Drive and Beacon Avenue stood a house under construction—one of those ginormous butt-ugly McMansions put up by Wall Street arbitrageurs and hedge fund managers who liked to flex their muscles by tearing down a perfectly good old house to put up a kajillion-dollar replacement. The frame was up, but the house was otherwise unfinished and, naturally, unoccupied, which made it a good place for Bonnie to stow her Jeep.

She approached the house with her headlights off, eased past it into the backyard, and parked behind the huge hulking pile in a muddy plot. Parking on the street would be too risky; there was always the chance Pascal would double-cross her by avoiding the boardwalk and simply prowl the neighborhood until he found her ride, then lie in wait until she returned.

For all she knew, he might even have anticipated her choice of a hiding place for the Jeep. The McMansion was the only house under construction in the vicinity of the rendezvous point. He might have expected her to park behind it. He might be scoping her out right now, ready to plug her when she got out of the car.

Damn, she was being super-paranoid about this. She wished she could convince herself she was being unreasonable. But Pascal had her spooked, and she couldn't shake it. She was on high alert as she stepped out of the Jeep.

Nobody shot at her, which was a nice change of pace.

Around her neck she carried the binoculars from the glove compartment. She found a ladder tilted against the side of the house and climbed to the roof, negotiating the slippery rungs with care. Raindrops struck at her like nails. Despite the poncho, she was quickly soaked to the skin.

On the roofline she crouched low, leaning into the rain, and tipped the binoculars to her eyes. The gusting wind threatened to whip her off her perch. The sky was a spread of blackness crisscrossed intermittently with jagged spears of lightning.

Two blocks south sat the sprawling bulk of what had once been the Victoriana Hotel, now the Victoriana Assisted Living Community, a marble-and-plaster wedding cake. Directly across the street from the Victoriana lay the town pavilion, built on the boardwalk, dating to the 1930s. It was a big old block of brick and concrete adorned with tile murals contributed by WPA artisans, with an Olympic-sized saltwater swimming pool, drained nightly, and a snack shop that served up greasy undersized hamburgers at six bucks a pop. It also offered an observation deck crowned by an ornamental tower that provided a panoramic view of the pool, boardwalk, and beach.

The tower was the perfect place to scope out the territory and spy an approaching figure. If Pascal was up there, he would see her coming a hundred yards away.

She knew he would have had no problem getting into the building. The pavilion's main door was secured after dark with a pitifully inadequate padlock that wouldn't stop a bicycle thief.

She zeroed in on the tower, playing with the focus. It took her three passes before she glimpsed a stir of movement.

A solitary figure, shifting his position from the northeast corner to the northwest.

Clever bastard. With a good scope and true aim, he could take her out before she even crossed the street.

She studied him a few minutes longer, until he moved to the southwest corner. Apparently he rotated his position at regular intervals. His walk was stiff, uneven, and he favored his left leg. Maybe he'd been hurt worse than she thought. Nicked in the knee and lamed. She hoped so.

Smiling, she gave him the finger.

She climbed down the ladder, considering her options. She couldn't approach via the streets, the boardwalk, or the beach. But there was another way.

She left the binoculars in the Jeep, along with her phone and her beret; being stylish wasn't a top priority now. She held on to the fanny pack containing the Glock and spare mags, but didn't bother with the Osprey silencer this time. Reluctantly she left her trusty carbine behind also. The way she was going, she couldn't afford any encumbrances.

A block north of the McMansion was the Brighton Cove Surf & Racquet Club. In common with all the exclusive private clubs in this area, it did not boast Bonnie Parker as a member. That fact didn't stop her from scaling the low wall and dropping down into the tennis courts with a splash.

She'd played tennis once. Sucked at it. Hit the damn ball so hard she busted a string on the racquet. Her instructor said she had anger issues. Like she didn't know.

A pedestrian passageway led from the club to the beach, passing underneath Ocean Drive. She made short work of the locked door, then crossed the street below ground, invisible to the watcher in the tower. It was nice to be out of the rain for a minute.

Then she emerged onto the beach, facing clouds of sand flung at her by the stinging wind. Somewhere in the wet darkness, the surf thrashed and moaned like a dying thing. She took cover behind a dune tufted with windblown dune grass, sandwort, and evergreen bushes, then adjusted her fanny pack so it rested against her hip, leaving her belly clear. On elbows and knees she wormed under the boardwalk and began crawling south, toward the pavilion.

The boardwalk straddled a series of concrete trestles ten feet apart, arches of stone mounted on pairs of thick pillars. The trestles curved low, and sand drifted up against the pillars, making for some tight spaces. Once or twice she had to stop and dig out a path, scooping up handfuls of wet sand.

She found herself wishing she'd spent more time at the gym. Or any time, really. Well, she was getting a serious workout tonight.

She kept going, yard after yard. Whenever she raised her head, she bumped into one of the crossbeams. The planks that served as the boardwalk's surface were fake wood, some plastic compound supposedly strong enough to survive nor'easters and hurricanes, but the crossbeams were real timber, old and weatherworn, and they left splinters in her hair. Rain dripped through cracks between the boards, leaking under her hood and down her shirt collar, raising stripes of gooseflesh on her back.

Staying busy had kept her apprehension at a manageable level, but it flared up now, as she found herself in the dark, damp, claustrophobic space, inching toward a man who had nearly snuffed her a couple of times already. She told herself she had the edge on him. She knew his position, and he had no idea where she was. While he watched the terrain around the pavilion, she would creep up underneath the boardwalk, then enter the pavilion and take him by surprise.

Decent strategy. She ought to be feeling good about her chances. But he had outthought her before. He had anticipated the GPS tracker on his car. He had somehow guessed that she would rig a tripwire on the farmhouse stairs. He had waited for her on Old Road. He was always a step ahead.

That was the thought she couldn't break free of. Every time she believed she had the advantage, he proved her wrong.

If she was wrong this time, then each yard of painful progress brought her closer to a bullet. Or to something worse. Pascal, after all, was a man who enjoyed inflicting pain.

Kill or be killed. Her motto. Her mantra. Her epitaph, someday.

She shouldn't live like this. No one should. But she didn't know any other way.

Des had been mistaken when he said she missed her parents. But he was right that she'd lost something. She'd lost her sense of safety, her trust in the basic decency of the world. She'd lost the luxury of being able to relax and let down her guard, ever.

Since that night fourteen years ago, she had lived like a wild animal—and even now, half-civilized, she could revert to savagery at any time. She knew it. It troubled her. Scared her, even.

Still, there was one saving grace. Last January, in the snowy twilight of the Pine Barrens, she had experienced a moment of vulnerability.

Kurt Land had needed killing, but at the last moment, she'd flinched from the job. Sure, she'd left him to die. She'd been certain he was finished. But she hadn't pulled the trigger while she looked into his eyes. That was a line she couldn't cross. She was not entirely devoid of conscience. Not wholly a bloodthirsty predator that killed without compunction.

A small thing, but she had hugged it tight on sleepless nights, and it had warmed her. A little.

And now it turned out that her one concession to human frailty had kept Kurt Land alive. She should have taken care of him when she had the chance. Holding back, surrendering to pity, was a luxury someone in her line couldn't afford.

Kill or be killed. No middle ground, no gray area. Kill or die. That was all there was.

She had been lying to herself to think it could ever be any other way.

30

Pascal was pleased with the conversation. He had let the girl believe he was reluctant to do battle. Naturally it had not occurred to her that he had kept the cell phone turned on solely in the hope that she would call with just such a proposition.

Kurt the rat was in position, as was Pascal himself. Together they would give the girl quite a welcome—and quite a good-bye.

Ordinarily he would have wanted to keep Parker alive in order to find out where the Kirbys were. But he had learned to take no chances with her. He would deal with her quickly and decisively, then locate the Kirbys on his own.

Beneath the black leather gloves his hands tingled, but not with cold.

With anticipation.

***

Bonnie was well along the boardwalk now, having groped and struggled through three blocks of wet, clinging sand. There was a cut on her left hand where she'd scraped a broken bottle, and a tatter of newspaper pasted to her shoe, trailing her like a ribbon of toilet paper from a restroom. All in all, she'd had better nights.

But she was almost there.

The pavilion's observation deck flared out over the boardwalk, which meant she could emerge from hiding with no risk of being seen. Unless, of course, he had abandoned his post and taken up a position by the door. She didn't exactly relish the prospect of emerging from cover only to meet Pascal face to face. At the very least she needed her firearm at the ready.

Rolling onto her side, she fumbled at the fanny pack lying hard against her hip. She unzipped the pouch and peeled away the Velcro strap that held the gun in place. In the stillness and close confinement, the soft tearing sound seemed terrifyingly loud, a sure giveaway of her position.

Then the gun was in her hand, and she felt a little better. She crawled to the edge of the boardwalk, sat up, and raised her head, scanning the boards in both directions.

Empty. The flat expanse stretched into darkness, a dim line of streetlights fading away in a mist of rain and sea spray.

He wasn't down here. Must still be in the tower.

The pavilion door, she noted without surprise, hung ajar.

She gripped the boardwalk's railing and hoisted herself up, then stood, distantly aware of the ache in her joints from the long, hard crawl. Silently she crossed to the open door and went inside.

She found herself in a small lobby adjacent to the snack shop. Directly ahead she recognized the staircase leading to the basement locker rooms. To her right was another stairway, which rose to a landing where a steel ladder offered access to a trapdoor in the tower. Lightning flickered through the trapdoor, propped open as if in invitation.

As long as she made no noise to betray herself, she could climb the stairs and the ladder, pop up through the opening, and take out Pascal before he could react.

Stealth—then speed. It ought to work.

Hell, it pretty much had to.

***

She was here.

Pascal saw her clearly as she stepped into the lobby, clad in a shapeless raincoat that dripped on the floor. For the past quarter of an hour he had crouched on the stairs to the cellarage, smelling saltwater and mildew and rot, and watching the door.

He had known she would reconnoiter the area and spy the sentry in the tower. And he had known she would find a way to reach the sentry without being seen. She was resourceful, this

Bonnie Parker, and reckless enough to tread where a more sensible adversary would not go.

She climbed the other staircase and began to scale the ladder in the dark. Her gun was in her hand. She thought he was up there, and she expected to take him by surprise.

Soundlessly he crept up the basement stairs into the lobby. He would wait until she was at the top of the ladder, reaching for the trapdoor, in a position of maximum vulnerability. Then—one silenced shot, and she would tumble down the shaft, dead before she hit the landing, the vinyl poncho covering her like a body bag.

She would never know what happened. He felt a bit sorry about that. He would have liked her to know.

***

Bonnie had nearly reached the top rung of the ladder when she heard the heavy tread of a footstep overhead. He was shifting his position again.

She paused, listening to the clack-clack-clack of his uneven stride.

Something about that stride bothered her. He'd been wounded, obviously. Shot in the leg ...

But the bloodstain on the farmhouse door had been at shoulder height. And the trail of blood in the parlor had been consistent with evenly spaced footfalls.

Pascal hadn't been wounded in the leg. Which meant ...

He wasn't the man in the tower.

She spun on the ladder. Below her, movement in the lobby. She fired down. The unsilenced Glock roared in the darkness, spitting purple muzzle flashes. In the flicker a dark figure dived for cover, rolling onto the basement stairs.

The guy above her was probably armed, too. Bracing her feet against the steel rails, she slid down the ladder firepole-style. As she descended the staircase to the lobby, she aimed two shots at the trapdoor and two more toward the basement. Another two shots— one high, one low—provided cover as she sprinted out the door. From the basement stairs came an answering shot, carefully aimed, striking the door frame inches from her head.

Then she was outside, on the apron of the boardwalk fronting the pavilion. The only available cover was the colonnade of brick pillars holding up the observation deck. She ducked behind the nearest one, the poncho flapping at her hips.

Someone shot at her from the pavilion doorway. The bullet struck the pillar, chipping flecks of brick. She fired back blindly and retreated to the next pillar, closer to the beach.

Couldn't stay here long. If both men were armed, one of them could pin her down while the other worked his way around to the side and picked her off.

Staying topside was no good. She needed to go below the boardwalk again.

She snapped off two more rounds, then swung under the railing and dropped to the beach. She burrowed beneath the boards and crawled north, away from the pavilion, putting distance between herself and her pursuers.

Pursuers, plural. Who the hell was the second man, and where had he come from? She'd pegged Pascal as a loner. He'd been alone in his motel room, alone at the Kirbys' house. How'd he find himself a playmate in the middle of the night?

At least under the boardwalk she should be safe. They might come after her, but as long as she watched for any intrusion, she would have the edge. The western side of the boardwalk lay flush against the dunes, affording no access to the crawlspace. If they came, they would come from the eastern side—the beach. She only needed to stay alert.

She had elbowed her way pretty far along now, far enough that she was no longer screened from the rain by the observation deck. Silvery threads of rainwater streamed like tinsel through cracks between the boards. The top layer of sand was wet and cold, like a thick crust of mud over the dryer, looser sediment beneath. She dragged herself forward a little farther, then stopped.

By her count she'd expended nine rounds, emptying more than half the magazine. She removed it and stuck it in her pocket, then pressed in a fresh one. If she had to fire, she wanted as many shots as possible.

She lay there, straining to hear any sounds besides the smash of thunder, the wet lash of rain, and the groan of the surf.

There was nothing. They might not be after her, not yet.

But they would come.

***

Pascal—on the hunt and feeling fine.

He was unconcerned about the failure of his original strategy. Something had alerted Parker to the deception at the critical moment. It was unimportant. One must always be prepared to improvise. Was it Napoleon who said that no plan of battle ever survived one's first encounter with the enemy?

His new friend Kurt seemed less philosophical about this turn of events. Stationed in the lobby, trading shots with Parker outside, Pascal had glanced behind him and seen the rat clearly—his eyes swimming in his blanched face, his Adam's apple bobbing beneath the mat of tangled beard, his shoulders hunched and stiff. Everything about him spoke of blind panic. He had expected to witness a quick and easy kill. Instead he was caught in a firefight.

Well, let him tremble. Parker was all that mattered. She was still nearby, hiding below the boardwalk, imagining that she was safe. But he had an advantage over her, one she did not suspect.

He only had to find her and put an end to things.

31

Huddled in the cold, drenched with rainwater, Bonnie waited, listening.

Past the noise of the storm, she heard the low creak of a board. A sound like a slow, cautious footstep.

She lay immobile, letting seconds tick by as fingers of rain probed through the cracks and poked chilly fingertips into her scalp.

Another creak, closer than the last. It vibrated through the boardwalk, releasing a trickle of grit from the crossbeam above her face.

He was coming this way. Moving stealthily, on the prowl. Moving directly toward her, as if he had zeroed in on her position.

But it didn't make sense. Her couldn't hunt her from above. Couldn't see her, couldn't possibly have any idea where she was.

She was trapped under the boards, with barely enough space to roll over, unable to move faster than a crawl. Her only hope was that he was as blind as she was, but he wasn't. Somehow he knew just where she lay.

Another step. He was close now. Less than ten feet away.

One man, not two. Just one of them was hunting her, and she knew which one it had to be.

He stopped. She waited through a long moment of howling wind and punishing rain.

Very softly, one of the boards creaked, but this was a different sound, a long drawn-out wheeze. Not a footstep. More like someone shifting his weight, altering his stance by a few degrees.

Panic flashed through her, and she knew she had to move, move *now*.

She flung herself sideways, rolling away, and there was a soft percussive noise and a spray of sand and splinters as a shot impacted the ground where she'd lain a moment before.

She started moving, blindly elbowing her way into the dark.

Above—the tread of his shoes on the boards. Tracking her, following her progress.

He knew where she was. Somehow he knew. He could fire at her whenever he wished. And she couldn't shoot back because she had no way to pinpoint his position. She might as well have been disarmed.

Not good, Bonnie. Not an ideal situation to be in.

The footfalls stopped again. This time she didn't hesitate.

She dived to her left, scrambling away from two muffled pops that dropped a rain of splinters on her back.

How could he keep finding her? Did he have X-ray vision, for God's sake? Could he see right through the planks?

She scrabbled at the ground, clutching up handfuls of loose sand as she drew herself forward. Her heart shuddered in her chest, banging at her ribs. She wasn't used to being prey.

She knew he was still somewhere above her, remorselessly keeping pace. She couldn't outdistance him, and if she left the cover of the boardwalk, she would be exposed against the beach with no cover, and he would gun her down, an easy score.

Reverse course, then. Crawl backward, see if you can shake him.

She gave it a go, backing up, glad to be trying something, glad to be thinking. It was hard to think when you were scared, and right now she was more goddamn scared than she had ever been in her life.

She had time to hope she might have lost him, and then she registered a soft scuff on a board, perilously close, and she veered to her right.

The gun coughed again, blowing another hole in the planks,

showering her with dust.

God *damn* it, he was still on her ass.

The shots were quiet; as before, his weapon was fitted with a suppressor, and he must be shooting light loads to keep the velocity subsonic. There were limits to a silencer's effectiveness, but the shots were muffled enough to pass for firecrackers or coughs of thunder. They got a little louder each time as the suppressor wore out, but at the rate he was closing in on her, he wouldn't need many more tries.

So think, Bonnie. Stop shivering, damn it, and think your way out of this mess.

She crawled aimlessly. Sweat and raindrops blurred together on her face like tears. Her teeth were chattering. It would be lights out for her in the next thirty seconds or so. She didn't like it. Getting killed was a real pain in the butt.

The worst thing was that she didn't know how it was happening, how he could see her. It made no sense. She was invisible.

Invisible—like the infrared beam in the farmhouse. And yet somehow he'd known it was there.

An infrared beam ...

She got it.

It wasn't anything supernatural. He was using night-vision gear.

The son of a bitch could see her body heat through gaps in the boardwalk.

And that meant there was no place to hide.

***

Pascal was cautious. Of course he enjoyed every advantage. He owned the night. The night-vision headset he had carried in his satchel was his secret weapon—an ITT Exelis binocular system, head-mounted, with an infrared illuminator. He had picked up the equipment in Europe, paying 10,000 euros.

The infrared goggles, like insect eyes, perceived a band of the electromagnetic spectrum alien to human vision. The warmth of the girl's body showed up on the 40° display as a faint green iridescence, flickering in the cracks between the boards.

He had turned off the Beretta's laser targeting assist. The laser beam might give her a target. The same professional caution made him keep his distance from his quarry. If he got too close, she might be able to determine his position and squeeze off a lucky shot.

He was content to play it safe. Guided by his enhanced vision, he fired from a distance, hopscotching nimbly from plank to plank, catching glimpses of her body heat, a feeble luminescent trail. She was clever, always changing course, zigzagging like a cockroach. The rain gear she was wearing dimmed her heat signature. The rain itself was another complication; it smeared his goggles, blurring his artificial vision, while flashes of lightning briefly whited out the display.

It was difficult work, tracking the girl—like chasing threads of St. Elmo's fire on the shifting deck of a storm-tossed vessel.

But he would score a hit before long. It was purely a matter of time.

He glanced at the pavilion, now well behind him, and made out the green glow of Kurt the rat by the doorway to the lobby. The man was waiting, watching, afraid to get too close. His only purpose had been to wriggle like a worm on a hook, luring this one particular fish. Now he was merely a distraction, to be dispatched when this was over.

First things first. Parker.

Though he had grown to respect her, he could not deny that it was her time to die.

***

Bonnie scrambled to the nearest trestle and huddled behind it, trusting the stone arch to conceal her. She had to make herself invisible. She was playing hide-and-seek, and if she lost this game, she wouldn't get to play again. It hardly seemed fair, though—her in the dark, and him with his goo-goo-googly eyes.

Still, she couldn't have been showing up very clearly on his infrared display, not with the boardwalk blocking most of her heat signature. If he lost track of her, he wouldn't know where to pick up the search—

Champagne corks started popping around her. He was firing again. She hadn't lost him. He was shooting at her position, and only the concrete mass kept her safe as she clung to the cold stone and the sand erupted like geysers. The fusillade went on and on.

Then it ended. His gun must be empty. But he would reload. Then all he had to do was circle around to the side for a clear shot.

Evasion wasn't working. Escape was impossible. Basically he was going to nail her for sure unless she changed tactics.

So stand and fight. Her only option. Hell, she was better on offense than defense anyway.

She rolled onto her back, pointing the Glock's barrel upward, unable to aim because she had no target. She pulled the trigger. The pistol kicked in her hands. She fired through the boards, her gun barking, the hollow-point rounds blowing holes in the fake wood.

The reports boomed in the confined space. She pumped out eight shots and paused, not wanting to blow her whole wad on one try.

He might be moving overhead, but if so she couldn't hear it over the furious chiming in her ears. She allowed herself to hope he'd been wounded—killed, even.

Then the sand erupted again. He was answering her attack with a new barrage of shots. She spun behind the trestle, blinking rain and grit out of her eyes, shooting back until her gun was empty, seeing nothing but muzzle flare, while her eardrums threatened to burst under the insane noise, and she heard her own voice screaming, *"Stop it!"*—the cry audible only inside her skull.

Her plea was useless. It wouldn't stop, it would never stop ...

But it did.

He must have emptied his gun again. But he would have more ammo. He would never run out.

She tried to come up with a plan of action, but suddenly she was all out of ideas. The gunfire had robbed her of night vision and most of her hearing. She was effectively blind and deaf, and she was up against an adversary who could see in the dark.

If she left cover, she was dead. If she stayed put, she was dead. Any way she played it—dead.

***

Pascal dumped the Beretta's empty magazine and inserted a new one. The procedure was automatic to him. He had done it thousands of times, often practicing blindfolded.

With his next attack he would get the girl—assuming he had not killed her already.

The phone in his pocket thrummed. Her phone, set to vibrate so the ring tone would not betray him in the dark.

Curiosity prompted him to lift his goggles and pluck the device from his pocket. He lifted it in a gloved hand and read the name on the display.

Slowly, Pascal smiled.

***

Bonnie heeled her last fresh magazine into the Glock, her hands shaky, her fingers slick with rain. The gun was barely more useful than a pacifier at this point. She couldn't tell where Pascal was, couldn't fire with any hope of scoring a hit. She could only wait to die, as she had waited in the motel bathtub as a kid.

Kurt Land must have felt like this when she stood over him in the Pine Barrens, her gun angled at his chest in the sun's last rays. The fear she'd read in his face—it was her fear now.

Now she knew why she hadn't shot him. He had been too much like her. Too much like the surprised and helpless victim she would have been, if the man in the motel room had pulled back the shower curtain and seen her cowering there.

She thought she had better get away from the trestle. Pascal knew her shots had come from there, and he would be homing in on her.

Leaving cover, she scrambled south a few yards until she blundered into a high drift of sand, wet and clammy. Cold.

Cold was what she needed. Pascal was tracking her body heat. Anything that disguised her heat signature would make her harder to see.

She shoved the Glock into her waistband and dug into the pile, scooping out handfuls of sand. As the cavity enlarged, she burrowed deeper inside, until the hill collapsed, blanketing her.

Talk about digging your own grave, a voice in her head quipped.

She told it to shut the fuck up.

The sand was thick and chilly, and in combination with the waterproof poncho it might—*might*—be enough to obscure her infrared display. Under the best of circumstances, all Pascal could possibly see was a faint ripple of heat through the cracks. The rain and lightning had to be a distraction, and now she was smothered in natural camouflage.

And if he saw her anyway ...

Then she might have time for one or two more shots before he took her out. She tightened her grip on the gun, hoping Pascal would make enough noise to give her something to aim at.

If she had to shoot again, her next rounds would be the last she ever fired, and she intended to make them count.

***

The phone call was brief and businesslike, devoid of emotion. Pascal appreciated that. He made the necessary arrangements and clicked off.

This new development left him with little time. He must be going. Bonnie Parker had become a strictly secondary concern.

But surely he could spare another few seconds to finish the job. He would kill her with his next few shots, then leave her body under the boardwalk to gather flies and sand crabs.

He lowered the goggles, immersing himself in an electronic field of view, and scanned the boards for a last look at the warmth radiating from Bonnie Parker's living body—a body that would not be living much longer.

He saw nothing.

She was gone.

He paced the boards, peering in all directions. She had to be close by. He had lost sight of her for only a minute. How far could she crawl in that time?

But she was not there. God damn it, *she was not there.*

He could not abandon the chase, not when he was so close. But he had no choice. Parker was not his priority. She never had been.

Perhaps if he gave his pistol and night-vision gear to Kurt, the rat could finish things for him. Even such a useless weakling ought to be capable of dispatching a trapped and nearly helpless adversary.

When he turned to the pavilion, this small hope died. The shimmering green fleck in the center of his vision was the figure of a man darting south on the boardwalk, then vanishing down an access ramp to the street.

The rat had fled. The latest exchange of gunfire must have unnerved him completely.

That, then, was that. He could not spare the time to nose out Parker now. He had wasted too many precious seconds as it was.

She would live. So be it. He begrudged her nothing. She had put up a good fight, and she deserved to keep her little life.

He turned and broke into a run, heading for the exit that would take him to the parking lot across the street.

32

Bonnie didn't know why she was still alive.

She shouldn't be. The sand couldn't conceal her anymore. By now her body heat must have leaked through and become visible to Pascal's infrared scope, which meant gunfire ought to be streaming down.

So far it hadn't. Somehow she was still breathing. She'd heard no footsteps, nothing that would give her a target.

Why didn't he just shoot? Why drag it out?

Come on, you son of a bitch, get it over with.

She shut her eyes, willing him to fire.

Nothing happened.

And gradually the idea came to her that he might be gone.

She didn't believe it. It would be a kind of miracle, and she didn't believe in miracles. Anything that seemed too good to be true was a scam. Her whole life had taught her that.

He was still up there, maybe hoping to lure her out so he could inflict a nonfatal wound and commence a new round of Q&A.

But more long moments dragged past, and still ... nothing.

She began to think he really had checked out. Maybe he thought he'd killed her in his last volley. But he would have confirmed it. He was a pro. A pro always got confirmation.

Well, no. Not always. She hadn't confirmed it with Kurt Land, had she?

She pushed her head out of the sand pile.

"Pascal?" she whispered. Her throat was sore, as if she'd been shouting, and the word was scarcely audible.

She tried again, louder. "Pascal!"

Nothing.

"Hey, *asshole!*"

No reply, either in words or bullets.

Even so, she didn't move. It felt warm and safe under the sand, and part of her wanted to stay here, just stay and rest. Sleep ...

Screw that. She wasn't swooning like a goddamned débutante.

She dug herself free, crawled to the edge of the boardwalk, and emerged into the open. Slowly she stood in the rain and looked around, the Glock traveling with her gaze.

Pascal wasn't there.

He had gone away, and she was alive. It made no sense, but she couldn't argue with it.

She was exhausted, wiped out. And a mess—splinters in her hair, rips in her poncho, random cuts on her arms and legs from crawling over shards of seashells and glass bottles.

She wondered if she really had the heart for this job. Maybe she should get her GED, go to community college, become a veterinarian or something.

The rain coursed down around her, washing some of the sandy paste off her poncho. The hood had fallen off her head, and her hair was a ragged mop.

She made her way to a wooden staircase and climbed up to the boardwalk. Her legs were shaking, her knees watery. Her only thought was that she ought to be dead. Pascal had outplayed her again. He'd held all the cards. He could have finished her. Why didn't he?

Maybe he'd heard a siren. Even in the clamor of the storm, someone who lived near the beach might have heard her unsilenced gunshots and called it in. But there were no sirens. There was nothing but the crackle of thunder, the drumbeat of rain on the boardwalk, and the crash of breakers on the beach.

She looked down. Brass shell casings littered the planks. They glittered in bursts of lightning. Each one represented a bullet that could have made her dead.

A few yards down the boardwalk glittered something bigger than a shell casing. Her stolen cell phone.

"Hey, Sammy," she said, picking it up. The smooth plastic case felt like the handshake of an old friend.

The phone must have slipped out of Pascal's pocket unnoticed. Or maybe he had noticed, but had been in too much of a hurry to care.

Though the screen had a jagged crack, it still lit up when she pressed the power button. She checked the call log. The most recent incoming call had started nine minutes ago and had lasted forty-two seconds.

The name of the caller: Alan Kirby.

She stared at the screen, trying to understand.

"Alan?" she breathed. "*Alan* called him? What in the name of fuck is going on?"

Her hand moved. She punched in Alan's number. His cell phone rang five times and cycled to voicemail.

She tried Des's home number, a landline—he didn't own a cell. The house phone rang and rang. No answer.

And then she was running.

Running north through billowing sheets of rain, running for her Jeep, not knowing what had happened, but praying she wasn't too late.

33

Sometime under the boardwalk things had stopped making sense. It was like one of those sci-fi movies where some poor schmuck falls into a wormhole or whatever and ends up in a parallel universe where the Nazis won World War II and the Kardashians have talent. Bonnie tried to puzzle it out as she slammed the Jeep into reverse and skidded out from behind the McMansion.

Alan had called Pascal, or at least someone using Alan's phone had called. Okay, start there. She already knew Pascal had one ally, the decoy in the tower. What if he had others? What if he was part of a team, a hit squad, and while she was messing around with him at the pavilion, his buddies were tracking down the Kirbys?

She had pegged him as a lone wolf. But the guy in the tower proved otherwise, didn't he? Alan and his friends had sent a team to rescue Mariana Ortiz. Why couldn't the Colombians have sent a team to exact revenge?

Say Pascal was part of a team. The other team members found the Kirbys. They called Pascal, using Alan's phone, to tell him the job was done. Or they made Alan call for some reason.

Either way, Pascal had to clear out. He couldn't wait around to finish her off. His partner amscrayed too. All of them heading for the Millstone County airstrip, maybe—she'd heard Pascal reserving the pickup on the phone. He hadn't specified the number of passengers. He could have been arranging transportation for his whole team.

It had to be something like that. None of it rang true to her, but she could only assume her intuition was leading her astray. She'd proceeded on the false assumption that she was up against one man, when in fact she was up against three or four or God only knew how many. She never could have won. She could only let the Kirbys get killed.

And Des too. Her best friend. Her only friend. He must be dead with the others.

Rage seized her, and she made a silent promise to track down Pascal, no matter what it took. Track him to Chile, to that place in the mountains—what the hell was the name of it? San Alfonso. She'd seen pictures of his villa. She would recognize it again. She'd break in at night and shoot the bastard dead.

But it wouldn't bring back Des. Or the Kirbys, formerly the Walkers. They were gone for good.

She pulled to a stop in front Des's house. The lights were on, and the front door hung ajar. Not a good sign.

No neighbors had stirred. Whatever had gone down inside the house had been quiet, anyway. She could hope the killers took their victims in their sleep. No waking up, no final pleas or screams. Just a silenced round to each victim's head. Like her parents, Tom and Rebecca, slain in the motel room while she listened from the tub.

Pascal's Lexus wasn't in sight. Her Jeep was the only vehicle parked on the street. She was almost certain the bad guys were gone. But she was through making assumptions.

She grabbed the Ruger carbine from the rear of the Jeep and approached the front door, making no sound, ready to let loose if anyone opened fire on her.

The door was swinging in the wind and rain. She pushed it inward and stepped across the threshold.

Nothing seemed out of place in the living room. She headed down the hall. The guest room was probably where it had ended for the Kirbys. Their bodies—all three of them—would be inside, sprawled across the bed, or possibly huddled in the bathroom if they had retreated in there to make a stand.

Panic room, she thought bitterly. What a stupid, stupid idea.

Like you could stop Pascal or any man like him with a goddamn bathroom door.

She took a breath and entered the bedroom, tensing for the sight of blood and death.

The room was empty.

Bedroom, bathroom—empty.

The bed had been hastily unmade, and she could see the imprint of little A.J.'s head on the pillow. Otherwise, there was no sign that anyone had even been there.

"Weird," she whispered, not getting it. She was still in that parallel universe, and things still weren't making sense.

She began to nurse a small seedling of hope. Maybe Pascal's friends had taken the family alive. She couldn't imagine why. And she didn't know where that would leave Des. Even if the Colombians wanted all three Kirbys for some unfathomable reason, they wouldn't want him.

His bedroom was the next one down the hall. She knew if he was dead in that room, she would lose it, at least a little. She had trouble swallowing and realized the old expression was actually true—you really did get a lump in your throat.

Pushing past her fear, she entered the room. Des's bed was mussed, but no worse than the Kirbys'. His chair was nowhere in sight, and neither was he.

She retraced her steps along the hallway and checked out the kitchen—nothing—and the den—ditto. When she opened the door to the garage, she was almost unsurprised to see that Des's van was gone.

They'd cleared out. The Kirby clan and Des. He had to be driving; nobody else could handle the van with its customized controls.

Had the bad guys forced them to leave in Des's van? No way. Even in a parallel universe that one wouldn't fly.

She was shaking her head in confusion as she returned to the living room. When she glanced into the dining area, she saw a large, heavy sheet of paper torn from one of Des's sketchpads lying on the table.

She took the paper in her hands. The sheets contained a few brisk lines of florid handwriting and a signature at the bottom.

Bonnie read the note, then read it again. And she understood.

She understood a whole lot of things.

34

Pascal drove through the rain, his high beams cutting the darkness. In the twin cones of light, each falling raindrop was a slender, glittering icicle.

Ahead, a figure solidified out of the night. A female form taking shelter under a maple tree at the corner of First and Garfield.

Mrs. Alan Kirby, he thought, his lips parting in the flicker of a smile.

He eased to a stop and unlocked the passenger door, then waited, letting her come to him.

Head lowered against the rain, she left the protection of the tree and ran to the car. With her hand on the door, did she hesitate? Perhaps for a heartbeat. No longer.

Then she was inside, settling into the passenger seat, pulling the door firmly shut.

She turned to him. Her face was lit in the glow of the ceiling lamp. Her hair was blond now, and she was thinner than he remembered. But nothing essential had changed.

"Guinevere," he said tenderly, stroking her cheek.

She fell against him, hugging his chest and weeping. In his ear he felt the warmth of her breath in time with the kiss of a single whispered word:

"Lancelot."

35

Bonnie was still staring at the sheet of paper in her hand when the hum of an engine rose in the driveway. Reflexively she tightened her grip on the Glock before identifying it as the sound of Des's van.

She left the house and met the van as it pulled into the garage. Des was at the wheel. Alan rode shotgun, his eyes staring, his face empty. The kid was in the backseat, sound asleep.

She yanked open Alan's door and said, "You didn't find her."

It wasn't a question.

He shook his head. "No. But we found this."

He handed over his cell phone, wet with rain.

"We figure he made her drop it," he added lifelessly. "He probably assumed we could track it. Which we could, with GPS. We used Desmond's netbook."

"Where was it?"

"Two blocks east. On the sidewalk."

Alan climbed out of his seat, then reached into the back and lifted his son in his arms. He carried the boy into the house. Bonnie followed. Behind them came the whir of the ramp that would allow Des to get out on the driver's side.

"He hasn't had her long," Bonnie said as they went down the hall to the guest room. "She called him less than twenty minutes ago."

"That's long enough," Alan breathed. He placed the boy in bed and tucked him under the covers. "She must have placed the call from outside the house so we wouldn't hear. That's why she took the phone."

"Right. And it had to be your phone, because it had my number in its memory. She knew he had my cell. She was just waiting for the chance to get hold of the phone and make contact." Bonnie hesitated. "In the note she said there'd been too many deaths."

Alan nodded. "It's what she was saying all along. She argued with me about it after you left. She said Pascal wouldn't stop until he had her. She had to give herself up. Sacrifice herself for us. Because she was the one he really wanted." He looked at her. "You saw the note. How she signed it."

"Yes." She had seen the graceful looping signature at the bottom of the page: *Mariana*.

"She never did like the name Cynthia." Alan managed a sad little laugh.

Bonnie remembered her first impressions of Cynthia Kirby. Fashionably thin—only it wasn't fashion; it was the ravages of cancer. Blonde hair—a dye job, she'd thought, and it was, but not for cosmetic purposes. For disguise. Her clipped style of speech—because she was educated abroad. Her stubborn refusal to take orders—because she was accustomed to fending for herself in dangerous places. Places like the farmlands of Colombia, and the women's prison in Bogotá.

"So the rescue mission was a success," she said, easing him away from the sleeping child.

"A partial success. They got her out. But Hector Bezos and two of his men were captured during the raid. The others got Mariana to safety. Most of what I told you was true," he added almost apologetically.

"*Most* doesn't cut it, buddy boy. Pascal was after her all along. Not you."

"I don't know if I was a target or not. He did kill Herb and Amy, after all."

"But only because he was tracking Mariana. He went to Maine first in the hope that she was hiding out there. When that didn't pan out, he interrogated Amy and used the emails to trace Mariana's location. By then he would have known she was with you."

"Herb told him, I'm sure. Or Amy did. They didn't know what names we were using now, but they knew we were together."

She led him out of the bedroom, down the hall to the living room. "What about Caroline? A.J.'s mom?"

"She died before all this happened. Before I ever heard of Mariana. Died of cancer."

He said it simply, but there were volumes of meaning tucked into the words. He had buried his wife, then learned of another woman with cancer, a woman he'd never met, a woman wasting away in a prison cell. He hadn't saved Caroline, but he could save this other woman, if he pulled out all the stops.

And sometime during the events that followed, he'd fallen in love with Mariana Ortiz. Fallen in love from afar, romanticizing her, idealizing her. She was the symbolic substitute for the wife he'd lost, and when she arrived in the US, he made his feelings known, and won her.

"And now I've lost her," he whispered, as if reading her thoughts.

"Not yet."

"What the hell does that mean? Are you crazy? He *has* her. Fuck, he's probably killed her already!"

In the guest room, A.J., startled awake, began to cry. "Mommy …"

It occurred to Bonnie that when he called for his mother, it was Caroline Walker he really wanted, not the dye-job stand-in.

She rested her hands on Alan's shoulders. "Keep your voice down. Get a grip, okay?"

He stared dumbly at her.

"Look, Alan—or Jeffrey, whatever—you've gotta focus. This son of a bitch has your lady, but if he wanted to kill her, he would have done it right there on the street. He took her alive for a reason. She's worth more to him that way."

"You don't know that."

"Yeah, I do. In your house he had a clear shot at me, but hesitated. Now I know why. He saw a woman at the top of the stairs, but he couldn't be sure which woman it was. I'd changed my clothes. I wasn't wearing a hat. For a second he thought it might be Mariana in his sights. And he held his fire."

"Okay, but … why would he want her alive? Why …?" Alan shut his eyes, answering his own question. "Oh, Christ. You think he's taking her back. Back to the Colombians. To prison and torture—"

"He'll have to get her out of the country first. He can't have left yet. He's on his way to Millstone Airport right now."

Des spoke up, surprising her. He had rolled in so quietly she'd been unaware of his presence. "That airfield's been closed for years."

"Which makes it perfect for a clandestine takeoff. I'm not guessing about this. I heard him make the arrangements. I just didn't know he was planning to bring a guest."

"You heard him? He said Millstone Airport?" Alan's eyes were wild. "We have to go there."

"Nuh-uh, chum. *We* aren't going anywhere. This is a solo mission."

"She's my wife—"

"Yeah, and that's your kid crying in there. You go play daddy. I'll deal with Pascal."

"But—"

She pressed a finger to his lips. "No backtalk. This has been kind of a bumpy night, and I'm in no mood."

His shoulders slumped. "All right. Just get her back. Please."

"Will do. Now go comfort the little shaver. That goddamn bawling is getting on my nerves."

He retreated down the hall. She and Des watched him go.

"Parker," Des said, "you sure you can handle this?"

"Not really. But it looks like I'm committed."

She moved past him to the front door. His voice stopped her. "Did you see it?"

She looked back. "Yeah, Des. I saw it."

He wheeled up to her. "And you're still going?"

"You bet I'm going." Impulsively she stooped and kissed his cheek. "Leave a light on. This won't take long."

She left the house and plunged back into the storm.

36

Pascal was happy. Altogether and unabashedly happy, perhaps for the first time in his life.

He had completed his quest. He had found his holy grail.

"I never thought you would come for me," Mariana said as he guided the Lexus down the highway. "I thought you'd forgotten me long ago."

"I never forgot."

"Even after I ran out on you like that? It was … so cruel of me."

"I never blamed you. I understood."

"Did you? How could you understand?"

Pascal had given the question much thought and had arrived at clear conclusions. He did not look at her as he spoke. He directed his gaze at the rainswept highway, alert for the airfield somewhere ahead.

"You were afraid," he said. "It was one thing to enjoy the things we did together, when it was only your pain and my skill. But I made the mistake of letting you watch me with Diaz. That was what frightened you, was it not?"

"Yes …"

"To see it done to an unwilling victim—it is a different matter from one's own voluntary participation. I should have realized that. I should have anticipated …"

"It was my weakness. You have no need to apologize. Anyway, I was wrong."

"You need not say so."

"But it's true. I learned that much in prison. They tortured me —and others. I heard them. Sometimes all day long, or all night— the screams."

She was quiet for a moment, perhaps hearing those screams again. He let the silence linger.

"But there was nothing unusual about the men who did it. They were just ordinary men doing a job." Her voice was low and thoughtful. "It's human nature, isn't it? I flinched from it, but only because I lacked the strength to acknowledge the plain truth."

"What truth?" Pascal asked gently.

"We are all torturers and killers at heart. We repress our deepest instincts, and suffer for it. Only those who face up to their true nature can finally be free."

The words were better than any he could have hoped to hear from her. Better than the words he had heard her say in his many imagined versions of this conversation.

His heart was full to overflowing. He knew a great and all-enwrapping peace.

"I have missed you greatly, Guinevere," he whispered.

"We should never have parted."

"That is behind us now." He slipped a gloved hand around her wrist. "We shall never be apart again."

***

Bonnie hit the highway at seventy miles an hour, distantly concerned about the risk of hydroplaning on the wet road, but not really giving a damn. Her friend Pascal had a plane to catch, and she intended to make sure he missed his flight.

She would disrupt his travel plans, all right. And she would bring Mariana Ortiz back to her husband so they could be together for whatever amount of time she had left.

Alan had lost enough already. He'd lost his first wife, his career, even his name. She was damned if she would let him lose Mariana too.

And as for Pascal ...

"Should've aced me when you had the chance, you son of a bitch," she said through gritted teeth. "Because it's my turn now."

***

Pascal walked with the pilot in the pelting rain, the two of them lugging his bags from the parked Lexus to the plane. The pilot was a thirtyish American with a ponytail and an earring, features that did not inspire confidence. It seemed likely he had tattoos also. Well, this would be Pascal's last contact with the degenerate culture of the North American continent. He supposed it was appropriate that the last American he would see on United States soil was so perfectly suited to his role.

"Getting pretty late," the pilot was saying. "I was starting to think you wouldn't show."

"There were complications. One complication in particular cost me a considerable delay."

The pilot nodded toward the Beechcraft turboprop on the runway. "You sure the woman's okay in there by herself? She won't run off?"

"Never." Pascal smiled. "Or at least—never again."

As they reached the baggage bay at the rear of the plane, he looked back, his gaze sweeping the row of hangers behind him. There was a chance Parker had overheard his phone conversation in the motel. He doubted she could get here in time to stop him.

But he had underestimated her before.

***

The gate to the airfield should have been padlocked, but as she approached it, Bonnie could see that it was standing open, leaning crookedly, blasted nearly off its hinges by the impact of a speeding vehicle. She doused her headlights and breezed through, the Jeep's tires spraying up fans of puddled rainwater.

Beyond the gate, a long winding driveway sloped gently downhill, leading away from the highway. She killed the engine and coasted down, hoping she wouldn't lose traction on the wet macadam.

Millstone Airport had been closed years ago, the ramshackle

buildings abandoned to field mice and millipedes. No lights burned in the buildings or on the field. She pulled into a parking lot ringed with the dark, squat shapes of hangars and eased the Jeep to a stop.

She slipped out, shutting the door softly. The carbine was still riding on her shoulder, the Glock tucked in her fanny pack. She had just one magazine for the carbine—twenty-five rounds, no more—but that ought to be plenty if she conserved ammo. She had a feeling this wasn't going to last long, one way or the other.

The runway was just past the nearest hangar. She crept along the side wall and looked out on a rain-puddled spread of cracked tarmac tufted with brushy weeds.

The black SUV was slant-parked thirty feet away. Beyond it was a small plane, a six-seater. The doors to the cabin and the aft baggage bay stood open. A man who was probably the pilot was shoving Pascal's duffel into the bay while Pascal stood at his side. Mariana Ortiz was not in sight. She had to be inside the plane.

Neither of them was looking in this direction. The SUV offered the only cover on the blank stretch of runway. She bent low and sprinted for it.

Crossing the tarmac, she was utterly exposed. If the pilot or Pascal turned, she was going to be caught in a firefight without cover or concealment.

Nobody turned. She reached the vehicle and crouched behind it.

She was pretty sure she could nail one of the two men at this distance. But probably not both, at least not before the survivor had time to return fire.

And it had to be both, because the pilot was carrying. A sidearm jutted out of the holster on his hip.

There wasn't much time for her to make her move. Hunkered down behind the SUV, she tried to figure out her best play.

***

The pilot caught Pascal scanning the darkness again. "Expecting trouble?" he asked.

"I always expect trouble. How soon may we take off?"

"Just got to finish loading this stuff, and we're airborne."

Pascal took a last look around, then ascended the airstair and stepped through the cabin doorway.

***

This was her chance. With Pascal aboard the plane, the odds had improved considerably.

She still didn't want to shoot from a distance. She could get the pilot with the carbine for sure, but the noise would alert Pascal and start a gun battle. If she used the Glock with the Osprey silencer, she could do the job quietly, but she wasn't willing to bet she could bring down the man with a pistol shot in the rain.

So what was the alternative? She could maybe figure some way to sneak onto the plane. If she hid among the baggage while the pilot was doing a last perimeter check, then waited till he took off and was occupied at the controls ...

Yeah, right. Then she could shoot him and Pascal, and while the plane went into a nose dive, she would parachute to earth with Mariana in her arms.

Fuck that. What the hell did she think this was, *Charlie's Angels*?

It was possible to overthink a situation. Sometimes you just had to go on instinct. And her instinct was telling her to get up close and personal with this asshole, and do it now.

She left the cover of the SUV and ran at the pilot while he crammed the satchel into place. He heard footsteps and started to turn and she clocked him on the side of the head with the carbine's buttstock, and he went down in the groaning heap.

Nice. Nothing like cold-cocking a guy to get his attention.

Question was, had she gotten Pascal's attention too? If so, she could expect to receive fire as soon as she climbed aboard.

Had to risk it. She was pissed off and out of options.

The luggage bay was divided from the cabin by a particleboard partition. Pascal's suitcase, satchel, and duffel bag were arranged inside. The duffel was the only item big enough to provide her with cover.

She hoisted herself into the bay, trying to strike a balance between stealth and speed, hoping any noise she made would be mistaken for the pilot manhandling the baggage.

One way or the other, it would all be over in the next few seconds.

***

Pascal felt the faint rocking of the plane as if a heavy bag had been thrown into the bay. This was odd, because the duffel was the heaviest bag he had, and he had seen the pilot stow it earlier.

He looked out the window. The pilot was not there.

***

Bonnie slid behind the duffel, hugging the floor, and waited for Pascal to fire.

No shots came. It looked like he hadn't heard her KO the pilot or sneak aboard.

Okay, so much for skulking around. The next part was all about sudden violence and the element of surprise.

She took a few quick shallow breaths like a diver preparing to submerge. Ready?

Ready.

***

Pressing his face to the glass, peering past a smear of raindrops, Pascal saw the pilot—or his legs, at least. Motionless, spread-eagled on the asphalt.

He had been knocked unconscious or killed.

The girl was here.

***

Bonnie kicked at the partition, knocking it free of the wall, and jumped over the luggage into the cabin. The carbine led her, the long barrel gleaming, wet with rain.

She kept her finger lightly on the trigger, ready to squeeze and release, not wanting to fire off a long burst because the risk of killing Mariana was too high.

***

Pascal heard the noise behind him and rose from his seat in

one liquid motion.

He was glad she had come. He had not wanted to leave things unresolved between them. And though she had earned the right to live, he would be happy to grant her a hero's death.

***

Dim lighting in the cabin, a narrow aisle with gray carpet and twin lines of running lights. Mariana on one side, Pascal on the other, both facing forward.

He moved faster than she expected. He was out of his seat before she cleared the luggage, and he was pivoting to face her as he drew the silenced Beretta from his shoulder harness.

The gun came up, clutched in a black leather fist.

She fired first.

Two shots, the shortest burst she could manage. Two .22 rounds that arrowed down the aisle and slugged into Pascal's chest, on the left side, below the heart.

Black blood suffused his shirt like a spreading ink stain. He opened his mouth as if to speak, but no words came out, only a froth of blood bearding his chin.

The Beretta tilted in his grasp and dropped. It hit the floor a half second before he did. His knees unlocked, and he crumpled against his seat, slumping sideways.

Mariana screamed. *"Pascal!"*

Bonnie closed the distance with him and snatched up the Beretta, jamming it into her waistband. She took a step closer, the carbine raised in case Pascal tried making some sort of move, but one look at his face told her that he was all out of moves, now and forever.

Mariana whirled on her, rage and grief skewing her features. "You goddamned fool. He was no threat to me. He *loves* me!"

Bonnie met her eyes. "I know."

***

Pascal was dying. He felt no fear, no anger. There was only a certain regret. He would have savored these next months, had he been permitted to have them. But it was all right. One performance had ended; another would begin. There were other lives to come. Better lives, perhaps. He could hope so.

He did not hate Bonnie Parker. He had been given more than enough opportunities against her. But she was good. And he was getting old. Ten years ago, or even five, he would have beaten her. But this was a young man's game, and he was a young man no longer.

In a haze of light, Mariana knelt by him. Tears stood in her eyes, making them suddenly too big for her face, a doll's eyes. She reached for his hand.

"Good-bye, my dearest," Pascal whispered.

A sound escaped her, an animal wail.

"Take off my glove," he said, every word an audible strain. "Flesh on flesh."

Obediently she peeled off the black leather glove and cast it aside, then entwined her fingers with his.

"It is good," Pascal said, "to feel your touch."

Now it was not only his hands that were cold, but his whole body. His blood was a river of ice, his skin a carpet of snow. The gray light of winter was settling over his vision, leaving him in a frigid twilight. Even the breath in his lungs was cold, breath that choked him until he coughed it up in a red mist.

He shivered. His teeth clacked. That was not good. It might be mistaken for fear. He looked at Mariana, trying to tell her that he was not afraid, but she was not there.

Nothing was there.

***

Bonnie watched, unimpressed, as Mariana knelt by Pascal, lying limp and pale in the aisle, his chest shuddering. She hugged him, rocking his body in her slim, shaking arms. Bonnie waited until she was sure that the movement was purely the woman's and that Pascal had stopped moving for good.

Then she leaned in and plucked his wallet from his back pocket. Silently she began counting out $2500 in large bills.

Mariana stared up at her with the purest hatred she had ever seen. "What are you doing?"

"Getting paid."

When she had tallied up two grand with plenty more to go, she decided to stop counting and just take it all. Screw it, a job like this had to have some perks.

She stuffed the bills into her pocket and tossed the wallet aside, then crouched by Pascal and ran her hands over his body, checking the damage. She found no exit wounds. The two .22 rounds had tumbled inside him, tearing up his vital organs. That was good on two counts. One, it had made him die faster, and like a scorpion who could sting with its last twitch, he was harmless only when he was dead. Two, it meant there was no damage to the plane. The crate could still fly, once the pilot woke up. And she wanted the plane out of here. If it stayed, there would be questions that neither she nor Alan Kirby wanted to answer.

Mariana was still on her knees, weeping over her lover.

"Cry me a river," Bonnie muttered. She grabbed the woman by her shoulder, not gently. "Out. We're leaving now."

Mariana shook her head, not in refusal but in sorrow and disbelief. "You knew? You *knew*?"

"Like I keep telling people, I have a way of figuring things out. Sometimes it takes me a little longer than it ought to. But the note you left—it told the story."

"The note said nothing about my past."

"No, but the handwriting matched the poem your lover-boy had been carrying around as a keepsake."

Mariana looked down at Pascal's lifeless body. "You kept my poem?" she whispered fondly. "Kept it all these years?"

"Yeah, he was the last of the great romantics. Anyway, that's when I knew he wasn't on a paid assignment. He never wanted to hurt you. He just wanted you back."

"If you knew all that, why come here? Why not let me go with him?"

"Because he didn't deserve happiness. And neither do you." She gave Mariana's shoulder another tug. "Get up."

Listlessly she obeyed. Bonnie pushed her ahead and followed, toting the carbine, with Pascal's Beretta wedged in her waistband.

Outside, the pilot was beginning to stir. She disarmed him, just on general principles, and kept walking.

The rain still hadn't let up. It mixed with the tears streaking Mariana's face.

"Cut it out," Bonnie said, irritated. "Pull yourself together."

Mariana looked away. Bonnie jerked her around and slapped her.

"Fucking quit it," she snapped.

"I can't even cry for him?"

"That's right, sister. No tears for killer."

"You're a killer. Maybe there'll be no tears for you when you die."

"I'm not expecting any."

The SUV was unlocked. Bonnie took a moment to check the interior. Castoffs from Pascal's surgical supplies littered the passenger seat. On the backseat was her handbag, with her wallet inside. She wondered whether Pascal had left it for her to find, or as a gift for the police, a way to make her life more complicated.

She retrieved the purse but took care to touch nothing else in the Lexus. She couldn't leave any fingerprints here. The cops would be all over this scene like stink on a monkey.

Actually, she was pretty much counting on that.

"I do have cancer, you know," Mariana said as they left the runway, heading for the Jeep. "It's in remission, but it will return."

"Yeah, so I figured."

"We would not have had more than a year or two together. Perhaps much less. And you couldn't allow us even that?"

"Sorry, sweetie. Guess I'm not that sentimental. Besides, there's the little matter of your husband. Remember him? Dweeby guy, kind of a loser, but he means well?"

"What about him? I never loved him. I married him only out of gratitude. Or pity."

"Or pragmatism, seeing as how you were deathly ill, and you

needed someone to lean on."

"It's not that I don't appreciate what he did."

"Sure, you appreciated the hell out of it, but that wouldn't stop you from leaving him high and dry as soon as your old flame made a reappearance. When I told you the hit man was named Pascal, your little heart must've gone pittypat, huh?"

"I didn't need to hear his name. As soon as you said he was from Chile—I knew."

"Well, like you said, the heart has its reasons, no matter how fucked up they might be."

"You're an evil, unfeeling bitch."

"Yeah, I get that a lot."

They reached the Jeep. Mariana slid in on the passenger side, Bonnie got behind the wheel, donning her beret for the first time in hours.

She started the engine and pulled away, using her headlights this time.

"You don't understand," Mariana said, her tone a curious mixture of petulance and grief. "You think he was a monster. He wasn't. He was a sensitive man with an artistic soul. A connoisseur and a gentleman."

"Yeah, he was a peach. And you were his lady love—the one who liked pain."

"He told you about that?"

"It came up in conversation."

"I felt shame. And fear. Fear of what I was, or what I might become. That's why I left him. I returned to Colombia and organized the farmers. Not out of idealism. I wanted … redemption."

"I'm betting you didn't find it."

"I didn't need it. I only needed to accept the truth about myself. Now I have. And so have you, I think. You're cruel, aren't you? Like me. Like him."

Bonnie didn't answer.

"You're cruel," Mariana said again. "You could have let me go with him to Chile. He has a home in the mountains. We would have lived in isolation, bothering nobody."

"Yeah, it would've been a fairy-tale love story, all right. Lancelot and Guinevere in their magic castle. Except for the part about Herb and Amy being dead. And Alan and the kid—what were Prince Charming's plans for them?"

"When I reached him on the phone, I insisted he must not hurt them."

"Sure, you never wanted to hurt anybody. And your boyfriend's not evil, just misunderstood."

"Why do you even care? You did all this for my husband? Do you even like him?"

"Not really."

"Then ... why?"

"Because he tried to do something decent. He put it all on the line for you. It was stupid as hell, and it backfired big-time, but he still thinks it was worth it, because he's married to a fucking saint. He doesn't see what a stone cold bitch you are. Love is blind that way. So you're gonna go back to him and make him happy. You're gonna be a faithful, loving wife, and never breathe a word about Pascal."

"You want me to live a lie?"

"Why not? You've had plenty of practice."

"You should have let us go," Mariana said in a voice so low it was almost a moan.

"Save it, princess." Bonnie lit a cigarette. "This fairy tale has a different ending."

37

The rain had slowed to a steady drizzle and the eastern horizon was brightening with dawn when Bonnie's Jeep pulled up to Des's house. She checked the time on Sammy's broken screen. It was exactly six AM.

Just about twelve hours ago she'd been eating scallops at the Main Street Diner. She thought about that as Alan came running out of the house. He paused on the porch just long enough to spot Mariana in the passenger seat, then bounded down the wheelchair ramp.

"Get in character, honey," Bonnie said with a nudge in Mariana's ribs. "And remember—you're happy to be here."

She wasn't too worried about the woman's performance. With Pascal dead, Alan was the only man she had left. She'd married him because she needed him. Well, she needed him again.

Then Alan was at the door of the Jeep, tugging it open, pulling his wife into his arms, clutching her tight. The two of them stood in the rain, locked in a tight embrace.

"I thought I'd lost you," he was saying. "I thought I'd never see you again."

On the porch, Desmond rolled into view, observing the scene without visible reaction. She had a good idea how he was feeling. He'd recognized the handwriting too.

"Did he hurt you?" Alan asked.

"No."

"And he's …?"

Mariana hesitated. "Dead," she whispered. She was crying

again, but that was all right. To Alan they would be tears of relief.

Bonnie found the whole spectacle more than a little sickening. She was afraid those scallops might make a return appearance if she watched any more of it. She climbed out of the Jeep and joined Desmond on the porch.

"There they are," he said, "the happy couple."

"Yeah. Ain't love grand?"

"I'm still surprised you went after her, knowing what you knew."

"Sometimes I surprise myself."

"I take it hubby still doesn't suspect."

"Nope. And he never will." She shrugged. "I almost admire stupidity like that."

"How does Mrs. Kirby feel about things?"

"Let's put it this way. Those aren't tears of joy on her face."

"You could have let Pascal get away, I suppose."

"No, I couldn't. Some men just need killing. He was one of them."

"Simple as that?"

"Yeah, Des. For me, it's as simple as that."

Alan and Mariana approached, arm in arm. Alan wore a bemused, almost beatific smile. Mariana's face was slack, her eyes vacant.

"How long do we have, you think?" Alan asked as he climbed the ramp.

Bonnie didn't get it. "Come again?"

"Until they send another one after us. The Colombians."

"Oh, I don't think you'll have to worry about that. Turns out Pascal was working freelance. The Colombians didn't hire him. Nobody did. So there shouldn't be any other bad guys in your future."

"You mean—we don't have to keep running? We can stay here?"

"You can stay. Pascal wouldn't have given his info to anybody else. And since Herb and Amy were the only ones who knew about you, the trail is cold."

Alan bowed his head, a humble, almost boyish reaction. "You've given us everything."

"Yes," Mariana echoed coldly. "Everything."

Bonnie smiled at her. "Just seeing you two together is my reward. Well, that plus my balloon payment. You'll be getting a bill. A damn big one." She caught Mariana's glare and added cheerfully, "What can I say? I'm just a working girl."

Alan led his wife inside. Bonnie looked at Desmond.

"You get any sleep tonight?" she asked.

"No more than you. I suggest we both take a good long snooze."

She turned away, staring into the rainy dawn. "Nice thought. But I got something else I gotta do."

"Can't it wait?"

"No. I don't think it can."

It was true, what she'd told him. Some men just needed killing. And there was still one left.

38

First things first. She needed the .38 in her safe.

She drove home, parking at the curb because she didn't expect to be inside long. The sun was rising through the drizzle, making another glorious Jersey morning. Mrs. Biggs was probably up already. Her day seemed to start around the time the birds woke up.

Bonnie entered the house and went immediately to her bedroom, where she retrieved the murder gun, snug in its Ziploc bag. The bag went into her fanny pack under her poncho, along with a pair of gloves and a folded-up garbage bag.

Time to go. She retraced her steps through the house, opened the door, and frowned.

"Crap."

Two of Brighton Cove's finest stood in the doorway. Apparently they'd been just about to knock.

A black-and-white Dodge Charger bearing roof lights and the seal of the Brighton Cove PD was double-parked alongside her Jeep. No doubt the prowl car had been hiding in the alley across the street while the cops awaited her return.

She recognized them as Hendrys and Jepson, whom she thought of as Heckel and Jeckel. Both of them were tall, broad-shouldered, crew-cut, and dull. Taking their cue from Maguire, they'd never been friendly toward her, which was probably why they'd been put on stakeout duty near her house.

"Yo, guys," she said.

"Ms. Parker," Heckel said in that unsmiling, judgmental way cops had, "the chief would like to talk with you."

"Didn't realize he was so lonely. You should tell him to get a pen pal or something."

"We need you to come with us," Jeckel said.

"Is refusal an option?"

"It wouldn't be advisable," Heckel said.

She wasn't entirely surprised. Dan had made it pretty clear he suspected her of involvement in whatever had gone down in the motel. And in his haste to depart, Pascal could easily have left something of hers behind. She only hoped it was something she could explain away.

She also hoped the cops didn't think of searching the Jeep. Pascal's Beretta and the pilot's sidearm were both hidden under a blanket in the backseat. For that matter, if they gave her a patdown, they'd find the fanny pack under her poncho, bearing the gun that killed Jacob Hart.

All in all, the timing could have been better.

"Fair enough," she said. "Thing is, I don't like sitting in the backseat of a patrol car. Makes me feel like a felon. Mind if I follow you there?" They exchanged glances. "I won't skip out on you. Scout's honor."

Jeckel shrugged. "You can drive yourself. But no funny business."

No funny business? Was the department recruiting cops from the 1940s now?

She got behind the wheel and followed the Dodge, while surreptitiously undoing the fanny pack. When it was free, she shoved it under the seat. Now if they patted her down, they wouldn't find anything but baby fat.

The police station was an ugly-ass brick building off Main, situated next to the firehouse, where a sign in the shape of a giant thermometer charted fundraising progress toward the purchase of a new engine. Her two uniformed buddies escorted her to a small conference room that doubled as an interrogation room on those rare occasions when there was anybody worth interrogating. Like now, for instance.

She sat in the straight-back chair, leaving her poncho on and letting it drip on the floor. With any luck, it would mildew the carpet. Then again, judging by the smell in here, the damage was already done.

"He'll be with you in a minute," Jeckel said.

"Just sit tight," Heckel said.

"And don't try anything," Jeckel said.

"I was hoping to try parasailing this weekend. Are you saying that's out?"

Heckel and Jekyll seemed confused by the inquiry. They didn't answer, merely left the room, shutting the door. Hard.

The thud of the door in the frame reminded her of what Lizbeth had told her about Dan Maguire—how much he'd enjoyed slamming the door on his long-suffering dog.

Bonnie had no doubt he'd take even greater pleasure in slamming a cell door on her.

***

Dan Maguire had a good feeling about this. He was pretty damn sure that itch of his was about to get scratched.

The hat was the key. Evie Papadopoulos, roused from slumber, had reluctantly identified it as an item she'd sold Bonnie Parker a couple of months ago. A sales slip in her files confirmed it. Evie was a bear about recordkeeping.

Dan had given a lot of thought to how he would play the interview with Parker. He needed to catch her in a lie, just once. Then he would have the leverage to extract some admissions. He would get her to say she'd been in room thirty-two of the Coach House last night. Once he'd placed her at the scene, he would grill her until she told him everything that had gone down, or until she lawyered up.

He let her stew in the interrogation room for a good ten minutes. Too bad the room didn't come equipped with a two-way mirror or a hidden camera. He would have liked to watch that bitch sweat.

She had to be feeling the heat now. He'd been after her for

months, and finally he was closing in.

When he couldn't wait any longer, he picked up a large paper bag that he'd kept in his office and marched down the hall to the interrogation room. He opened the door and found her with her feet up on the table and a cigarette in her hand, blowing smoke rings at the ceiling.

"There's no smoking in this building," he said.

"Could've fooled me. I've been smoking like a chimney for the past five minutes."

"Put it out, Parker."

She stubbed out the cigarette on the table, leaving a circular burn mark.

"And put your goddamned feet on the floor." He glared at her. "Your father may have raised you to be an outlaw, but I'm setting the rules now."

"You mean you want to be my daddy?"

"Parker—"

"I'm flattered and all, but I'm a little old to be adopted."

"Shut up and listen to me."

"There are lots of Chinese orphans who need parents. You could look into that."

"Shut the hell up!"

The meeting had gotten off to a bad start. He sat down opposite her, placing the bag ostentatiously on the table, and tried to regroup.

He studied her. She appeared disappointingly unruffled, but it had to be an act. "That poncho's looking a lot worse for wear," he said.

She shrugged. "You try getting by on a PI's salary."

"You've been out all night, haven't you?"

Let her deny it. Hendrys and Jepson would testify she hadn't come home till sunup.

"No law against that," she said, disappointing him.

"What were you up to?"

"Sex orgy."

"Good. Then you'll have witnesses."

"Okay, you got me. There was no orgy. I drove up to Sandy Hook and watched the storm."

"All night?"

"I conked out in my car for a while. Guess the rain put me to sleep."

"You were alone the entire time?"

"Natch. You think I sleep in my car with strangers?"

"I don't know who you sleep with. Your account doesn't exactly ring true."

"It's what happened. Just another boring night in my boring, ordinary life. Why are you so interested in my whereabouts, anyway?"

"I'm not convinced you've been up to anything so innocent, either before or after I stopped you on the highway."

"You're getting to be a real hard-ass, Dan. This police chief gig has gone straight to your head."

He sat back in his chair. Her story was preposterous, yet in its devilish simplicity it was impossible to disprove. He was momentarily alarmed. His quarry might slip away after all. Then his gaze traveled to the paper bag.

Time to play his trump card.

He reached into the bag, hesitated for maximum dramatic impact, then took out the powder-blue bucket cloche and slapped it down on the table. "Recognize this?"

"Hey, that's my hat."

This was not what he'd wanted to hear. He'd wanted her to say she'd never seen the hat before, wouldn't be caught dead wearing the thing. Then he could pull out a copy of the sales slip and nail her with it.

"So you do recognize it," he said belligerently, trying to recapture the offensive.

"Sure. Where'd you find it?"

"Where do you think?"

"I'm guessing at the Roach House, 'cause that's where I lost it."

He could hardly believe his good luck. She'd just put herself in the motel. "So you're saying you lost this item at the Roach—I mean, the Coach House last night?"

"Not last night. Last month. And I guess *lost* isn't the right word. It was pinched."

"Pinched?"

"Lifted. Snatched. Swiped."

"Someone stole this hat?"

"That's what I'm saying."

All right, he saw her strategy now. But it wouldn't work.

"Why don't I believe you?" he said slowly.

"Because you have a suspicious nature?"

"I think you lost your hat there last night. I think you were present in room thirty-two of the Coach House when some crazy shit went down. I want to know what happened."

"And then you'll prosecute me for, what, participating in some crazy shit? I don't think that's a felony. In Jersey, it may not even be a misdemeanor."

"We'll consider the legal ramifications once we know all the details. You can help yourself a lot by cooperating."

"Sure I can. You're all about helping me, aren't you, Dan?"

"Were you in the motel or not?"

"Last night? Nope. But it looks like my hat was."

"And how did it get there?"

"Probably on top of some hooker's head. Like I told you, it was stolen last month. I was working a case at the Roach House. Taking pictures of a husband who was there in the company of someone other than his wife. I prefer not to give any names. A certain borough councilman would prefer it that way too."

"Stick to the point."

"The point is, the hat was filched from my Jeep while it was parked there."

"And you're claiming a hooker stole it?"

"That's how I always figured it. That place is pretty much crawling with skankaroos, and we gals like our hats."

"Was anything else taken?"

"Pack of cigarettes and some spare change. It was strictly a smash and grab—except there wasn't any smashing, 'cause I'd left the Jeep unlocked."

"And it just so happens that whichever party girl took your hat was in room thirty-two last night?"

"I dunno. Maybe. Was the hat in plain sight or tucked away somewhere?"

"It was found under the bed," he said reluctantly.

"Then I guess it could've been there for days. Weeks, even. It's not like there's any maid service in that dump. When do you think was the last time anyone looked under the bed?"

This still wasn't going the way he'd hoped. He decided to try a psychological approach. "You can lie to me all you want, Parker."

"Thank you."

"But I know what's really going on with you. Let me tell you exactly what happened last night."

"This oughtta be good."

"I think you finally pissed off the wrong people. Somebody with a grudge lured you to that motel, where the occupant of room thirty-two—a mystery man with a Latin American accent—put you in the tub and subjected you to electroshock torture. Maybe for interrogation. Maybe just for kicks. You got away somehow. He fired off a shot as you fled."

"I hope he missed. Did he?"

He ignored her. "Later you cruised past the motel to see if the police were there. That's when I stopped you. You made up an obvious lie about meditating on the beach. I think you spent the rest of the night hunting for this man."

"Did I find him?"

"You tell me."

"That's a really great story, Dan. You could write it up and sell it to *Reader's Digest* or something. But I already told you how my hat got into the room."

"Right. It was stolen. So I assume you filed a police report?"

He knew she hadn't.

"Nah. You guys have more important things to do than chase after my stolen merchandise."

"Do we?"

"Sure. Those bribes and kickbacks ain't gonna take themselves."

He felt a sharp pain in his hand and realized he had squeezed it into a fist. "You didn't report the theft to the police. There's no paper trail. Is there any reason I should think your story isn't complete bullshit?"

"You can ask Lizbeth."

"Who?"

"Lizbeth, the waitress at the Main Street Diner. I eat there all the time. You know her?"

"Yeah, I know her." He'd grown up next door to her. She'd been an annoying little squirt, and time had done nothing to improve her. "What about Lizbeth?"

"I'm pretty sure I mentioned losing the hat to her. That would have been right after it happened."

"And she'll vouch for that?"

"You might have to jog her memory. I remember we got to talking after I had sort of a sneezing fit and she brought me a Kleenex. There was too much pepper in my soup. I said the chef needed to tone it down, because it nearly knocked the hat off my head. That's how we got talking about hats."

"Is that so?"

"Just tell her we were talking about pepper. That ought to do it."

"Talking about pepper."

"You got it."

Something about this story struck Dan as wrong—not just as a lie, which it undoubtedly was, but some kind of inside joke at his expense.

"I'll ask her," he said. "If she doesn't back up your story ..."

"Why wouldn't she back it up?" Bonnie Parker asked with a

blank-faced innocence that infuriated him.

There was a knock on the door. He was almost relieved at the interruption. "Yes?"

"Chief, something's come up." The voice was Jepson's.

He rose from the table and stuck his head into the hallway. "What?"

"Could be another link to the motel case," Jepson said in a low voice.

Dan stepped into the hall, closing the door, and motioned for Jepson to continue.

"Highway patrol just called in. Something weird went down at Millstone Airport. Someone in a rented SUV blew through the gate, knocked it pretty much off its hinges. Vehicle was abandoned. It looks like someone took off in a private plane."

"And you figure it could be the guy from the Coach House? Why?"

"They found medical stuff in the car. Bloody swabs, stuff like that. You know, like someone cleaned out a wound.Could tie in with the gunshot in the parking lot."

Dan didn't want it to play out that way. He wanted the foreigner to be the shooter, and Parker to be the intended victim. That was how he'd reconstructed it. But he could have been wrong. It was possible—just possible—that Parker hadn't had anything to do with the Coach House at all.

"Okay," he said wearily. "Canvass the neighborhood around the airfield and see if anyone noticed a plane coming in or leaving. Maybe we can establish some kind of timeframe. Are the state troopers going over the vehicle?"

"That's the plan."

"See if we can get the same bag-and-tag brigade that worked the motel. They might pick up something that can link the car to the motel room. Carpet fibers or some goddamn thing."

Jepson nodded. Dan released a long and heartfelt sigh, then reentered the conference room. He found Bonnie Parker leaning against the wall, inches from the door. She was blowing smoke rings again.

"What did I tell you about smoking?" he snapped.

"That it's bad for my health?"

"Put out the goddamn cigarette. And not on the table."

"You're the boss." She stubbed it out on the door, leaving another burn mark, then dropped the spent butt on the carpet.

He realized she'd been close enough to the door to listen through the plywood. "Were you eavesdropping?"

"Yup." She grinned. "Sounds like your boy's flown the coop. Literally."

"I still say you were involved."

"How about an alternate theory? Let's say this dude comes to town to do some wet work. He's a pro, hired to do a job. He tortures some poor schmoe in the motel room. The victim gets away. Maybe the pro is wounded in that episode, or maybe it happens later. Either way, he tracks down his quarry and finishes the job, then takes off on a private plane."

"How do you know he finished the job?"

" 'Cause a pro wouldn't leave unless he'd gotten it done. A hit isn't something you just walk away from."

"I guess you would know."

"Bottom line, Dan, my version makes way more sense than yours. You got nothing to hold me on. Which means I'm free to go."

She didn't wait for confirmation. She brushed past him in her wet, dirty poncho, soiling his shirt.

He got in a parting shot. "This isn't over. I'm still going to talk with Lizbeth."

"Remind her about the pepper."

Something stirred in Dan's memory. He gave Parker a hard stare. "You know, I had a dog named Pepper."

"Did you? Hope you treated her right. I like dogs. Big fan."

"How about dogshit? Fan of that too?"

She sniffed the air. "Is that what that is? I thought you were trying a new cologne."

"I know you were in that motel room, Parker. Your story's crap. Even if Lizbeth confirms it, I still know you're lying to me."

"And she's lying too? Everybody's lying?" She shook her head, assuming a sorrowful expression. "Paranoia's not a good look for you, Dan. You should lay off the detective work. Stick to those jaywalking geese."

He fumed, having nothing to say.

At the door she paused, looking over her shoulder. "Hey, can I get that hat back? I like it."

"It's evidence."

"Maybe I can fill out a claim form or—"

"Get out, Parker. Just get the fuck out."

She left. Dan sat in a chair and slumped forward, his head in his hands, feeling like all the air had been squeezed out of him. The interview had not worked out as planned. Nothing with Parker ever did.

And now that itch was back, more insistent than ever, and he didn't know if it would ever get scratched.

39

It was a short drive from the police station to her office. Bonnie took care to ensure she wasn't followed. She wouldn't put it past ol' Danny Boy to stick a tail on her.

She parked in her usual spot. The alley, paved with crunchy sand pebbles, ran perpendicular to Main Street and was bracketed by her building on one side and a retail establishment on the other.

She retrieved her fanny pack and strapped it on under the poncho, then left the Jeep, moving quickly. If her assumptions were correct, this was the moment of maximum risk. But she was counting on Kurt Land not to be watching the alley. By now he must be familiar with her schedule, and ordinarily she never showed up this early.

She made it inside without incident and climbed the stairs to the second floor. Her key let her into her office. As usual, the place smelled of old carpet and musty third-hand furniture. She'd done nothing by way of improvement except tack a couple of posters to the wall. One of them was a reproduction of the famous shot of the original Bonnie Parker posing on the grille of a roadster, a gun in her hand and a stogie in her mouth. It was the stogie that had most scandalized public opinion of the day. The other was a shot of Clyde and Bonnie's last car, the one that Frank Hamer's posse had shot to pieces on a rural road. She had bought it as a reminder of where her own road was likely to lead.

Des had tried to reassure her by saying she was not like her namesake. Well, maybe not. History's Bonnie was a blond hellion with bright blue eyes, her head filled with unrealistic dreams and bad poetry. She'd been a waitress slinging hash in Cement City, Texas, until Clyde Barrow, all five feet five and 140 pounds of him, offered her a more exciting life. The result was a multi-state crime spree, several deaths, and a great deal of wanton violence. It all ended badly, as it had to.

In the words of a Texas lawman, Bonnie Parker was "a two-gun girl, as tough as the back end of a shooting gallery." She was in some ambushes and survived most of them, though the last proved fatal. Up to the end, she was a survivor—desperate, half starved, crippled from a car wreck, but going on, until the guns mowed her down and she couldn't go on anymore.

Still, she'd been memorable. A newsreel poster at the time shouted: *Bonnie Parker—modern tigress, fast shooting, cigar smoking, blond Jezebel!*

There were worse epitaphs.

She turned away from the posters and carefully approached the window that looked out on the alley. The building across the way hosted a shoe store on its ground level. Its second floor was taken up by rented rooms.

Bonnie had never thought much about the people who lived in those rooms. She was thinking about them now.

Only two windows above the shoe store looked out on the alley. One of them was open a few inches. Faded curtains flapped in the damp breeze. The other window appeared to belong to an unoccupied room. The curtains were pulled back, exposing bare walls and no furniture.

If her theory was right, the first room was where she would find Kurt Land.

Kurt knew things about the shooting in the alley that only an eyewitness would know. She was guessing he'd staked out her office, repeating his old habit of obsessive surveillance. He'd watched her come and go, just as he'd watched Jacob Hart.

She left her office and exited the building via a rear door, then made her way to the other building. That one had a rear door also. Locked, but she bumped it and got in with no difficulty. Near the staircase, a row of mailboxes hung on the wall. She scanned the names affixed to the boxes with plastic labels.

The name on unit 2A was BOWMAN.

Cute.

Before going upstairs, she pulled on the gloves she'd taken from her house. Black leather gloves. She flexed her hands, watching the leather stretch.

She took out the Beretta.

Pascal's gun. Gloves like his.

I'm a killer too, she'd told Cynthia Kirby, alias Mariana Ortiz.

She climbed the stairs in the half-light trickling through high, curtained windows. The upstairs hall was lined with rooms on both sides. She went to room 2A and turned the knob. Locked. Bumping it would make too much noise, but the door had no deadbolt, and the beveled edge of the lock faced the hall. Easy enough to pop it open with a credit card.

She entered the room, and there he was, Kurt Land, snarled in a tangle of bedsheets. Beer cans littered the floor by his bed. He had drunk himself asleep.

His shirt was on, and his trousers were off, exposing a pair of Jockey briefs, not clean, and an ugly brace on his left leg. Bonnie saw that brace and thought of the man with a limp in the pavilion's tower.

And she knew. She couldn't make sense of it, but she *knew*.

Kurt Land had been Pascal's partner tonight. His decoy.

She shut the door and explored the room. It was a sad little hole. Hotplate, can opener, cans of Beefaroni and pork and beans. No toilet; she'd passed a communal bathroom down the hall.

She found no diary, no handwritten notes of any kind, and no computer. There was a cell phone, the one he'd used to call her. She put it in her pocket. The call log would include her number. Nothing else in the room would tie him to her.

She removed the .38 from its Ziploc bag and placed it carefully in a bureau drawer. Dan Maguire didn't know it yet, but the mystery of who shot Jacob Hart was about to be solved.

On the cold radiator by the window sill lay a pair of binoculars and Kurt Land's most recent acquisition, a PSE Mach-12 compound hunting bow. No surprise. Kurt was a bow hunter, after all, and Dan had told her that Starkey's had been robbed of this exact item two nights ago. She'd never had any doubt about who'd stolen it, or who its intended target was.

The bow could easily be aimed at the window of her office, where she would be seated at her desk. In his last phone call he'd bragged that she would never know what hit her.

She ran her gloved fingers over the wide bowhead, barbed like a miniature harpoon. It could bring down a deer. It would have sunk deep between her shoulder blades, killing her instantly if she was lucky, or not so instantly if his aim was not quite true.

The window was open just enough to let in some air without admitting too much of the rain that had fallen throughout the night. She wanted it shut. Even a silenced gunshot would produce some noise.

She lowered the window. It squealed in its frame, and Kurt Land stirred.

Bonnie pivoted toward him, the Beretta ready. He wasn't quite awake yet, but he was coming around.

Quickly she groped under his pillow, then patted down the sheets until she was satisfied he had no hidden weapon within reach. Then she waited for him to wake up.

He had grown a beard and dyed his hair darker, but the face was the same one that had stared up at her from the snowy ground in January. His eyes, when they opened, were the same shade of hazel. She remembered thinking that the eyes of the dead lost their color. Maybe it was that thought that had stopped her then.

It wouldn't stop her now.

He registered her presence with slow comprehension, his vision coming into focus along with his mind. He saw the gun in her hand, and the black gloves, and she wondered if he was reminded, if only for a moment, of Pascal.

"Oh, fuck," he whispered.

She smiled. "Hey, Kurt. How's it hangin'?"

He didn't answer. Presumably he knew the question was purely rhetorical.

"You know, you're like a bad meal, buddy boy. You keep coming back on me."

"Fuck," he said again. A shudder moved through him, and he kicked off the covers with a convulsive movement of his legs.

"Once I figured out it was you on the phone, you really should've vamoosed. You had to know I'd find you before long."

He made a low whimpering sound. She'd never heard a man whimper before—like an animal, like a beaten dog.

"But maybe you had no place to go, huh? You look like a guy who's pretty much run out of options. Cash all gone?"

He chewed his lip and didn't answer. His Adam's apple bobbed in his throat.

"Rent in Brighton Cove's pretty steep," she said, "even for a glorified broom closet like this. I'm guessing you had some extra cash squirreled away."

"A few thousand. You can have it. What's left of it. Just take it."

"I didn't come here to rob you, Kurt. You and me—we got other business."

She raised the gun just slightly, for emphasis. She saw him flinch as if struck, saw the muscles of his face twitch in panic, and she knew how Pascal had felt when he administered shock after shock.

"Where was your stash, anyhow?" she asked. "It wasn't in your townhouse. I would've found it when I tossed the place. You knew I'd been there, right?"

He managed a shaky nod. Tears glimmered in his eyes.

"Sure, you knew," she went on, "because your safe deposit key was gone. The only other people who had a reason to search your townhouse were the police—you being a missing person and all. But if the police had looked inside the safe deposit box, they would've found the photos, and Jacob Hart would have been charged with corrupting a minor, statutory rape, whatever. And there was nothing in the news about that."

"Right ..."

"So where'd you keep the cash?"

"With a friend."

"Yeah, I don't believe you, buddy boy. I don't think you have any friends."

"He used to be a friend. He always kept cash around ..."

"You ripped him off, is that it? Broke in and lifted his wad from its secret hiding place?"

"I was desperate."

"Hey, no need to justify yourself. You were in a bad way, I know. Bet those bullet wounds messed you up pretty good, huh?"

"It took three surgeries."

"And you still can't walk right. I heard you clomping around like Peg-leg Pete in the pavilion."

"I don't know ... what you're talking about."

"Yeah, you do. You were Pascal's little helper. You tried to set me up."

The room filled with a sudden ammonia smell. She looked down at his briefs and saw a widening yellow stain.

"And when the going got rough," she said, "you ran off like a scared little girl."

He tried to speak, but his voice seemed stuck in his throat, trapped by panic. She had never seen anyone so nakedly afraid.

"He's dead, by the way," she added. "Pascal, I mean."

He made a retching sound. She thought he was pretty close to throwing up on himself.

"You hear me, asshole? Pascal's dead."

"I—I don't know any Pascal ..." He might have wanted to say more, but he choked up again. Chewing, chewing at that lip. Drawing blood.

"Save it. It's a little late for bullshit."

He dipped his head, acknowledging defeat. Saliva dribbled out of his mouth, spotting his chin. "You ... you really got Pascal?"

"It was him or me. Turns out, it was him."

His throat jerked, and a mouthful of undigested beer spilled out of him in a viscid stream, spattering the sheets. He stared down at the mess in dumb incomprehension.

She ignored the mess. "I take it you were watching my office the night Jacob Hart dropped by for a visit. Don't deny it, okay? You'll just piss me off."

"I saw it. Had a … ringside seat." He looked up, and his mouth tugged itself into a sickly smile. "I really thought he was going to get you."

"He took his shot—literally." She nodded at the crossbow. "Looks like you were about to take yours."

He shook his head and went on shaking it. "No, it wasn't like that."

"Sure it was. You were all set to use that bow the next time I showed up in my office. On the phone you pretty much said my days were numbered."

"That was just talk, just—I was drunk, I didn't know what the fuck I was saying …"

"You knew. It took you long enough, but you'd finally worked up the nerve to do it."

"I'm not—I couldn't …"

"Maybe if I hadn't gone fishing yesterday, you'd have taken me out already."

He chuffed ragged bursts of breath. His shirt was pasted to his skin. "You can't prove that."

"Kurt, Kurt, Kurt … I don't have to prove a goddamn thing. You see a jury here? It's just you and me, buddy boy." She tightened her grip on the Beretta. "And soon, it'll be just me."

"You can't do it!" Crying shamelessly, all dignity lost. "You couldn't do it before, in the woods. And you can't do it now."

"I made a mistake before." She took a step closer to him. "But here's the thing, Kurt. I learn from my mistakes."

He pushed himself away. His head bumped against the wall, and he glanced around frantically, as if suddenly aware that there was nowhere to run.

"Don't," he said. The plea was squeezed out from between bloodless lips. "Just ... don't."

Tears streaked his face. He clasped his hands in supplication.

"Don't," he said again.

She fired once into his temple at point-blank range.

His head snapped to the side. His eyes were wide and startled. A thick ooze of blood ran slowly down his face from the hole in his skull.

It had been easy, even face to face. She didn't know why she had hesitated in the Barrens.

There must have been a reason, but she could no longer remember what it was.

40

Though Pascal's silencer was degraded after repeated use, the shot still hadn't been loud enough to wake the neighbors, especially with no one next door. Most of the spatter had gone on the wall, but there was some blood on her poncho. It was no big deal.

She unfolded the garbage bag from her fanny pack and filled it with the crossbow, arrow, and binoculars. She retrieved the Beretta's expended shell casing, though it carried no prints, simply because it was the kind of precaution a pro would take.

The hallway remained empty. She descended to ground level and left via the rear entrance, then hopped the low wall to the alley and climbed back into her Jeep. She took care to obey all traffic laws as she drove away.

A mile from the scene she parked behind a Rite Aid, not yet open for business. She peeled off the gloves and added them to the garbage bag, then ditched the bag in a trash bin, taking care to bury it under other refuse. She smashed Kurt Land's cell phone to pieces and tossed the pieces into the bin, after removing the SIM card.

In another dump bin, this one behind an A&P, she disposed of the bloodstained poncho and the SIM card, having first crushed the card under her tires.

All that was left was Pascal's Beretta. She wiped it clean, then drove to the lake where she'd gone fishing yesterday. Screened from the road by trees, she flung the pistol far out over the lake. It vanished with a plop, disturbing some sleepy ducks.

By now it was after eight o'clock, and the rain had stopped.

She headed over to Atlantic Avenue, parking down the street from the home of Mr. and Mrs. Andrew Wright. At eight fifteen, their daughter Sienna bicycled down the driveway, racing west toward the highway, where she had a job at the Donut Hutch.

Bonnie watched her go. She looked like any ordinary fifteen-year-old girl. Her hair was tied back in a ponytail, and her lean, athletic legs pumped the pedals. She was probably happy.

Jacob Hart was dead, but Bonnie continued to keep watch over Sienna Wright, just to be sure there was no backsliding into another bad situation. She didn't need Des to analyze her motives. She'd been fourteen when she was traumatized by the murder of her parents, and she'd spent much of the next year hunting the killers and taking them out. There had been no normal upbringing for her. This girl still had a chance.

She sat at the curb until the bike was out of sight. Then she put the Jeep into gear and headed back toward the ocean.

She had one more stop to make.

***

The housekeeper at the Hart residence actually flinched when Bonnie opened the door.

Bonnie smiled. "Yeah, me again."

"She not see you."

"You haven't even asked her."

"She already tells me, she not see you *ever*."

"Well, now, that's just rude."

The door started to close. Bonnie elbowed it open and stepped inside, bypassing the housekeeper with a quick sidestep. She was tired, and she wasn't taking any crap.

"You cannot come," the housekeeper said.

"Try and stop me."

The woman thrust out her lower lip and hunched her shoulders, and for a moment it looked as if actual fisticuffs were about to commence.

"It's all right, Nilda." The voice was Gillian Hart's, and it came from the top of the stairs. "I'll take care of it."

Nilda retreated, sulking.

Gillian descended the stairs in silky slow motion, lean and elegant, like that old-time movie actress, the one who got it on with Bogart. What the hell was her name?

"Lauren Bacall," Bonnie said, remembering.

"What did you say?" Gillian reached the bottom of the staircase. She stood there in a pink nightgown and fuzzy slippers that somehow managed not to look comical.

"Nothing. Did I get you up?" Sammy's display screen read 9:02.

"I've been up for some time. I rise with the sun and take breakfast in my room."

"Really? I rise with the morning zoo crew and take breakfast over the kitchen sink."

"I assume you have some purpose in coming here again."

"You and me have some catching up to do."

"We caught up yesterday."

"A lot has happened since then."

Gillian looked her over. "I'll say it has. You look like you've been put through the wringer."

Bonnie wasn't exactly sure what a wringer was, but she doubted the expression was intended as a compliment. "Yeah, whatever. Is this really where you want to talk?"

Gillian hesitated, doubtless aware that Nilda was listening somewhere nearby, then turned to her left and started walking. "Come into my parlor."

Said the spider to the fly.

Bonnie followed, noting that the fuzzy slippers made absolutely no noise even on hardwood floors. Burglars ought to wear the damn things.

The parlor was an oak-paneled room decorated with historical photos of Brighton Cove and an impressive collection of scotches.

Gillian shut the door for privacy. "Well?"

"The first thing you need to know is that there's about to be a break in the Jacob Hart case. Your husband's shooting will be solved in the next few days."

Gillian smiled. "Then it appears you're in trouble. After all, you told me yourself that you did it."

"Me? You must've heard me wrong. Kurt Land did it. Turns out he wasn't as dead as I thought."

"Is that so?"

"He planned it all out. Made himself disappear because otherwise he'd be an obvious suspect, given his known animosity to your husband. He rented a room in downtown Brighton Cove. It just happened to be across the alley from my office. Pure coincidence. It's a small town, you know."

"So he had no connection with you?"

"Nah, I never even heard of the guy. Anyway, he lured Jacob to the alley and shot him with a thirty-eight. The same thirty-eight that's now stashed in his room, just waiting to be found, along with his dead body. Really dead this time."

"You know none of that is true."

"Doesn't matter what I know." Bonnie lit a cigarette. Gillian was sufficiently distracted not to object. "What matters is what Officer Friendly of our neighborhood police department knows. The story I just told you is how it's going to look to him."

"You're saying Kurt Land actually was alive all this time?"

"Yup."

"And now you killed him?"

"Didn't say I killed him. Who knows how it happened? But what it looks like is a professional shooter from Latin America was hired to snatch Kurt Land and torture a confession out of him. Somehow Kurt got away, but the bad guy tracked him to his room and finished him there. The bullet in Kurt's head will match another bullet fired at the motel where the torture took place, which ties everything together quite neatly, don't you think?"

"Nobody will believe such nonsense."

"Wrong-o." She took a deep breath of smoke. "Everyone who matters will believe it. It explains not only your husband's demise but a whole bunch of other things. And it puts me in the clear. You, though ... not so much."

Gillian narrowed her eyes. "What do you mean by that?"

"Think it through, Mrs. H. Who would hire a pro to avenge your hubby's death? Whose business has a ton of Latin American connections—all those authentic south-of-the-border fixin's you import? The authorities will be taking a good long look at you."

"You expect *me* to be charged for *your* crime?"

"I don't expect you to be charged with anything. First, because there won't be any proof, and second, because people like you don't do time for murder. No charges, nothing formal. Just a lot of whispering and innuendo. Oops, there goes that good name of yours—you know, the one you were always so anxious to protect." She took another hit off the cig and found it good.

"And what's to stop me from ... from ..."

"From pointing the figure at yours truly? Come on, ask me a hard one. You can't tell what you know without implicating yourself in a murder-for-hire plot. Do you enjoy irony, Mrs. H? 'Cause there's a buttload of irony here. You're gonna be widely suspected of hiring an assassin to kill Kurt Land. And you can't say a word in your own defense without admitting that, on a prior occasion, you—wait for it—*hired an assassin to kill Kurt Land.* That's what some people might call poetic justice."

Gillian looked suddenly unsteady. She sank into the nearest chair, her face unnaturally rigid. "And you're doing all this just because my husband ambushed you? I had nothing to do with that."

"Fair point. But that's not why I'm doing it."

"Why, then?"

"Because you set me up, Gillian," she said, using the woman's first name for once.

"I ...?"

"Yeah, you. You had a meeting with Alan Kirby, aka Jeffrey Walker, yesterday evening. He knew you through his nonprofit work in New York. He'd come to you once before, when he was in trouble. You bankrolled his family's change of identity and helped them relocate here. You were their guardian angel. Which was nice of you. The Kirbys probably couldn't have swung it on their own."

"You don't know what you're—"

"Save it. Yesterday he came to you again, and as usual he was in a sweat. His friend Amy was dead, and the killer had just checked into the Coach House, which meant he was breathing down Alan's neck. Poor Alan didn't know what the hell to do. You told him to hire me."

"What if I did? Is that so wrong? You should be grateful for the work."

Bonnie took another drag and coughed out a laugh. "Oh yeah. My thank-you note's in the mail. You weren't doing me any favors, girlfriend. You wanted me to go up against a seasoned hitter who, for all you knew, had been sent by the Colombian government. Maybe I'd get lucky and take out the bad guy. But I think you were counting on it to go the other way. And if that meant things didn't work out so well for Alan and his family—well, I think you hate me way more than you like them."

"That's crazy. You're paranoid. Delusional."

"I don't think so. You pretty much gave the game away with that little good-bye speech you delivered. Remember? How one of these days I'd come up against somebody better than Jacob. And then you'd be visiting my grave."

Gillian said nothing.

"That wreath you bought—you might have meant it for your dear departed, but I'm thinking you came up with another use for it around the time I dropped by."

"You damned bitch," Gillian whispered.

"Sticks and stones, Mrs. H. You fucked with the wrong gal, and now you wind up on the receiving end of all those pointing fingers. Get used to it. Your family name will never be the same. Me, on the other hand—I'm coming outta this mess just fine. I might even get an apology from Dan Maguire, though I'm not holding my breath. The cops will take me off their list of persons of interest and put you on it. They'll know you're dirty, and as for me—I'll be clean."

Gillian rose stiffly from the chair. Her former grace and elegance were gone, and she looked suddenly old. She fixed Bonnie with an ice-cold stare.

"You may be a lot of things, Miss Parker. But you're not clean."

***

There was nothing more to say after that. Bonnie let herself out. She left the house and crossed Ocean Drive to the boardwalk. She leaned on the railing and watched the sun.

It was cool for August, the surf still rough. Clouds scudded past, the whitecaps matching their tempo. But behind the clouds there was blue sky.

Gillian might have doubts about the fix, but Bonnie had looked at it from every angle, and she knew it would hold up. The only possible hitch was Kurt's time of death—shortly after the plane's departure from Millstone Airport, when, according to her scenario, he should have died a little earlier. But she wasn't worried. For all she knew, there were no witnesses to establish exactly when the plane had left. More to the point, Kurt's remains probably wouldn't be found for a couple of days. He had no friends, and no one would come calling on him until somebody noticed the smell. By then, an accurate time of death would be impossible to determine.

To the south, she could see the pavilion in a haze of distance. Squinting, she made out a couple of uniformed cops. Someone must have spotted the shell casings and bullet holes from last night's firefight. Another piece of the puzzle for Dan Maguire. But that was no problem either. Hell, maybe Kurt Land's prints would turn up at the scene. He'd been there, after all.

It had all worked out. She was tired now, and hungry. Ravenous, in fact. She figured she would stop at the Main Street Diner, and chow down on their eggs Benedict. But not quite yet. She was too restless to sit and eat.

She started walking north, away from the pavilion. The wind beat at her face. Joggers huffed past. Kids flashed by on bikes, reminding her of Sienna Wright. The sight of them made her feel good, but the feeling faded as she thought of what Gillian Hart had said.

You're not clean.

Bonnie couldn't argue. She knew who she was and what she was. Since midnight she'd made two men into corpses. There had been other men before them. And there would be more.

She wore hats and made small talk and tipped waitresses. She looked and acted like any other person. But she was not like the others. She could shoot a pleading man in cold blood. And feel nothing. Nothing at all.

She was a killer—hard as a bullet, sudden as a shock, and, always, cold around the heart.

Author's Note

As always, I invite readers to visit my website at michaelprescott.net, where you'll find news items, information on my books, and other good stuff.

The lines of verse that serve as an epigraph for *Cold Around the Heart* are excerpted from a poem written by the real Bonnie Parker, which was found among her personal effects after her death. I've taken the liberty of altering a couple of words in the last line, which originally read, *For they know they can never be free.*

My thanks to Diana Cox of www.novelproofreading.com for her careful proofreading of the manuscript. Any remaining errors are mine.

—M.P.

Also by Michael Prescott

Made in the USA
Lexington, KY
22 May 2013